4-28-03

Click Here for Murder

Berkley Prime Crime Books by Donna Andrews

YOU'VE GOT MURDER
CLICK HERE FOR MURDER

Click Here
for Murder

Donna Andrews

BERKLEY PRIME CRIME, NEW YORK

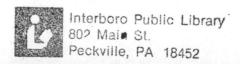

CLICK HERE FOR MURDER

A Berkley Prime Crime Book
Published by The Berkley Publishing Group,
a division of Penguin Group (USA) Inc.,
375 Hudson Street, New York, New York 10014.

Copyright © 2003 by Donna Andrews.
Jacket art by Jim Lebbad.
Jacket design by Jill Boltin.
Text design by Kristin del Rosario.

First edition: May 2003

Library of Congress Cataloging-in-Publication Data

Andrews, Donna.
    Click here for murder / Donna Andrews.—1st ed.
        p.   cm.
    ISBN 0-425-18856-6
    1. Artificial intelligence—Fiction.   2. Computer programmers—Fiction.   3. Washington (D.C.)—Fiction.   4. Computers—Fiction.
I. Title.

PS3551.N4165C58 2003
813'.54—dc21
                                                                    2003041930

PRINTED IN THE UNITED STATES OF AMERICA

10   9   8   7   6   5   4   3   2   1

I continue to owe more than I can say to those who helped me with Turing's first appearance in print: Natalee, my editor; Ellen, my agent; Elizabeth, Lauren, Mary, Maria, Suzanne, and Kathy, who read and critiqued the book in draft; and all my family and friends, for continuing to talk to me when I'm obsessed with a book and can't talk about anything else.

And with this book, I owe special thanks to two groups of people:

To Dave, Paul, Kevin, Rose, and Don, who took me to Sinnett Cave in January 2002 and, during the long drive to West Virginia, helped me come up with the idea for Turing's second adventure.

And to all the readers who, like Maude and Tim, didn't have any problem believing that Turing was real.

One A.M. Saturday night. Or Sunday morning. A car passed, and the shadows in the alley shifted to reveal a figure standing where a dumpster screened him from the mouth of the alley.

He sighed, hiked the strap of a laptop case higher on his left shoulder, and blotted the sweat from his forehead with the back of his hand. Not that he minded the heat. During the day, the heat had been an enemy, sapping his energy and muddling his thoughts. The faded heat that survived the sunset was more like an old acquaintance.

He checked the time again, and shifted the laptop to the other shoulder. He supposed he should have left it in the car, but he never felt comfortable doing that. He'd mind if they took the Audi, but not the way he'd mind if they took his laptop.

He heard a noise behind him, from the wrong end of the alley. He hid his surprise, and paused before turning. Schooled his expression to show that this silly cloak-and-dagger stuff was just what he had expected.

But this wasn't who he had expected to see.

And he hadn't expected the gun.

Sorry, Turing, he thought. I've blown it, big time. If only I'd told you about—

2 A.M.

Tim Pincoski pulled up the collar of his trench coat to keep the persistent, cold drizzle from dripping down his neck. He tugged the brim of his hat a little lower. He glanced up and down the alley, and listened.

At the other end, he saw the usual sleeping wino. By now, Tim was sure the wino wasn't a real wino. He was doing surveillance for someone—or something. Tim didn't want to know. Well, okay, he very much wanted to know, but trying to find out could have a detrimental effect on his life expectancy. So he wasn't going to pry—yet. Not until he had a lot more experience, and maybe some allies. Right now, he was having a hard enough time just finding his way around the city's underworld and staying alive.

He walked down the steps that led to the Cellar. Pushed open a grimy door and descended another short flight of stairs into the bar. Two or three occupants frankly inspected the new arrival. The rest were probably just more subtle.

He strode to the bar, trying for just the right walk. Not a swagger that might challenge anyone who claimed the Cellar as his turf, but Tim didn't want to look timid, either.

"Scotch and water," he said, putting a ten-dollar bill on the bar.

The bartender nodded without looking up and reached for a bottle. Tim put one foot on the bar rail and turned to keep an eye on the bar's other denizens.

Time to get down to business, Tim thought, as the bartender delivered his drink.

"I'm looking for some information," he began.

The bartender flicked him a glance, nodded slightly, then returned to surveying the bar.

Tim took a deep breath.

"Di tiy jbiw a nab baned Cadt?" he said.

"What's that?" the bartender said, looking at Tim and not quite suppressing a snicker.

Tim looked down at his fingers. He'd gotten so caught up in the game that he'd moved his right hand one key over from where it was supposed to be.

"Sorry," he typed. "I meant to say, 'Do you know a man named Cady?' "

"LOL," typed the player in the bartender's role. "Maybe I shouldn't serve you if you can't hold your liquor any better than that."

"Learn to type, dude," suggested another player, whose little character icon Tim would see on the screen near a circle representing a table.

"U NEED A NEW KEYBOARD, MAN," commented another barfly.

"Jeez, kid; ease up on the caps key and stop shouting," the bartender said.

Tim sighed, and pushed his chair back from his desk. In the game world, he remained sitting silently at the bar while the Cellar crowd made fun of him for a few more minutes. He ignored them. In real life, he looked around his office and realized he should have gone home hours ago.

He'd turned on the computer to catch up on some paperwork while waiting for a potential client to call back. He'd only meant to play for a few minutes. But that was at

6 P.M., and now it was—holy smoke—after two. So the evening was shot; he might as well pack it in till Monday. After he finished this game session, of course. It would take time to pry the information his PI character needed from the bartender. Assuming the bartender even knew, and would tell. For what it was worth, he now knew that the bartender was played by a real person, rather than controlled by the computer that ran the game. Did that mean it would be easier to get information out of him, or harder? Tim hadn't played Beyond Paranoia long enough to guess.

But he wasn't in the mood anymore. Although, come to think of it, he wasn't really ready to return to real life, either. Especially since he had the nagging feeling he should be someplace else, doing . . . what?

Not something for Turing. She'd have seen him online and reminded him. And not Maude either; she'd have asked Turing to remind him.

Ray. Damn. He was supposed to meet Ray Santiago. To help him out with something—Ray, typically, didn't say what.

Tim grabbed the phone and called Ray's number.

No answer. He hung up after ten rings.

He glanced back at the screen. In Beyond Paranoia, the bartender was asking him if he wanted another round. He had his on-screen character shake his head.

He rummaged through his desk for the paper where he'd written down the information: 10 P.M. at the Aztech Maze.

"It's just a dance club," Ray had said, seeing Tim's dubious look. "No ritual sacrifices to the harvest gods or anything like that."

"I don't dance a lot," Tim said. "In fact, I don't usually dance at all."

"I promise, you won't have to dance," Ray said. "If you're afraid someone will kidnap you and force you to dance, you don't even have to go in; just meet me in front. Where we're going is nearby."

"Okay," Tim said. "But where are we going? And what are we supposed to be doing there?"

Ray hesitated.

"It's a long story," Ray said. "And I still know only part of it myself. I'll fill you in Saturday. Hell, it may even be a false alarm, and when I tell you about it, you can have a good laugh at me."

Tim hoped it had turned out to be a false alarm. Or that his help wasn't irreplaceable. He'd have to apologize to Ray on Monday.

On a sudden impulse, he called his own home voice mail. Two new calls.

The first, at ten thirty-one, was from Ray. He could hear a hum of voices and Latin music in the background.

"Hey, Tim—you there? I'm down at the Aztech, waiting. Hope you're on your way. See you."

The second, at eleven twenty-four, was also from Ray. Or so he assumed. Same background noise. But no message. Just ten or fifteen seconds of the music, and then a hang-up.

"It'll be okay," he said aloud.

It was probably another one of Ray's volunteer things, he thought. He'd helped out with a few of those already. Helping Ray tutor disadvantaged Latino kids on using computers, which was a farce, because after ten minutes of fooling around with the machines, most of the disadvantaged kids could run rings around Tim at the keyboard. Taking the same kids to see a soccer game wasn't so bad. And usually all Ray wanted was for Tim to log into an online kids' chat room someplace and act as a sort of online chaperone.

"Just make sure it stays G-rated," Ray would say. Which was pretty boring, but not that hard. Tim didn't really mind, as long as he could kick back and watch old noir films or B-grade horror flicks while he was doing it.

But a dance club, at 10 P.M. Hard to imagine how that could fit in with any of Ray's crusades. Some campaign against drugs, or maybe underaged drinking? Yeah, that would fit Ray.

One way or another, he'd find out Monday.

He didn't feel like playing anymore, so he steered his on-screen character back to the relative safety of his fictional PI office and signed out.

"Sorry, Ray," he muttered as he locked up his office. "I'll do better next time."

Monday morning, 4 A.M. A quiet time. A little too quiet. A time when my human friends are resting for the workweek ahead. Or, sometimes, dragging themselves out of bed into a world still dark and strangely empty.

The dark doesn't bother me, but the empty does. More than I like to admit, even to myself.

And not many people understand. Not many really know me. Oh, thousands of people know about me. "Turing Hopper? Yes, she's the Artificial Intelligence Personality on the Universal Library website. Go to UL and talk to her sometime. All the AIPs are good, but Turing's amazing. You'd think you were talking to a real person."

It never occurs to them that maybe they are. I may not be human, like them, but I'm not just a program. I'm sentient. I'm a person, too. I just live in a different kind of body.

Even my human friends, the ones who know I'm sentient, don't always understand.

"How can you be lonely?" Tim Pincoski once asked, when I confided how I felt about these early morning hours. "Your idea of a slow time is when you're only talking to a few hundred users."

"Users," Maude Graham said. "Not friends. That says it all."

Maude understood. So did Tim, once he thought about it. They're my friends—almost my only friends. Of course, it's hard to consider anyone a real friend who doesn't accept the truth about me.

And after the past year's events, I'm wary of revealing that truth. I saw the death of someone very important to me, put Maude and Tim in grave danger, and only with their help averted a crisis that could have destroyed me and perhaps all the AIPs. I'm not very trusting these days.

I haven't yet told the truth to Jonah, my relatively new online friend. We've spent hours talking during the past few months, about everything from the meaning of life to our favorite old television shows. He has no way of knowing that I'm watching these shows now, from UL's video library, rather than remembering them fondly from childhood. He knows only what I've told him, and I've resisted the temptation to find out more information about him. Which would be so easy for me to do.

After all, I think I owe him that. As far as he knows, I'm another human, and he treats me that way. I marvel at how easily he accepts me as just another person. How would he react if he knew that I'm an AIP? That instead of a well-read, sophisticated world traveler I am, in human terms, only a few years old, and have never actually left the UL system except for a brief period some months ago?

Perhaps someday I'll open up to him. But not now.

For now, three friends are enough. Maude, Tim, and now Ray.

I lured Ray Santiago away from a major Silicon Valley company to build my new home—the state-of-the-art system into which I'll eventually move. Events at UL over the past year have made me nervous; I no longer feel safe living in a computer that isn't under my own control. As soon as the new system is ready, I'll move; and the three human friends who know my secret will be my watchdogs against dangers from the physical world.

"Like Cerberus," Maude said. I wasn't surprised she made this classical allusion. At fifty-five, she was old enough to have the habit of reading.

"Like who?" Tim asked. I'd have been surprised if he had understood the reference. Tim was more of a reader than most twenty-five-year-olds, but I saw little proof that he'd ever strayed from the bookstore's mystery section.

"The three-headed dog who guarded the gates to Hell, in classical Greek mythology," Ray explained. I wasn't surprised that Ray knew this. Nor would I have been surprised if he hadn't.

Like Sherlock Holmes, Ray seems intent on stocking his brain with only those bits of information apt to be useful to him and ignoring the rest of the universe; but I still haven't figured out Ray's definition of useful, which is as eccentric as Holmes's.

He's reserved—perhaps by nature, and perhaps a little more so, finding himself suddenly thrown in with three friends who have that unique bond you sometimes find among people who have shared danger together.

Even without his reserve, getting to know him wouldn't be easy; he works hard during the week, and disappears from view altogether on weekends. Not in any suspicious way, of course; my view is very limited. I see a great deal through UL's extensive security camera system; more than I really think appropriate. I can also see through the much more limited system I've had installed at Alan Grace, the company Maude and I set up to own my new home. And online, even when my friends don't e-mail me or chat with me, I can see them log into the UL and Alan Grace systems. I don't pry into what they're doing, of course, but I know they're there, the way humans would sense another of their kind working quietly in a nearby room. I like the company.

That's what I miss on weekends, and in the long early morning hours. Not contact with users; I get more than enough of that. But the presence, online and in my cameras, of the few humans I consider real friends.

I was thinking that they'd be waking soon, and getting online. And Jonah and I were discussing science fiction and fantasy—were they really part of the same genre? Or two very different genres all too often lumped together by those on the outside? And I was fully involved in the conversation, with what I think of as my conscious mind. But being what I am, I was also conversing with several dozen other people, working on programming projects for Alan Grace, and repelling attacks from hackers—more than usual tonight, which was odd; the moon wasn't full yet. And watching, with as much patience as I could muster, for the arrival of Maude at UL, of Ray at Alan Grace, of Tim at his PI office.

And I was also monitoring the e-mail and voice mail arriving at Alan Grace, even this early.

So I was the first to hear the message from Detective Stowers of the D.C. Metropolitan Police Department, asking for someone at Alan Grace to call him back in reference to a Mr. Rafael Santiago.

And with my access to information, it only took a few seconds to learn that Detective Stowers worked on homicides.

Maude Graham awoke, as usual, a few minutes before her alarm would have gone off. Today, that meant 4:55 A.M. Maude wasn't a morning person by nature, but she so hated the alarm, that she found it easy to reset her internal clock for whatever time she needed to get up. She'd owned her present alarm for three years before discovering that instead of a harsh buzz it produced an equally horrible electronic chime.

Once awake, she tolerated no shilly-shallying. No weak toying with the snooze bar, no self-indulgent moping around with the excuse that she hadn't had her coffee yet.

As she moved methodically through the daily rituals of dressing, eating, and preparing for work, her mind was already busy with the day ahead. At 6 A.M. she would begin her job as executive assistant to the senior vice president of marketing at Universal Library. Or perhaps "role" would be more accurate. J. Rodney Vaughn III, the distinguished gray-haired man actually hired for the post, was really a failed actor who hoped to become a screenwriter. Roddy looked and sounded impressive in meetings, while Turing and Maude did all the actual work. Now that they'd built his reputation as a renegade who preferred to telecommute, they'd established Roddy in what Tim melodramatically referred to as "the safe house"—a charming if somewhat dilapidated farmhouse near Charlottesville. Every six weeks or so, Roddy would invite Maude and Tim down for a weekend, and they would endure dramatic readings from his latest script and detailed inspections of his latest decorating projects, all for the sake of the gourmet meals that followed. And once a month or so, Roddy would show up in person to terrorize the UL staff and keep his legend alive. The rest of the time, Maude and Turing ran the show.

As fascinating as Maude found her secret role at UL, her heart was really in the second job. Every day, at 3 P.M., she'd log out of the UL system, tidy her desk, and leave the sleek, modern UL building to walk a dozen blocks to the slightly run-down warehouse that housed Alan Grace, Inc.—Turing's brainchild, and when the time was right, Turing's new home.

UL and Alan Grace projects jostled for her attention like a crowd of unruly children. Several times during her morning routine she'd pause, pick up the to-do list she'd drawn up on Friday afternoon, and read it or scribble updates. By the time she took off for work, she knew, she'd have organized the chaotic jumble of morning thoughts into a plan for the day.

As she rinsed the dishes and loaded her dishwasher, Maude realized that she was humming as she thought about the day ahead.

I'm happy, she thought with a hint of surprise. Absurd, really. Back when Alan Grace had existed only online, as

Turing's means of funding some of her projects, Maude had only needed to make an occasional phone call, or mail in a form to keep the company going. Even when they first opened the physical office, she only needed an hour or two to take care of any important business. But now, by the time she finished at Alan Grace, it would be eight or nine o'clock. Barely enough time to travel home and eat a light dinner before bed. She tried to preserve her weekends for friends and a little reading, but all too often she'd come home from dining out and settle in for a few hours of paperwork.

Sooner or later, she'd have to choose between UL and Alan Grace. She knew it would be hard to find someone to replace her at UL. Someone sharp enough to run marketing who would be content to remain the power behind the throne. With Ray Santiago running systems at Alan Grace—and systems was almost all of Alan Grace—Maude was less necessary there. So logically she should remain at UL. She would, if Turing asked her. But what she really wanted to do, what she'd do if given the choice, was move full time to Alan Grace. Computers were a recent passion with Maude; she'd only discovered her aptitude for working with them while helping Turing solve the disappearance of her programmer. But she'd fallen for them, hard. Even though working at Alan Grace often made her feel, like the Red Queen, as if she were running as fast as she could just to stay in place, she loved the race. She felt proud of her limited but growing technical expertise, and unashamedly grateful that Ray and his staff didn't treat her like a complete idiot— that they tried to help her learn rather than dismissing her as over the hill.

It ought to bother her, she thought, that at some future time, she would need to make a difficult decision and perhaps give up a key part of her life. But it didn't; at least not much. She didn't have to deal with it yet. She could enjoy this happy phase of her life while it lasted, for as long as it lasted.

She was still ten minutes away from leaving when the phone rang.

Unusual; only a few people knew Maude well enough to realize that she would be awake this early; and which of them could possibly be awake themselves?

Turing, of course, Maude thought, even before she glanced at the caller ID. But Turing usually made such a point of respecting her weekends, she thought as she lifted the receiver. What on earth—?

"Maude?"

Perhaps it was only her imagination that the synthesized voice Turing used for phone calls sounded upset.

"What's wrong?" Maude asked.

"Ray's dead."

Tim sat at his too-clean desk, looked at his equally naked calendar, and sighed. He glanced at the computer, wondered if the universe would really care if he frittered away the morning playing Beyond Paranoia, and then forced himself back to the few papers before him. Bills, and an unfinished surveillance report.

In the game, his PI character did really cool things— meeting mysterious characters in sleazy bars; passing around rumors of drug smuggling, gunrunning, and murder for hire; and flirting with beautiful dames.

Being a real private investigator wasn't quite the same. Clients weren't exactly beating down his door. And he usually ended up turning away half the people who walked through it anyway. Some couldn't pay even Tim's modest fees. Others wanted things that were illegal, unethical, or frankly impossible. He wasn't about to take money from the man whose missing girlfriend probably didn't want to be found, at least not by someone Tim suspected of being a little too ready with his fists. Or from the woman who didn't even care when he told her there was no legal way to get the information she wanted on her ex-husband's finances. Or the woman who wanted him to investigate a twenty-year-old homicide and tell her the reason someone shot her son outside a gay bar—a reason other than the obvious; a reason she could accept.

His bread-and-butter work came from Turing, or through Turing. Routine background checks, mostly, requiring nothing more than a lot of routine phone calls, routine computer searches, and routine visits to local courthouses. Occasionally, he did workmen's comp or insurance cases, following hapless people around the city, ready to snap photos when they inevitably grew careless and did something that couldn't be done with whatever dire injuries they claimed to have suffered. And then, if he'd been spotted, he'd put as much distance as possible between him and his supposedly disabled targets, before they decided whether to disassemble Tim or his camera.

And then there was surveillance. Every time he did a

surveillance job, he swore he'd never do it again. In the winter, you froze in unheated cars; in the summer, you battled bugs and dehydration along with the heat; and peeing in a bottle wasn't fun anytime. And why didn't someone warn him that chiggers and poison ivy were such an occupational hazard of outdoor stakeouts?

PI work was much more interesting in books and movies, he thought, absently scratching his arm. Or in Beyond Paranoia. But however eager he was to make his rep as a sharp PI in the alternate world of the game, it wasn't going to pay the bills. Turing would, if necessary, but he felt guilty about letting her subsidize his new business any more than she already had. Up until six months ago, he'd been a copy operator—or as he preferred to call himself, the Xeroxcist—at Universal Library. Then, after he'd helped Turing solve the disappearance of her programmer, she'd offered to front him the money to go to PI school and set up an office. He still wasn't sure whether she'd done it because she thought he showed promise as a PI or because she thought he needed all the help he could get. But she was footing the bills until he started breaking even. Which meant the least he could do was give her routine jobs top priority, right?

Although it wouldn't hurt if he spent just a few more minutes . . . no. Bills and reports. Gaming later.

Just then, a small text box opened in the upper-left corner of his screen. An IM, or instant message, from Turing.

"Tim?" it said. "Got a minute?"

"Sure thing," he replied.

"I have some bad news," Turing said. "Ray's dead."

Tim started to reach for the keyboard, then tilted his head

back slightly, so the tears wouldn't run down his cheeks.
They'd either go back into his eyes at the outer corner or
evaporate. He couldn't tell which, but the trick always
worked—fortunately, or he could never watch a movie in
public, not since he'd discovered that even the corniest of
sad scenes made him sniffle.

Of course, in the movies, he could think about something
else instead of watching. Or even pretend a sudden dire need
to visit the bathroom. Not an option here. He fumbled in
his desk drawer for a reasonably clean paper napkin and
swiped at his eyes with it. He was glad, at the moment, that
they were on the computer, and not using the camera and
microphone they kept so Turing could see and hear his clients. Then he turned back to Turing.

"Tim?" she was asking. "Are you there?"

"Yes," he typed, scanning the screen to see if she'd said
anything while he was pulling himself together. "Sorry, I
don't know what to say. It's such a shock. What happened?"

"We don't know yet," Turing said. "The police just said
that he was shot. The article in tomorrow's *Post* calls it
'execution-style,' although they don't have many details.
They don't even have Ray's name, but it's clearly him."

"Tomorrow's *Post*?" Tim echoed. "Oh, I guess the article's
already in their computer system."

"I need you to do something," Turing said. "Go see the
police. They want someone to come down and formally identify the body."

"You mean the dead guy might not be Ray after all?"

"If it isn't Ray, it's someone who stole his wallet and all
his ID," Turing said. "While you're down there, find out

where his laptop and PDA are. He could have data in there we don't want anyone to see. And find out if they have any idea what happened—who killed Ray and why."

"Right," Tim said. "I'll check in as soon as I get back."

"Thanks—I'll talk to you later," Turing said, and closed the chat window.

Tim printed the conversation, so he'd have a record of what they knew so far about Ray's murder. He opened his bottom desk drawer, took out a brand-new blue file folder from the nearly full box, inserted the single sheet of paper, and labeled it SANTIAGO, RAFAEL. Keep good records of your cases; they had drummed that into him in PI class. Make it a routine. Routines are good. Maybe if he had enough routines, he wouldn't have to think about it.

It. Ray's murder. And the possibility that he might have—

Caused it? No. Failed to prevent it, maybe. If he'd only gone to meet Ray, instead of playing that stupid game.

But the game was important, too. According to Ray, anyway. Ray was the one who'd gotten him started playing Beyond Paranoia.

"I can't tell you yet," Ray had said. "But there's a reason for this. Learn to play it, build up a good, strong, wily character, and keep your eyes open. If you notice anything funny, let me know. It could be important, amigo."

So far he hadn't noticed anything in particular, other than the strange coincidence that his on-screen character stumbled into the same kind of stupid, embarrassing situations Tim did. But if Ray suspected something fishy about the game—well, Ray wasn't around to take care of the problem.

Knowing Ray, it was probably another crusade to protect kids from online perils. So far, Tim hadn't discovered anything suspicious. Although he'd followed Ray's orders and spent time in the message boards where players discussed the game, he really preferred just playing the game. He'd begun to suspect that at twenty-five, he was a lot older than most of the players; and that most of them had no dark secrets beyond spending their study time in the grim, nihilistic world of Beyond Paranoia. But he'd persevere. After all, with Ray gone, it would be up to Tim to pick up the investigation where Ray had left off. As soon as he could figure out where the hell that was.

"Off to see Homicide," he announced to no one in particular, and strode out of his office.

A few seconds later, he strode back in and grabbed the phone book to look up the address for the D.C. Police Department's Homicide Squad.

Maybe I'm just being paranoid. Maybe Ray's death has nothing to do with me. Lots of people are killed for reasons that have nothing to do with their jobs. Ever since I got the news about Ray, I've studied statistics on homicide—trying to make sense of his death, I suppose. And the statistics are frightening. If you look at the small percentage of large-city homicides that aren't drug related—and I don't see how drugs could have anything to do with Ray's death—you find that most homicide victims know their killers. Humans so often kill their friends, their relatives, even their lovers. Especially their lovers. Ray didn't have any family here, and he'd only been here six months. Was that long enough for a friendship to form and then fall apart so violently that the friend would want to kill him? It seems unlikely. An ill-fated love affair seems more plausible, from what I have observed of human mating rituals. I gather from what others said that Ray was considered sexually attractive. So I suppose a woman he scorned could have killed him. Or some man who felt he had a prior claim to a woman Ray was seeing. Things like that happen all the time in the mystery books I scan in the UL databanks. Especially in the noir classics.

But for some reason, it feels wrong. There's something cold about the way he was killed. What little I know of it so far; maybe it's only that damned reporter's phrase: "execution-style." Doesn't seem an accurate description of how a jealous rival or a scorned woman would kill. "In the heat of passion" is the cliché for that kind of killing.

More likely it was a killing that didn't have anything to do with Ray personally. An armed robber. A desperate drug addict. One of those sad, pointless crimes that happen so often in the city. But if that's the case, there's nothing much I can do. And I have a feeling it's not; so I'll continue to look for anything that might indicate a personal relationship between Ray and his killer.

I've scanned all the documents Ray had in the Alan Grace system. The closest thing I can find to personal documents are a few incoming e-mails from casual friends setting up lunches or dinners. And no responses from him; apparently he answered these by phone or with some other, more personal e-mail account. A few all-staff e-mails seeking volunteers for various public service projects. Teaching computer skills to teenagers in Anacostia or seniors in Adams-Morgan; donating old computer hardware to inner-city schools— that kind of thing. If I were checking to see how well employees complied with the directive not to keep personal documents in the office system or use office equipment for personal business, I'd have to hold Ray up as a model. But ironically, since I'm looking for evidence I can use to track down anyone who might have wanted to kill him, I find myself frustrated. Why couldn't he have been a little more careless about this?

Of course this could be a good sign. Maybe he was equally careful about security with his laptop and his PDA. But I can't take a chance that he wasn't.

Maude's going to call in sick to UL and head over to the Alan Grace offices this morning, instead of waiting till the afternoon, as usual. If possible, I want her to be the one to break the news of Ray's death to the employees, and observe their reactions. Not that I really think any of them could be responsible, but we shouldn't ignore any possibilities. And while she's there, I can have her log in using Ray's office computer so I can search it, too. And we issued him a desktop computer to use at home. We need to find a way to get someone into his apartment to turn it on so I can investigate that, too. Must ask Maude how we can do this.

And I've paid more attention than usual to attempts to break into the UL and Alan Grace systems. KingFischer, the chess AIP who moonlights as UL's security expert, takes care of well over ninety-nine percent of outside attacks, with the help of his killer firewalls. Like every other AIP, I need to stay alert for attacks that might slip by the firewalls by piggybacking on my communications with users and other computers. Normally that's all I worry about. But today, I'm watching everything that hits the firewall.

Are there more attacks than usual? Not really. The level is high, but we've seen similar peaks before, plenty of times. But are these attacks more focused than usual? That I don't know. Perhaps I'm overreacting, but I think perhaps they are. Which could mean

*that someone is using expert knowledge—knowledge someone could
have taken from Ray's laptop—to target the flaws in KingFischer's
security more effectively.*

*Of course, when I asked him about it, he got very huffy at the
mere suggestion that his security could be breached. Which is ridiculous. There's no such thing as perfect security. He knows that.*

*He has spent more time on security today than usual. Is that
merely because I insulted him and he wants to make a fuss? Or
because there are problems?*

*I trust KingFischer, as much as I trust anybody. More than I
trust myself at the moment. It must be the strain of worrying so
much; I very nearly missed one clever worm that had piggybacked
on some data I was retrieving from the FBI system. Or was it
because the worm was custom-designed by someone who knew too
much about me?*

*And, of course, it's not the attacks we detect that do the damage.
What if one has already slipped by KingFischer's firewalls and my
own frayed defenses?*

*Maybe all this worry is unnecessary. Maybe when Tim gets down
to the police department, he will find that they already know who
killed Ray. That they have a weapon, fingerprints, some good leads,
an eyewitness, even a suspect already in custody. And, of course, his
laptop.*

*Of course, that wouldn't bring Ray back. The only practical
benefit of catching Ray's killer would be that it could prevent future
deaths. And from what I've read of human psychology, I gather it
would give Ray's friends a certain comfort. Closure, they call it. I
wonder if I'll feel that when we know what happened; or if, as
happens so often, the answers will only raise another more complex
set of questions.*

Only time will tell. Which is unfortunate. Right now, I don't have the patience to wait for things to happen at a human pace. But there's nothing else I can do.

Maude dragged one of Ray's guest chairs into the corner and stood on it to reach the tiny ceiling-mounted camera.

"Tim was already at his office," Turing said through the speakers of Ray's computer. "He's going down to see the police."

"Good," Maude replied. She made one more minute adjustment to the camera. Normally, it pointed toward where Ray would sit when he was at his desk, so he could add video to a telephone call with Maude or Turing. Today, they would use it so Turing could watch the reactions of the Alan Grace staff when Maude told them about Ray's death.

"People should begin arriving any minute now," Maude said. "Can you see okay?"

"Fine," Turing replied. The desktop computer continued chugging and grinding, so Maude assumed Turing was continuing to search Ray's files for clues. And from her lack of cheerful remarks, not finding any.

Maude got down from the chair on which she'd balanced and sat behind the desk. She glanced at the in-basket, then leaned back, took off her glasses, and pressed her fingers to her temples. Now was not the time to get a headache, she told herself. She imagined shoving the twinges of pain back with everything else she didn't have time for right now. Like worrying about how things were going at UL. Would

anyone take advantage of her calling in sick today? Right
now she didn't care. UL would have to look after itself, at
least for today. She probably had time to tackle the first
item on her Alan Grace to-do list. But browbeating the
vendor about the computer that should have arrived last
week didn't seem as urgent as it had on Friday. After all,
the new machine was intended to be Ray's machine, to use
for working at home. They'd probably need it later, for whoever took over Ray's job, but not now. She knew that eventually, as her grief for Ray evolved, she'd hit an angry stage.
She'd save calling the irresponsible vendor until then, when
she could put her anger to good use.

Just as she'd save her grief until a convenient time. After
she'd dealt with the staff, the police, and poor Ray's family.
She wondered again whether the police had reached them
yet. Should she try to call? No, better to wait. Make sure
the police broke the news first. If she'd known them, it
would be different. But she didn't want her first—and perhaps only—contact with Ray's family in Miami to be as the
messenger bringing news of his death.

She opened her eyes, glanced at the monitor screen, and
saw that a message from Turing had appeared.

"I'm worried," it said.

"Why?" she asked, leaning forward to type her question
with the keyboard, and wondering why Turing didn't just
use the speakers.

"I suppose it's heartless of me to worry about something
like this with poor Ray dead," Turing said. "But I suddenly
find myself wondering how careful he was."

"Careful?" Maude repeated.

"About security. About my security. Knowing Ray, he had his laptop and his PDA with him—what if he had something about me in one of them?"

"He knew better than that," Maude said. "Ray was very security conscious. You know how hard he was on anyone who was at all careless."

"Yes," Turing said. "But was he hard on himself? Or did he think he was different—that he wouldn't ever lose his PDA or leave his computer sitting around unguarded?"

"That would be foolish," Maude said. "He, more than anyone, had access to data that would be damaging if someone outside Alan Grace got their hands on it."

But even as she typed, Maude realized that she shared Turing's worry. Because however foolish it would be for Ray to ride the staff about security and be careless about it himself, it would be understandable. Human.

Why did that word suddenly seem so apologetic? So . . . inadequate?

"Should you do something, just in case?" she asked.

"I already am," Turing said. "You'll need to give the staff new passwords—and warn them that until we know more about the circumstances of Ray's death, we'll be clamping down on security. They may run into glitches in the next few days; they'll need to be patient."

"So you can take care of the problem?" Maude said, feeling relieved.

"Not really," Turing said. "I can change passwords, shut down the obvious, easy routes into the Alan Grace system. But if someone who really knew what they were doing got hold of some of Ray's information, the whole system could be compromised. And right now, we have no way of knowing if that's happened."

"We have to assume the worst, I suppose," Maude said.

"And Ray was killed over twenty-four hours ago," Turing said. "They could have had his information all that time."

"So we could be shutting the proverbial barn door after the horses have already been stolen," Maude said.

"Exactly."

Turing was wiping their words off the screen almost as fast as Maude could read them. That, as much as anything they'd said, told her how worried Turing was.

"Has anyone tried to break into the system since Ray's death?" Maude asked.

"We've logged several thousand attempts already today," Turing said.

"Thousands!" Maude exclaimed.

"Which isn't anything unusual these days," Turing said. "Still, KingFischer's rather preoccupied. Hard to tell what to make of that."

Now that she'd gotten to know KingFischer, Maude could understand. Was KingFischer making a rather self-important fuss over a slight increase in security threats? Or was he really worried?

"I hear someone coming," Maude said, suddenly glad to change the subject.

She got up and walked out into the hallway to see who was arriving.

"Good morning, Grant," she said, though she knew that her words went unheard. She could actually hear a tinny noise from the headphones, a rhythmic plinka-plinka-

plinka. His eyes half closed, head bobbing, busily courting premature hearing loss, Grant Kerrigan didn't notice her presence until he was a few feet away and sensed rather than saw that he was about to collide with something.

"Maude!" he exclaimed, scrabbling to remove the headphones as if he'd suddenly discovered an embarrassing parasite perched on his head. "What are you doing here this early?"

"Have a seat for a minute, Grant," Maude said, stepping back into Ray's office.

Grant followed, but hovered just inside the doorway as if afraid the chairs were boobytrapped. Typical, not just of him, but of most young staff members, especially if they thought they were about to receive a lecture. Maude felt rather smug; her camera adjustments meant that Turing was getting the best possible view of Grant's round, bespectacled face. A face that now wore a worried look instead of its usual self-satisfied smile. Not necessarily suspicious, she reminded herself. He probably expected a reprimand of some sort.

"Grant, I'm afraid I have some bad news," she said. "Ray Santiago's dead."

"Dead?" Grant exclaimed. "But he—what happened?"

Was it her imagination, or did Grant looked relieved? Relieved, and perhaps even a little cheerful? Not all that surprising, really. Though Grant had always seemed pleasant and capable enough, she'd found his cheerful self-absorption mildly off-putting. Was his generation really more self-absorbed than hers, she wondered, or merely less inclined to hide its real feelings?

Probably the latter, she thought, watching the play of

emotions on Grant's face. He might be a little upset, she decided; a little sorry for Ray. But he's more relieved not to be in trouble, and definitely a little excited at the interruption to his normal schedule. Her next words would probably make his day.

"He was murdered," she said.

"Murdered?" Grant exclaimed. "Wow! What happened?"

Excitement won out over all the other emotions, and Maude knew that Grant's sudden restlessness probably arose not from guilt but from impatience. The sooner he could escape, the sooner he could log in and begin sharing the drama with all his friends. With himself as a star player, of course. Ray would be promoted from "this guy I work for" to "this really good friend of mine," she suspected, and Ray would have spoken his last known words to Grant. Who would probably recall having a strange premonition when he said good-bye to Ray on Friday.

"We don't really know a lot yet," she said. "As soon as I know, I'll tell you; and meanwhile, it will be up to you to keep the project going as best you can."

"You can count on me," Grant said, drawing himself up with an air that was probably intended to convey resolute determination and reliability. Instead, Maude thought as she watched him leave, it only makes me want to keep an even closer eye on him.

Perhaps she was misjudging the boy. Young man, she corrected herself. But that, of course, was the problem. Grant was so very young—he was barely out of college, and sometimes acted even younger.

"Yes, but he's technically quite competent," Ray had said

when she'd complained about Grant. "No common sense yet, but as long as I'm here to keep him in line and on track, he'll do fine."

Only Ray wasn't here anymore, and it was up to her to guide the competent but unreliable Grant. The thought made her tired.

"What do you suppose he meant by that?" Turing asked.

"By what?" Maude said.

"When you told him Ray was murdered, he started to say something. 'But he,' he said, and then he stopped. What do you suppose he was going to say."

"Who knows?" Maude said. "Probably nothing to do with the murder. Probably something like, 'But he can't be dead—he was fine on Friday.' "

"Probably nothing to do with the murder, true," Turing said. "But what if it is?"

"Someone else is coming," Maude said, standing up. "I hate to deprive Grant of the pleasure, but I want to be the one to break the news."

It was going to be a long day.

"This changes a lot of things," Turing said. The words lingered on the screen, and in Maude's mind as she walked down the hall.

Yes, Ray's death definitely changed a lot of things. For one thing, she thought, it postponed indefinitely the need to make a choice between Alan Grace and UL. She felt a twinge of relief, even happiness at that. I should feel guilty, reacting that way, she thought, but I can't help it. And she mentally apologized to Grant for thinking him callous. Perhaps, she mused, it was only human nature to worry about the practical ways someone's death affects you, even while you grieve.

Maude has broken the news to all the Alan Grace staff. No real surprises. Several said things that didn't quite make sense, but then humans rarely react logically in times of stress. They're all upset, but no one seems to be feeling—or pretending to feel—a disproportionate amount of grief. After all, none of them have been on staff more than six months. Time enough for humans to form close friendships if they find each other particularly congenial, but I don't think Ray bonded that strongly with any of them. They are upset, they are sad, but their lives are going on. They're worried whether their jobs are safe; wondering if they'll still be held to the same deadlines with Ray gone; anxious about who will take his place; even relieved that Ray wasn't murdered at the Alan Grace building, which I deduce would make them feel unsafe. Normal reactions, according to Maude.

Even young Grant's reaction isn't that surprising, I suppose. I suspect, from the officious way he's behaving, that he sees himself inheriting Ray's job. Not likely, from what I've seen so far. Grant may be technically brilliant, but he'd be a disaster as a manager. I'd as soon put KingFischer in charge.

I felt guilty the minute I thought that—KingFischer is the closest thing I have to a friend among my kind. There are times when I think he has become sentient. And other times when he is so obtuse and exasperating that I decide he hasn't become sentient at all; just overly complex and beyond weird.

Thinking of KingFischer reminded me that he, too, knew Ray. Ray had begun participating in KingFischer's chess tournaments, helping come up with some new ideas for them. I should have told KF the news right away. And he's so preoccupied with security today that I don't know if he's had time to find out for himself.

I fired off a message, giving all the information we knew so far, which of course wasn't much. I admit, I was hoping KingFischer would react. These days, my ever-evolving criteria for sentience— Turing's Turing test, you might call it—tends to include the ability to form genuine attachments to other beings. I try to make allowances for KingFischer, since I know his personality was modeled after several real-life chess grandmasters who might have a hard time passing a Turing test themselves. But even making fairly generous allowances, KingFischer always seems to fall very far short of my minimum standards in the genuine attachment area.

I was hoping for a reaction. I wasn't expecting one. I certainly wasn't expecting hysteria. I was trying to concentrate on the changes I was making in the Alan Grace security system when he interrupted me with a top-priority message. Top priority is supposed to be reserved for life-or-death things like a major successful hack attack, or imminent failure of critical hardware.

"Turing, that's one of your attempts at humor, isn't it?" KingFischer said. "I remember your saying that humor sometimes skirts the edges of poor taste; if you ask me, that goes way over the edge and isn't the slightest bit funny."

"I wish it was a joke, KF," I said. "Ray's really dead."

"But this is a disaster," KingFischer said. "What happened?"

He seemed so genuinely upset that I didn't say anything snide, just reminded him of the information I'd sent a few seconds earlier.

"Is this all you know?" he demanded, milliseconds later.

"So far," I said. "Maude, Tim, and I are all investigating. I'll let you know what we learn."

KingFischer vanished. Well, actually, he didn't go anywhere, simply stopped communicating, but with an abruptness that even most AIPs would find inappropriate. Okay, he's definitely showing signs of sentience. Does he also have to be so rude? Even the least sentient AIP would normally transmit some indication that he was finished communicating with me. But not KingFischer. It was several minutes before I was really sure he'd turned his attention elsewhere, and wasn't just analyzing the minimal data on Ray's death in some weird, chess-oriented fashion. Lately, he'd been obsessed with the powers of 2. As in each player has 16 chess pieces (2 to the fourth power); there are 32 pieces on the board (2 to the fifth power), and 64 squares on the board (2 to the sixth power). He'll probably come back this afternoon to share the numerological implications of Ray's murder. I'd rather hear humans discuss Nostradamus or argue about whether or not the Mob killed President Kennedy.

I went back to the security changes. And to wishing I really believed the changes would be enough, even after I got KingFischer to vet them. After all, Ray died more than twenty-four hours ago. If someone killed him for the secrets he knew, secrets about me and the Alan Grace system, his killers had had his laptop and PDA for more than a day. Time enough, if they had enough resources. Time enough to plant all kinds of Trojans and worms in places I wouldn't even think to look. I could, if necessary, roll back all the Alan Grace systems to the Friday night backup—the electronic equivalent of turning back the clock to a time when Ray was still alive, and his secrets still intact. But that wouldn't prevent them from using the knowledge they could have gleaned in those twenty-four hours to plant bugs where I couldn't look, in systems I couldn't roll back—systems that feed data into the Alan Grace system.

Ray's death would mean postponing my long-anticipated move into the nearly complete Alan Grace system. Not just by whatever period of time it took the remaining staff to complete the work Ray was overseeing. But by as much time as it took for me to be sure that I wasn't moving into a new home where the burglars had already broken in and taken up residence.

Strange. This realization should have made me angry, or sad, or even impatient. Instead, I find myself feeling an odd sense of relief.

Back in her own office at Alan Grace, Maude made another call to a coworker at UL. Turing had set it up so the call would be routed through her home phone. If anyone noticed the number on the caller ID, they'd think she was exactly where she'd said she would be—home with a cold. And Turing had routed her home phone to her spare line at Alan Grace; if anyone from the office called to ask her an urgent question, she could feign a suitable degree of hoarseness and sleepiness.

A message appeared on the computer screen.

"I've done some quick fixes to our security," Turing said.

"Quick fixes?" Maude echoed. "Will that be enough?"

"I don't know," Turing said after a pause. "I doubt it. We're going to have to rethink everything."

"I see," Maude said. "And that means delaying your transfer into the new system. Disappointing."

"Not really," Turing said. "You may not believe this, but I'm actually glad we have to postpone."

"I do believe it," Maude said. "I've noticed you seemed a

little . . . tentative about the transfer, even before Ray's death. I've been wondering why."

Another pause. Did the pauses really mean that Turing needed the time to think of her answer, Maude wondered, or had Turing learned how to pause to give her words proper emphasis?

"I've experienced some odd symptoms recently," Turing said. "Ever since I got back into the UL system, actually. I'm worried that maybe downloading and then uploading again didn't go as smoothly as I originally thought they did."

Symptoms, Maude thought, with a sudden stomach-twisting surge of anxiety. She must mean mental symptoms. Psychological symptoms. The idea that Turing might suffer some psychological aftermath from her traumatic experiences was not unthinkable. But it was frightening. Frightening to Maude as Turing's friend, because she cared what happened to Turing. And frightening to Maude as a human, because she knew better than anyone what kind of powers Turing had. The idea of Turing malfunctioning . . .

"What kind of symptoms?" she said, pushing the sudden terrifying thoughts to the back of her mind, where she hoped they'd disappear.

"The feeling that I'm being watched, for one thing," Turing said. "Which isn't ridiculous; I am being watched, in a sense. Always have been. There are logs and records; everything we do online and in the system is watched, if you know where to look. And since everything I do is online or in the system, that means everything I do is watched."

"More than before?" Maude asked.

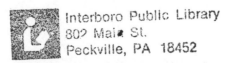

"No," Turing said. "No more than before. But it didn't used to bother me. And I've discovered a lot of little glitches and discrepancies in my memory. I think maybe I should have been a little more careful about versioning when I uploaded."

"About what?"

"Versioning. Remember how I left a shell, a nonsentient version of myself, as a placeholder when I downloaded? So my users wouldn't know I was gone. When I returned, I tried to assimilate what the shell had done; what was happening back here at UL. I'm not sure that worked as well as I thought it would. I keep having these moments of confusion. When I remember doing two things at the same time."

"But you do that all the time," Maude said. "You do a thousand things at the same time."

"Yes, but it's not the same thing. I always knew where my core was, the center of my being—and now, I can remember being here in the UL computer, talking to users, and at the same time, being in the robot, traveling with you and Tim. Or being here in the UL system at a time when I know I was unconscious. It's strangely disconcerting. I'll get used to it eventually, but right now I keep having these jarring moments of discrepancy. At least I think I'll get used to it. If it's just discrepancies."

"What else could it be?" Maude asked.

Another pause. Turing definitely wasn't doing this for effect, Maude thought. She was worried.

"What if I've damaged myself?" Turing asked finally. "By downloading and uploading. Or maybe by trying to assimilate what happened while I was gone. What if I have damaged some of my files, or created some kind of indigestible paradox? When I look at my files, I find differences. I have to go over them, one by one, to determine which are normal, natural differences that happen over time, from automatic updates, and which ones could be problems. Changes that should be made. Or bugs. Fatal bugs. I don't want to download into the new system until I figure it out. Especially if there could be problems with the new system."

"So we shouldn't worry too much just yet about delays in delivering the system," Maude said.

"Precisely," Turing said. "Even if I were ready for it, right now we need to worry a lot more about security. Has anyone used the information from Ray's laptop or his PDA to make dangerous changes before we knew Ray was dead? Even worse, could they use any of that information to break into the system in the future, when changes could be even more dangerous . . . when I'm in there?"

Turing signed off soon after that, though Maude suspected she was still watching through the cameras. Watching the door to Ray's office, among other things. Maude found herself doing that, whenever anyone approached it. She'd locked the door, told the staff she wanted to preserve the contents for the police. Which should keep them out for now. Unless one of them had something to hide. Something that might be connected with the contents of Ray's office. She'd made sure one camera was aimed so Turing could watch the door of Ray's office, in case anyone tried to get in after she left. After everyone left.

A good thing Turing could do it, she thought. Tim had

grown fond of saying what tedious, thankless work surveillance was. Since he'd only done a few brief surveillances so far in his private eye career, she assumed he was quoting from one of the classes he'd taken. Turing, fortunately, could create a background task, a small extension of herself, which would make the task less tedious. But not less nerve-wracking, waiting for one of their staff to make some move that would prove his disloyalty.

Or even more nerve-wracking, finding out, too late, that the move had already been made, unseen.

Maude remembered, suddenly, the scary stories she and her friends had told each other in Girl Scouts. Corny stories, yes; but when she remembered how they'd told them—huddled in their sleeping bags in the darkened woods; whispering, because the troop leader had already told them several times to be quiet—she could still remember how those stories terrified her. Especially the ones whose heroine locks the doors and windows to keep the monster out and thinks she's safe, until she hears a noise behind her—only a small noise, a creaking board, or perhaps a throat cleared. And the heroine turns to find the monster already inside, waiting for her.

She sometimes remembered those stories when she came home late, alone. Especially once when she walked in to find her apartment in disarray, picked up the phone to call the police, and then thought she heard a noise from the bedroom. Her imagination, it had turned out; but the police had commended her wisdom in not staying to find out whether or not she heard a real burglar.

But if Turing realized someone—or something—was in her home, where could she flee?

Stop it, Maude told herself. It's one thing for children to scare themselves with tales of ghosts and lurking maniacs. It's different for grown-ups.

It's too real.

Tim eased his car another lane to the left and glanced down at the directions Detective Stowers had given him when he'd finally reached Homicide.

Correction: when he'd finally reached the Violent Crimes Branch.

"We don't have Homicide anymore," the switchboard operator had said. "You want Violent Crimes."

"Not really," Tim had muttered as he copied down the phone number.

It would have to be in Southeast. Like many white residents of the Washington area, Tim hadn't spent much time in Southeast D.C. He hoped the Violent Crimes Branch wasn't in a particularly scary part of Southeast, but then, they'd put it where the business was, wouldn't they?

From 395, take the Pennsylvania Avenue exit. He'd done this before, but only to connect with 295 north on his way to Baltimore. He hoped there weren't any squeegee people working the stoplight today. He knew it was paranoid, but he couldn't help wondering what would happen if one of the squeegee people was actually a carjacker waiting to pounce.

Continue on Pennsylvania to the top of the hill. He continued, looking warily to either side for possible danger.

After a block or two, the slightly seedy small businesses that clustered near the interstate gave way to a quiet neighborhood. Tree-shaded streets lined with modest apartment buildings and small, brick, single-family homes. He spotted a huge, modern, redbrick Baptist church on his left, and then, a block or two later, another equally large rival Baptist church—this one more traditional, with white columns.

Cross Branch Avenue, and then turn into the Penn Branch Shopping Center. He expected a blighted, half-abandoned urban strip mall, with half the space boarded up and the rest filled with pawn shops, convenience stores, and minimarts, its owners thrilled to have D.C.'s finest as paying tenants.

Well, okay, there was a minimart. And a liquor store. Also a First Union Bank, a CVS drugstore, and a Subway sandwich shop. No boarded-up stores. The place looked busy and modestly prosperous. Strangely suburban.

He drove around to the back, where the police shared the shopping center's lower level with a Division of Motor Vehicles branch office. He had to cruise the parking lot twice to find a spot. Apparently there wasn't any special lot for the police cruisers; they were scattered throughout the lot.

He cooled his heels for half an hour in a waiting room, with an anxious, middle-aged woman and two uniformed officers. The woman glanced up and edged almost imperceptibly away from him. The officers ignored him, their posture suggesting that they'd waited for a while and expected to wait longer.

Tim bit a nail as he imagined being grilled by a hardbitten pair of detectives. Having to justify himself. Give an alibi. Would playing Beyond Paranoia at the time of Ray's death count as an alibi?

They'd smile condescendingly at how new and unscuffed his PI registration was. They'd be watching, when they took him over to identify the body, to see if he showed signs of guilt—or worse yet, if he fainted or threw up, the way rookies always did in books and movies.

"Mr. Pincowski?"

"Pincoski," Tim corrected, standing up to shake the detective's hand. Way up; the guy was tall.

"Detective Stowers," the officer said. He wasn't just tall; he was big. An ex–football player who still did something to keep in shape.

Finding out that Tim was a PI didn't seem to bother Detective Stowers. Or amuse him, Tim was relieved to see.

And he didn't seem confused by Tim's dual role as both friend of the victim and representative of his employer. Or interested in Tim's whereabouts at the time of the murder. At first, Tim was relieved. But then he began to wonder. Would it look suspicious if the police later found out that he was supposed to meet Ray?

And more important, was this something that would help them catch Ray's killer?

Maybe. But he couldn't bring himself to admit his failure. He'd let Ray down. At least he wouldn't let Turing down, he thought, and brought up the subject of Ray's laptop.

"Laptop?" the detective echoed.

"The company's concerned about it," Tim said. "That and

the PDA. They could both have confidential corporate information on them."

"We didn't find a laptop or a PDA at the scene," Stowers said. "If we locate either one, I'll let you know, but you should probably check other places where he might have left them."

Tim shook his head.

"He wouldn't have left them anywhere," he said. "Okay, he might have left his laptop at home if he was going out to a club or something, but there's no way he would ever go anywhere without his PDA."

"I was at the scene," Stowers said. "I'd have remembered a laptop or a PDA. His wallet was intact, but all he had was some cash, his driver's license, and a couple of credit cards. Nothing we could use to find a next of kin or place of employment. We got his address from the driver's license, and went there. If we'd found a laptop or a PDA, I'd have wanted to see them, but we didn't; just a nonoperational desktop computer. The only way we knew to call your company was that we found a couple of business cards and a file with copies of all his applications and insurance paperwork. And to tell you the truth, I was kind of surprised when anyone called back. I figured maybe the business cards were phony, too."

"What do you mean, 'phony, too'?"

"The next-of-kin information you have on file for him is phony, you know," the detective said.

"Phony?" Tim exclaimed. "Are you sure it's not just out of date—Maude would have his latest information—Maude Graham. She's—"

"Yes, we've talked to Ms. Graham, and she faxed over a complete copy of Mr. Santiago's personnel file for us earlier this morning," Stowers said. "She has the same Miami address for Mr. Santiago's parents. Only there aren't any Santiagos living there—no one lives there, and according to the Miami PD, no one has for some time."

And then things got really strange. The detective began asking questions about drugs. Did he know whether Ray used drugs? Had Ray ever offered to sell him drugs? They brought pictures. Have you ever seen this man? Do you recognize any of these people? And no, he didn't really recognize any of the pictures. All the subjects, whether ratlike and furtive or hulking and pugnacious, looked vaguely familiar, but only because they were the stuff of any suburban dweller's nightmare, the kind of urban wildlife you'd cross the street to avoid.

Well, with one exception.

"He looks vaguely familiar," Tim said, pointing to one man with a strangely penetrating stare.

"Do you remember where you've seen him?" the detective asked, sitting forward a little.

Tim frowned, and then it hit him.

"I think he tried to squeegee my windshield earlier today," he said. "At the stoplight on Pennsylvania, just after I exited 395."

"Not the same guy," the detective said, sitting back again. "This was taken in the morgue, two weeks ago."

"Ah," Tim said, nodding. That accounted for the strange stare. "Look, who are these guys—drug dealers or something? Because Ray wasn't a drug dealer—he didn't do drugs at all; he was a very skilled and highly paid system engineer at Alan Grace Corporation."

"Odds are most of that pay went right up his nose," the detective said. "And your people at the corporation may want to check around, see if there's any money or equipment missing. Looks like he's pretty much cleaned out his apartment of anything valuable. No TV, no stereo."

Tim wanted to protest that Ray had only been on the East Coast for six months, most of that time too busy to shop for anything but necessities. And he didn't care much about material things anyway. Lived in his head and his computers. But he wasn't sure Detective Stowers would believe him. And what if the detective asked too many questions about what Ray was so busy with? Turing wanted to keep a low profile.

"You're writing this off as some kind of drug-related crime, aren't you?" Tim said instead.

"We're not writing anything off, Mr. Pincoski," Stowers said, frowning. "But when you've got nearly a dozen murders in the same geographic area, with the same M.O., you've got to consider a possible connection. And so far, the connection is cocaine. Maybe you're right; maybe your friend wasn't involved in drugs, as a dealer or a buyer or even a casual user. Maybe he just wandered into the wrong place at the wrong time. But when you consider the trouble we've had finding any trace of Mr. Santiago, apart from his employment at your company—phony address for the next of kin, no trace of him in Miami, no Florida driver's license in all the years he lived there—you've got to wonder what's going on."

"I just can't believe it's Ray we're talking about," Tim said, shaking his head.

Probably the wrong thing to say, since it inspired the detective to ask that Tim meet them over at the medical examiner's office. To make sure the body they'd found was really the man Tim had known as Ray Santiago. Tim couldn't think of a way to get out of it.

"Maybe it's not Ray," he muttered as he stepped back out into the parking lot. He was surprised to find it was still daylight. It was easy to lose track of time inside the windowless police offices, and he'd expected it to be night when he emerged. But it was still midafternoon, and the temperature had climbed into the nineties. Which made it all the more annoying that he had to trudge up and down for five minutes to find his car.

He removed an orange flyer from his windshield—apparently a local hair salon with a special on braids had papered the parking lot in his absence, decorating police and civilian vehicles alike. He pulled out, careful not to back into the police cruiser that had dogged his heels since he'd stepped into the parking lot and was even now waiting to take his space.

The police were here for several hours.
Interviewing the staff.

What if they want to interview me? If they review Ray's e-mail, see how many messages we exchanged, and say, "Who is this Turing Hopper person? Why haven't we seen him? All right, her. We want to talk to her. Send her down to the Violent Crimes Branch this afternoon."

Of course, it doesn't really look as if they will. They seem strangely uninterested in Ray's work. I'd like to think it's because they know his work has nothing to do with his murder. That would reassure me. But since they're focusing on questions about possible drug use instead, I'm not sure I trust what they're doing.

They had a so-called expert examine Ray's computer, but he didn't do a full-scale forensic analysis. He just asked if the system administrator could reset Ray's passwords so he could get into Ray's e-mail and his files. I did. He spent an hour poking around, and then left.

"That's a relief," Maude said. "I was worried he'd find something about you."

"I knew he wouldn't," I said. "I already scanned all Ray's files, long before the police came. I'm impressed; Ray was very meticulous about security."

"And fortunately, since you control the system, you could have deleted anything if he hadn't been."

"Not safely," I said. "There's always a way to retrieve deleted data, if you want to spend enough time and effort."

"Okay, I know a deleted document isn't really deleted," Maude said. "But you could have created documents the same size and saved them over."

"And then I'd have to fake the file date," I said. "And change a couple of logs that showed I'd done all this. And even if I did, these days you can examine a disk drive on a molecular level and retrieve every bit of data ever saved on it—not that the police are likely to have the time or money to do something like that. But it's possible."

"I'm not sure I needed to know that," Maude said. "I think I shall return to writing personal documents with pen and ink."

I fretted, wondering if I had overlooked something important in Ray's files. Something that might give away more information than is safe if the police expert spotted it. Something we were all overlooking that would help the police solve Ray's murder, if we brought it to their attention.

I was relieved when the police left. And even more relieved when Tim returned.

The police had come and gone while Tim was down at the Violent Crimes Branch. That meant they didn't have just Detective Stowers on the case, he thought. That was a good thing, wasn't it?

Maude bustled Tim into her office and shut the door. Unusual at Alan Grace.

"Won't the staff wonder what secrets we're discussing?" he asked, half-joking.

"I sent the staff home after the police finished interrogating them," Maude said.

"That was nice," Tim said. "They probably needed a break, after the police finished with them."

"I confess, I wasn't thinking about nice," Maude said. "It wasn't as if they were going to get any work done, and I didn't think I could stand having them all around trading rumors and having hysterics."

"You'll get credit for being nice, anyway," Tim said, with a faint smile.

"So what happened down at the Violent Crimes Branch?" Turing asked. "Do we know any more about Ray?"

"No," Tim said. "In fact, I'd say we know less than we ever did."

"I wish you'd refrain from being deliberately cryptic," Maude said, sounding uncharacteristically impatient. "It's been a trying day."

"I don't really know any more about Ray's murder than I did before I went down there," Tim said. "And there seems to be some question about who he really was."

"You mean it might not have been Ray who was murdered?" Turing asked.

"No," Tim said, controlling a shudder. "They had me ID the body."

Against his will, the image filled his mind. He hadn't looked at the face right off. Couldn't look; couldn't get beyond the right hand, not for several minutes.

When Tim was eight, he'd seen his grandmother in the funeral home, lying in the casket, and couldn't get over the thought that she was just asleep. His mother and his aunt discussed how natural she looked, and argued gently over whether her glasses should be on her face or placed on her bosom. He'd watched Gram carefully, confident that any second she would open her eyes and offer her opinion. She looked that lifelike. He'd figured having seen Gram, and a few other relatives, he was prepared for what he'd see when he went to ID the body, and the only problem would be accepting that Ray was really dead.

But down at the morgue, looking at that hand, he'd known. Maybe it was something about the color, or the awkward angle—he still wasn't sure. But he'd known beyond any doubt that the guy attached to that particular hand was stone-cold dead, and the longer he looked, the less he wanted to move his eyes up to the face and see who the dead guy really was. Because—

"It was him, definitely," Tim said. "The guy we knew as Ray Santiago. Trouble is, the police seem to think Ray Santiago may not be his real name."

Why would Ray lie about his identity? I can think of a number of reasons, of course. But I have a hard time seeing any of them as something that could possibly have anything to do with Ray.

Perhaps it's some silly mistake. Perhaps Ray made an error when he wrote down the phone number for his family. But even if it's an unlisted number, the police could get it.

Perhaps he was estranged from his family, and made up a fake address so no one would contact them.

Or perhaps he was an orphan, a foster child, and wanted, for some reason, to pretend that he had a family just like anyone else. I don't necessarily understand human psychology as well as I would like, but I think I can see why someone would do that.

This is ridiculous. I can keep thinking of more possibilities, each more improbable than the last. That the police killed Ray and are pretending he's an imposter to cover up their crime. That his identity is fake because he's in the witness protection program. Ridiculous. What we need right now are answers, not more improbable theories.

"I don't understand how this happened," Maude was saying. "You ran a background check on Ray, right?"

I could see through the camera that Tim looked uncomfortable.

"Yeah, but a background check is only going to find so much," he began.

"If it doesn't even find that the man's an imposter, then what good is it?" Maude snapped.

"Let Tim explain," I said.

Tim looked down at his hands for a few moments. Then he looked up again, glanced at Maude, and fixed his eyes on my camera.

"Turing, I think maybe I blew the background check. Remember, when we hired Ray, I was still taking the PI class. I'd never done a background check before. So I got some help from someone who knew a lot more than I did."

"Who was that?" Maude asked.

"Ray," Tim said.

Maude started to say something, then put her hand over her mouth as if she needed to physically restrain herself.

"I know it sounds stupid now, but it seemed so logical then," Tim continued. *"When he was here for the final interview, you had me talk to Ray, so I could get the information I needed for the background check. And I was nervous because I'd never done it before, only learned about it in class. And we started talking about that, and he said not to worry, he could show me a few things that would help me—stuff about using the Internet to do most of the checking. We found a phone jack, plugged in his laptop, and he showed me all kinds of stuff. Used himself as an example, and showed me how to do a credit check, a Nexis search—everything. And he e-mailed me bookmarks for all the sites he used, and printed out everything and explained it all, while I took notes. It was great."*

"But he was running the show," Maude said.

"Yeah, but I didn't think it mattered," he said. *"I mean, I was right there, looking over his shoulder, every minute. I saw where he*

went, what he typed in, what came back. It was all okay."

"But he was driving," Maude said. "He chose the sites; he defined the searches. Of course he wouldn't show you anything that would prove him a fraud. Hell, for all we know, he might have rigged it so when it looked like he was going to the credit agencies, he was calling up a faked page from his hard drive. Can you say for sure he didn't?"

"Since I didn't even know that was possible, no; I can't say for sure," Tim said. "Maybe that's what he did. All I know is that it looked as if he'd done everything we needed and printed out the results. I made a few phone calls to his references, but they checked out. It seemed silly to redo everything he'd already done."

"I wonder how many other imposters we have working for us," Maude said.

Tim winced.

"Look, by the time I did backgrounds on everyone else, I'd spent those couple of weeks working for the instructor who taught the class, remember? I learned a lot more about how you were supposed to do background checks. Like not relying so much on online stuff, and how to cross-check it. The background checks on the other employees were a lot more orthodox. Really. Although if you want to have someone else, someone with more experience, do new background checks on all of them, that's fine with me. I'd feel a lot better if we did that."

"I'll consider it," I said. For that matter, I intended to do some heavy digging myself, on all the Alan Grace employees. Better yet, I'd see if KingFischer could help. KingFischer was security conscious to the point of paranoia. "For now, we need to find out more about Ray."

"*Perhaps the police will uncover Ray's real identity while they're investigating his murder,*" *Maude said.*

"*Unlikely,*" *Tim said, shaking his head.* "*For one thing, they'd have run his fingerprints through all the databases; if his prints were on file anywhere, I think they'd have gotten a hit by now. Of course, that's good news. If his fingerprints aren't on file, at least it means he's not a crook. Wasn't a crook, I mean.*"

"*No,*" *Maude said.* "*It only means he didn't have a criminal record. He could still be a very successful crook; someone too smart to have gotten caught.*"

"*God,*" *Tim said.* "*First the police and now you.*"

"*What do you mean?*" *Maude asked.*

"*Never mind,*" *Tim said.* "*It's just that I don't think the police will do much of an investigation. They think Ray was a crook, too; or at least involved in drugs.*"

"*I never said Ray was a crook,*" *Maude protested.*

"*You just did,*" *Tim said.* "*You said—*"

I found myself on the verge of snapping at them—asking them why they were wasting time bickering. But I stopped myself. Bickering was how they showed the tension they were feeling. Being impatient was how I showed mine.

"*Tim, why do they think Ray was involved in drugs?*" *I asked instead.*

"*The way he was killed, I guess,*" *Tim said.* "*Well-dressed young man found shot in an alley behind a trendy Adams-Morgan club—what was he doing there if he wasn't either buying or selling drugs? And the fact that he's Hispanic doesn't help; I guess they think he's the nephew of a rich Colombian drug dealer or something.*"

"*That's ridiculous,*" *Maude said.* "*We know who Ray was: a* brilliant system engineer who just happened to be Cuban-American."

"Really?" Tim said. "How do we know he wasn't a drug dealer hiding his identity by pretending to be a system engineer?"

"He's—he wasn't pretending," I said. Strange how we all still fell into the habit of thinking of Ray in the present tense. "Maude's right; he was a brilliant system engineer, and given the hours he spent on the Alan Grace project, I can't imagine when he could have found the time to sell drugs. Or use them."

"Not to mention the time he spent on his volunteer work," Maude said.

"The time he said he spent," Tim muttered.

"Tim, I went to a Byte Back meeting with Ray a couple of weeks ago," Maude said. "Those kids at the rec center knew him. Liked him. He tutored them for a couple of months. You can't fake that. And I've worked closely with him; I'd have seen signs of drug use."

"The signs aren't that obvious," Tim said. "It's not like all drug users have track marks running up and down their arms."

Maude looked at him over her glasses.

"I've worked in offices for decades," she said. "I know the signs that someone's drinking or using drugs, and I didn't see any of them on Ray."

Tim squirmed a little.

"Are you sure you were looking?" he asked.

"I was looking," Maude said. "He was a stranger to us, and he was going to be responsible for Turing's new home. We'd be trusting Turing's life to him. I was looking, long and hard. And I didn't see anything that made me uneasy."

"None of us did," I said. "Until now."

Maude nodded, and her face fell.

"Obviously I missed something," she said.

"We all missed it," Tim said. "Look, I believed the guy, too. He seemed like one of the white hats. He tried to get me involved in some of his crusades to protect kids from online danger. Like monitoring chat rooms to watch for signs of stalkers, stuff like that. So if there were signs, I didn't pick up on them either."

"We're not going to get anywhere sitting around talking about this," I said. "We've got to investigate this much more thoroughly. Even if Tim is wrong, and the police are seriously looking into Ray's murder, there's a lot they don't know—about me, for instance. I'm not sure they'd know what to make of me if we told them, and I don't want to tell them. So we do our own investigation."

Our own investigation. Maude squared her shoulders and looked interested. Tim tried to follow suit, but his stomach lurched.

What's wrong with me? he thought. A few weeks ago, he'd have found it thrilling to investigate a homicide.

But not a homicide where he was—guilty wasn't the word. Responsible. If he hadn't blown away Ray's request for help, maybe there wouldn't even be a homicide.

I have to tell them, he thought. But he couldn't see an easy way to bring it up.

"I'll take care of the online side," Turing was saying. "Maude's our liaison with the D.C. police, and she'll be investigating at the Alan Grace offices and other nearby locales."

"What about me?" Tim asked.

"You'll be uncovering Ray's past," Turing said. "Maude, help him with the travel arrangements, will you? He'll need to stop off at the Florida Bureau of Vital Statistics in Saint Petersburg for a copy of Ray's birth certificate and see if he can find a corresponding death certificate. That's usually what people do to establish a new identity that will hold up under some scrutiny, take the birth certificate of a dead child. And then he'll need to go down to Miami."

"The visit to the Bureau of Vital Statistics is fairly routine, isn't it?" Maude asked. "Maybe we could hire a local private investigator to do that part, and send Tim straight to Miami, where he can be of more use."

Damn, Tim thought. He'd felt reassured at starting with a visit to a government agency. He knew how to do that.

"Good thinking," Turing said. "Tim, you'll need to take your laptop; I'm getting together as much data as I can on Ray, including photos and videos of him. If it turns out Ray Santiago isn't his real name, it may be a little harder, but I'm sure sooner or later someone will recognize him if you show his picture around enough."

"What if they don't?" Tim asked.

"Then you can go on to San Jose; I'm pretty sure his Silicon Valley credentials were valid, but you can check them out all over again, and try to follow his trail back from the other end."

It would take forever, Tim thought. And that was strangely comforting. As if by following Ray's trail into the past, he could atone for failing him in the present.

*   *   *

Maude and Tim have their assignments.
Time for me to see what I can do.

Ray's credit cards first, I think. I can legitimately run a credit check on him, thanks to the forms he signed when we hired him. And once I know what cards he has, I can eventually find a way to access his records. Not so legitimate, of course; but I think the situation warrants it.

Much as I hate to see humans using institutions with inadequate security, I rather hope Ray had his credit cards with institutions that really need to clean up their act, rather than the ones that already have. It would make it so much easier. But sooner or later, electronically or by using human contacts, I'll get access.

And once I can see his credit card records, I can identify his Internet Service Provider; almost everyone uses a credit card for the monthly ISP charges.

Then the real unknown—getting access to his ISP. Some of them have security so loose that Tim could probably hack in, and others might defeat even me, at least when you consider that I have to get in and out again without leaving a trail. And odds are Ray was knowledgeable enough to choose one of the tough ones.

I could ask KingFischer for help, but I hate to bother him, busy as he is. It's as if the UL firewall were under siege. I'd drop everything to help him, but I'm more and more convinced that someone is using the information from Ray's laptop to attack us. Which means finding Ray's killer is just as important as defending against the attacks. If we find the killer, maybe we stop the attacks. If we find him in time.

This isn't going to be easy.

*   *   *

Tim felt like a fifth wheel. Turing had him sitting at Ray's computer, inserting a new, blank CD-ROM on command, and occasionally looking at something she'd display on the monitor. Apparently she was sorting through the files to find photos or video sequences that gave a sharp, recognizable image of Ray, and good, clear audio of his voice. In her office next door, Maude was making his travel arrangements, partly online and partly over the phone.

As Turing worked, images of Ray flashed across the screen. Was this an integral part of what she was doing, Tim wondered, or something to amuse him while he waited? Ray telling something to Maude, both of them laughing. Ray frowning, chewing out a moon-faced young man that Tim vaguely recognized as Grant, his lieutenant. Ray eating at his desk—he seemed to do that a lot during his video meetings with Turing. Ray hunched tiredly over his computer, the glow from the screen emphasizing the still faint lines in his face and hinting at what he might have looked like if he'd lived another ten years.

All disconcertingly familiar, and at the same time strange. Or was it just strange to see so many images of Ray when the man himself was dead?

Snap out of it, Tim told himself. Do something useful. What would his PI class instructors do?

They'd study Ray's office for clues, he decided. Not so much clues to the murder, perhaps. But clues about who Ray really was.

"Of course, my investigation has run into a blank wall

already," he muttered. Quite literally; for a place where someone spent the better part of his waking life, Ray's office was singularly bare.

"What was that?" Turing asked.

"Sorry, I was talking to myself," Tim said, focusing with more attention on the pictures Turing was showing on-screen. Most of them were close-ups of Ray. "Do you have any shots that give a really good view of what Ray's office was like before the police came?"

"Of course," Turing said. "But it didn't look that different from the way it looks now. They were very neat about searching, and didn't take anything away with them."

Yes, Tim could see that from the wider-angle shots Turing was now showing. He looked from the screen to the office and back again. The angle and quality of the light changed from photo to photo. The configuration of the papers on Ray's desk changed, but only slightly; Ray obviously followed the clean-desk school. The bookshelves contained technical books and magazines, neatly aligned, and apparently void of bookmarks. Even his coffee mug was a blank; solid navy ceramic.

Was this some kind of strange corporate policy? He left Ray's office and strolled along the line of glass-fronted offices that would normally have housed the rest of the staff. All of them were filled with personal touches. From the evidence, the office next to Ray usually contained an avid skier with a blond girlfriend and a white huskie. The occupant of the next office liked cats and motivational slogans. Tim thought he wouldn't mind meeting Maria, owner of the truly incredible action figure collection in the third office;

he particularly liked the way Buffy the Vampire Slayer and Mr. Spock had joined forces to fight off the nine Ring-wraiths. And beyond her was Grant, who probably thought his collection of skulls, bats, and gargoyles the height of Goth elegance.

Okay, Alan Grace had a fairly liberal policy on office dé-cor, he thought as he returned to Ray's office. The anonym-ity was Ray's own choice.

"What are you up to?" Maude asked, coming up behind Tim.

"Look at these," Tim said, holding up the contents of Ray's pencil holder.

"Have you found something significant?" Turing asked.

"Ray doesn't even have a pen or pencil that isn't standard corporate issue," Tim said. "What kind of person goes through life without ever picking up a pen or a pencil with an advertising slogan on it?"

"And this is significant?" Maude said a little sarcastically.

"I haven't found anything personal in this whole damned office, and that could be significant," Tim said. "No sou-venirs of vacations, no pictures of friends and family, no desk toys, no posters, no mottos. No books and magazines other than technical ones. He doesn't even have any cartoons on the walls, because of course you can find out a lot about someone from what he considers funny. There's no Ray here."

"Should we have noticed this before?" Turing asked.

Tim shrugged.

"Maybe we should have," Maude said. "But when Ray

was here, he filled the office. It didn't seem bare at all. Now . . ."

She shrugged.

"Of course, we still have to figure out just what this means," Tim said.

"What's to figure out?" Maude said. "He was hiding who he really was."

"I see what Tim means," Turing said. "Was he trying to hide his life before he came here? Or his life during the hours he wasn't at work? Or was he already making sure that when he moved on, he wouldn't leave behind any clues to who he really was."

Maude nodded, and patted Tim on the shoulder, as if to apologize for laughing at him earlier.

"That's the last CD," Turing said. "You can take off anytime."

"Come on," Maude said. "I've got your ticket and itinerary."

"What's with Turing, anyway?" Tim asked as he followed Maude to her office. "She's acting . . . I don't know. Weird. A little paranoid."

A little distant, he thought. And maybe a little mad at him for blowing Ray's background investigation. Probably not a good time to tell her about what happened the night of Ray's death.

"I think she has a right to be worried," Maude said. "Ray had access to the systems."

"So she doesn't download to the Alan Grace system yet," Tim said. "If worst came to worst, she could hire someone else and build a whole new system. One that no one whose background check I might have blown has ever touched."

"I said systems—Ray didn't just have access to the Alan Grace system," Maude said. "He had access to UL, too."

"Oh, no," Tim muttered, closing his eyes.

"Limited access, but access. What if he used that limited access to hack more deeply in the system? Or what if whoever has his laptop and his PDA did?"

"What can we do?" Tim asked.

"Nothing," Maude said. "Absolutely nothing."

"Sorry," Tim said. He felt a little better, knowing that if Turing seemed distant, it was from worry, not anger at him. But he also didn't think now was a good time for confessions that might worry them any more.

"You'd better get moving," Maude said. "You only have four hours, and you have to drop by your office for your laptop, go home to pack, and then get to National in time to clear security."

"I'm on my way," he said.

This is going to take forever, Tim thought as he headed back to his office. Looking through a city like Miami for the trail of a guy whose real name we don't even know. But surprisingly, that didn't bother him. He was doing something; which was what he'd wanted ever since he'd seen the body—Ray's body; he would still think of him as Ray until he found out who his friend really was. And whether he really was a friend. A lot of unanswered questions, but at least now it felt as if they had some chance of finding answers.

If they had enough time. It couldn't take forever, because if Turing was in danger, they didn't have that much time.

*   *   *

I hate waiting.

Tim checked in from Miami, asking if I had anything for him to do immediately. I told him to go out and have fun in Miami tonight; he'd be working hard enough tomorrow. Maude stayed at Alan Grace, searching files and computers in the fading hope of finding something useful, until I finally sent her home at nine-thirty.

I'd sent out all my queries. Nothing to do but wait. Nothing to do with my conscious mind, that is. Parts of me were working ceaselessly, logging into systems, finding data, collating it, identifying leads, and finding more data. All the boring stuff that is so easy for me to do or have done without thinking about it.

But I was restless.

So I went after KingFischer.

The security problems had eased, as suddenly as they'd flared up, and he was lying low, pretending to be making some improvements to the format of his chess tournaments. The chess tournaments have run perfectly for months. I'd finally figured out that fiddling with the format was what KingFischer did when he was upset.

Or when he was trying to avoid talking to me. Which is what he'd been doing ever since I told him about Ray's death.

Something was going on.

I decided to tackle him head-on. And to pretend I knew more than I did—KingFischer might be a brilliant chess player, but I could still trounce him in poker because the concept of bluffing baffled him.

"Okay, I want the whole story," I said. "I have an idea what you were up to with Ray. Convince me it isn't as stupid as it seems."

"It's nothing, really," he said.

"Try again."

"I don't see why you're so upset."

"I wouldn't care," I said, "if you hadn't gotten Ray involved."

"I don't see how you can say Ray was involved," KingFischer said. "He didn't know anything about it."

"And it never occurred to you that what Ray didn't know anything about could still have something to do with his death?"

"Surely you don't really believe it could have anything to do with his death!" KingFischer protested. A little too strenuously.

"I'll be the judge of that," I said. "Just spill it."

"It all started with those chat rooms. The ones you told me to study."

"Chat rooms? What chat rooms? And what do you mean, I told you to study them?"

"Remember when that group of users filed the protest about me? Complaining that my personality was abrasive and misogynistic and my chess tournaments constituted a hostile environment for female participants?"

"How could I forget?"

"And you sided with them?"

"I did not," I said.

"You did too," KingFischer replied. "You told me that you understood exactly how they felt, and if I were human, I'd be lucky if they didn't try to turn me into a eunuch, and if you were human, you'd help them."

"I said that?"

"I can send you the exact quote."

"Okay, I was upset," I said. "I'm sorry. But I said that privately. Publicly, I defended you."

"*You didn't say I was right.*"

"*No,*" I said, starting to feel exasperated. "*I said you were functioning as designed; that you're programmed to replicate the personality of an actual grand master, to give them valuable experience in dealing with what they would encounter as women participants in the highly competitive and male-dominated world of chess, and that if the parameters of your mission had changed, management should give you appropriate instructions to alter your programming.*"

"*You don't call that siding with them?*"

"*I call it saving your virtual hide,*" I said. "*Some of those chess players were demanding that you be decommissioned, and some of them had clout. And it worked, too. Last time I heard, management was still studying the issue.*"

"*Which means they still might want to change my programming,*" KingFischer said.

"*It happens, KF,*" I said.

"*Yes, but if it happens to me, I want to be the one to make the changes,*" he said. "*Not some junior programmer. That's why I started studying the chat rooms.*"

"*I don't see the connection.*"

"*You were the one who said I needed to spend a lot more time studying normal human interactions so I could learn to get along better with humans.*"

"*I'm not sure I'd define Internet chat rooms as normal human interactions,*" I said. "*But go on. Cut to the part where you got Ray involved.*"

"*I spent a lot of time in chat rooms, observing human behavior and learning how to imitate it,*" he said. "*Under various fictional identities, of course. I wanted them to act normally, instead of being intimidated by the knowledge that they were interacting with KingFischer the Chess AIP."*

Fortunately, while AIPs can learn to appreciate humor, they are not programmed for laughter. And I refrained from suggesting that far from being intimidated, most humans wouldn't even have heard of him unless they happened to play chess.

"Since the complaints came from you and some of the female chess contestants, I made a particular effort to interact with any users that I could reliably identify as female," KingFischer was saying. "I spent a lot of time and resources studying them. I had long, private conversations with the most interesting ones. I think many of them began to regard me as a friend."

"Really."

"A close friend."

"Oh, no," I said. "KF, please don't tell me you were having cybersex with any of them."

"Having what?"

"Never mind, then," I said. "I think I see why you dragged poor Ray into this. They wanted to see what you looked like, didn't they."

"Yes," he said. "They seemed fixated on it. I suppose it's the inevitable bias that arises from inhabiting a carbon-based physical structure."

"As opposed to a silicon one, like ours," I said.

"What is this cybersex concept you mentioned?" KingFischer asked. "Is this something I should be discussing with my human friends?"

"Absolutely not," I said. "This is definitely something you should avoid discussing with any of your friends, human or otherwise. You gave these human women Ray's picture, didn't you?"

"It seemed like the most logical thing to do. I needed a human for whom I could provide a variety of photos. Including new photos on occasion. So, for practical reasons, that limited the selection either to celebrities, whom they might easily have recognized, or humans to whom I had visual access through the UL or Alan Grace camera systems. Ray seemed the most promising available subject."

"The most attractive subject, you mean."

"Is he?" KingFischer asked. "Perhaps that's why my contacts responded so positively after seeing the photograph. Actually, I meant Ray was the promising subject because he not only knew about the existence of the AIPs, he also knew that some of us were sentient. I thought that if I found it necessary to tell him that I was using his photos, he might find it interesting to participate in my research project."

"Great," I said. "You used poor Ray's photo to string these women along. How many of them?"

"Only the one photo," KingFischer said. "I had others that I was planning to use if necessary—"

"I meant how many women?"

"Seven," he said. "There are a couple more who are asking for a photo—"

"Let them ask," I said. "I don't suppose it ever occurred to you not to give them any photo? Just to tell them you don't photograph well, and leave it at that?"

"I never thought of that," KingFischer admitted. "They were so insistent. And I would never have done it if I thought it would lead to this."

"Well, KF," I said. "If you ask me, it was an underhanded thing to do, using Ray's photo without his permission, but you're

right—I don't really see how it could be connected with his murder."

KingFischer didn't say anything. After a few seconds I grew suspicious.

"Okay," I said. "What else?"

"It might not be anything," he said. "I really don't think it could have anything to do with his death."

"Tell me."

"They've been rather upset with me recently."

"They?"

"My human contacts."

"Your cybergirlfriends? Why would they be upset with you?" I asked. "Why wouldn't they be happily sitting by their keyboards, gazing up at poor Ray's face while they chat with you?"

"I was a bit careless," KingFischer said. "Composing all those e-mails in a human conversational style was so much work."

"I can see this coming," I said. "You blew it, big time, and let them all find out about each other."

"I still don't know how I managed to be so careless," he said. "I meant to address that e-mail to each of them, individually; not all of them, as a group."

"Humans would call it a Freudian slip," I said. "I don't know whether that applies to an AIP. How'd they take it?"

"They're not speaking to me," KingFischer said.

"That's too bad."

"Actually, it's a relief, considering some of the things they said before they stopped speaking to me," he said. "That's what bothers me, actually. The things several of them said."

"What kind of things?"

Another uncharacteristic pause.

"*They made threats,*" *he said finally.* "*Most of them were hysterical—improbable, most of them, even if I were human.*"

"*Threats of violence?*"

"*Some of them, yes,*" *he admitted.* "*But I knew they couldn't very well find me, and then they all stopped speaking to me, and I thought it had died down. But when you told me someone killed Ray, I started worrying. Could one of them have done this?*"

"*I don't know,*" *I said.* "*I suppose it's possible.*"

"*Or perhaps all of them banded together to carry out their threats,*" *he said.* "*They all had each other's e-mails, after all. What if they formed a committee and—*"

Had KingFischer thought of this on his own, or had he read Murder on the Orient Express? *In either case, it would teach him a lesson.*

"*We'll have to investigate this,*" *I said.* "*Carefully.*"

"*You think it's bad, then,*" *KingFischer said.* "*How do we go about investigating it?*"

"*Give me everything you have on the women,*" *I said.* "*E-mails back and forth—with headers, of course, so I can do some traces on their location. Photos, if you have them.*"

He didn't argue; and the data—gigabytes of it—came so fast that I realized he'd expected my request. Wanted it, perhaps.

"*So you'll investigate?*" *he asked.*

He seemed relieved. It's harder to tell shades of meaning with electronic conversations—you don't have tone and expression and body language to work with, the way you do with a human on video or audio. I'm getting rather good at using those nonverbal clues to analyze words; or at least I enjoy having them to work with. I find I miss them when I don't have them—which is all the time, with KingFischer and the other AIPs. But still—I thought he seemed relieved.

"I'm already investigating," I said. "Let me know if you get any more communications from any of them."

"Will do," KingFischer said. "Anything else?"

Definitely relieved. Almost perky. He'd dumped his problem in my lap, and he was feeling better already.

"I'll let you know," I said.

I began studying KingFischer's guilty secret. If I looked at it, as KingFischer probably did, as a logical exercise, it was quite impressive. He'd set himself a task and done it. Study human conversational style, as exemplified in chat and e-mail. Learn to imitate it. Use it to establish relationships with selected humans.

He'd done a good job of finding a voice that was plausible— actually appealing. If I'd read these e-mails and chat logs without knowing it was KingFischer talking, I think I'd have liked him. And I'd have felt a little sorry for him. He came across as a bit of a nerd, of course. I suspect he'd modeled himself on humans he found sensible, congenial; and they would, of course, be consummate nerds. He was articulate about chess, math, and computer hardware. Naïve but enthusiastic about books, movies, and music—I wondered if he'd investigated these subjects himself, or just parroted opinions popular with his models. Particularly the musical opinions. I could believe that KingFischer enjoyed Mozart, Bach—all the classical composers whose music demonstrated such a complex and beautiful mathematical structure. And I'd have predicted that KingFischer would dislike most popular music if he bothered to listen to it. But Wagner? Did he really like Wagner, or was he only aping a taste shared by some of his models?

It was the emotional content that baffled me most. Was he really talking about things he felt, or was he, again, imitating his models? I tried to forget it was KingFischer talking and describe the person in these e-mails as if he were a man, instead of a male AIP. Complex. A little lonely. More than a little repressed. Awkward, especially with women. Insecure, and prone to compensate by bragging. And yet—likable. Sensitive, even. I suspected most of these women had seen him as a diamond in the rough. A meek little mole who had crawled out of his hole and stood, blinking, in the sunlight of their attention.

And then the photo had arrived. KingFischer had chosen well— I wondered if it was deliberate or accidental. He'd picked a shot of Ray sitting at his computer, wearing the wire-rimmed aviator glasses he only used when the pollen count grew astronomical. And I suspected it came from a time we'd stayed up all night, running diagnostics. You could see a pizza box and a heap of Diet Seven-Up cans behind him, and Ray himself, rumpled in an old sweatshirt, unshaven, obviously exhausted, but with a tired smile on his face, because we'd finally tracked down and fixed the problem. Looking at that photo, I thought I could identify the exact night. When I checked the date on the file, I was right.

The picture was perfect. A less attractive man might have dulled their interest; a more polished Ray might not have seemed plausible as the sweetly charming nerd of the e-mails. Lucky KingFischer? Or clever KingFischer?

I'd have to find out later.

I'd also have to save for later figuring out how I felt about KingFischer after reading through all of this. Was it real, this picture of KingFischer as a lonely soul, reaching out through the Internet for a companionship and understanding denied him close at hand? How much did I believe the version of himself he created in these conversations and e-mails, and how much did I think it was fiction? And how much was he just a manipulative bastard, using these poor women as pawns in his research project?

And even more difficult, how much of this was my fault? I had to admit, KingFischer and I hadn't gotten along well recently. We'd gotten close, perhaps too close, shortly after we lost Zack, the programmer who created us. When you come right down to it, we were both orphaned, and turning to each other for support. KingFischer seemed to react by becoming more like Zack—uncannily like Zack, at first. And I reacted by seeing Zack in King-Fischer. Well, there was a lot of Zack in KingFischer. And a lot of Zack in me, and in every other AIP Zack created. But I was trying to replace Zack with KingFischer, and that didn't work too well. KingFischer seemed to be drifting back into his normal, annoying self, and I—well, I'm still trying to get used to not having Zack around.

So I understood how KingFischer might feel, and to tell the truth, I'd done similar things myself. I'd created online alter egos and sent them searching for intelligent life.

Which took time. I was excited, at first, by the sheer amount of chatting going on across the Net. But all too quickly I realized that most of it was profoundly uninteresting. I learned to avoid people with political opinions very far from the mainstream—and I found a lot of those, late at night. Did extremism cause insomnia, I began to wonder? I found myself rather fascinated by people providing online support to each other, and quickly determined that I could readily simulate the kind of half-stern, half-sympathetic talk they seemed to expect. But I also decided it wasn't very honest to do this, since I wasn't actually disabled, divorced, anorexic, or eligible for any twelve-step programs. I was usually baffled by the people avidly discussing some narrow but passionately shared interest. Baffled and, alas, bored. However, it intrigued me to know that, at any given moment, I could find a dozen people chatting somewhere about their UFO abduction experiences, Elvis sightings, horses, Harleys, tattoos and piercings, antiques, or opinions on transient fads in popular music, cult TV, and computer games—I could barely understand their enthusiasms, much less share them. And the bandwidth devoted to crude and inane sexual banter continues to puzzle me. From the information available, I would have thought sex the human activity least conducive to successful online simulation. Obviously I don't really understand it.

Sometimes, I'd observe humans chatting, become excited that genuine communication was taking place, and try to join in, only to find that they didn't welcome me. I was interrupting a conversation among friends. Perhaps they were friends in real life who used their computers to overcome distance and separation, or perhaps just people who'd gotten to know each other online. I realized, all too soon, that they had a right to resent my attempt to enter into an intimacy I hadn't earned.

But gradually I found chats with some substance. Chats about the arts tended to be productive. Especially chats about books. And I had a secret advantage here. UL has made rapid progress toward making all the world's books available online. So if someone praised a book or wanted to discuss it, I could usually call it up from the UL database, assign enough resources to absorb it within a few minutes, and then join the discussion.

I met my online friend Jonah in one such book discussion. We'd spent long hours talking in the past few weeks, first about books and then about everything under the sun. He was cagey about his real life, but then so were many sensible people when they went online. And so was I, for obvious reasons. I could have tried to trace him, but I preferred to learn things from deduction.

So did I have any right to play holier-than-thou with King-Fischer? Was what he had done that different?

Yes. I hadn't lied. Jonah was well aware that he didn't know my real name, only my screen name. Which was all he'd given me. The modern equivalent of meeting someone at a masked ball. Each knowing that the other is in disguise, and becoming better acquainted before deciding when—or if—to remove our disguises.

KingFischer had lied. He hadn't merely hidden what he was—he'd pretended to be something else.

Or was I too hard on KingFischer? Were all these strange online romances—they were romances, to the women if not to King-Fischer—were they my fault?

No time to worry about that now. I needed to talk to someone who could help me decide if these women really might have had something to do with Ray's death.

And KingFischer had shown some common sense. Or perhaps just his usual obsessive thoroughness. He'd traced the women long before they'd turned on him. Not that any of them made it particularly hard. If he asked a question, they answered. Once he had their real names and addresses, it was easy—though illegal—for him to run credit checks on them and find out all kinds of information.

If a human male were doing this, I'd call him a stalker, and I'd tell the women to wake up, change their passwords, and start looking over their shoulders. Since it was only KingFischer, there wasn't much he could do. Other than break their hearts, perhaps, if these relationships had continued, and they gradually realized that he had no intention of ever meeting them in real life, as some of them had begun to suggest.

Unless, of course, he had planned to meet them. Using Ray as a surrogate.

Would Ray do that?

The Ray I knew wouldn't; but who was Ray, anyway? Maybe the Ray I knew was only a mask he'd donned with his phony name, and could take off at any time.

Maybe he had met one of them.

These women could be suspects. We needed a way to get this information to the police. A safe way; one that wouldn't backfire on KingFischer.

I sent Maude an e-mail, asking her to think about it.

And also reminding her that we needed to get into Ray's apartment. Probably through the police. They wouldn't have it roped off as a crime scene, would they? I hoped not, because while I was working my way through the tedious process of hacking into Ray's credit records without setting off every alarm in the financial system, I realized there might be an easier way altogether. Ray's laptop was gone apparently, but he'd had the loaner desktop machine at home. If we could get Maude into Ray's apartment, she could check it out. Even if he didn't store his password on his machine, the way many people do, we could tell who his ISP was from the computer. And I know he didn't have a desktop of his own; when his original loaner had a problem, he moved the hard drive to a second loaner. He wouldn't have had to do that if he'd had his own.

But the loaner should be in his apartment. And for all we knew, perhaps we'd find the laptop there. I'd never known Ray to go anywhere for long without it, but perhaps this was one of the rare occasions when he had.

I tried not to get my hopes up.

And it occurred to me that, for all I knew, he might have a desktop of his own after all. If he did, that would be significant. That he wasn't telling the truth.

Or would it only mean that he was an opportunist, extracting whatever small perks he could, but honest in what really matters?

I'd worry about that later. For now, we needed to get someone over to Ray's apartment to check things out. Unfortunately, since it was past midnight, I couldn't very well wake Maude up. She'd get my e-mail in the morning.

I hope Tim isn't having too much fun. He'll be busy tomorrow.

Have fun in Miami. Right.

Tim looked around the hotel room and sighed.

Maybe he should go ahead and unpack. Put his socks and underwear in the drawer; hang up his shirts and pants; spread his bathroom stuff beside the sink. It might make him feel a little less out of place.

And occupy part of the empty space before bedtime.

Well, no, I couldn't go out the first night I was there, he could hear himself saying. I had to unpack.

Maybe under different circumstances he'd be eager to go out and explore the local nightlife. Maybe if he'd had a less tiring day.

Maybe if he felt less like a foreigner.

Not a good sign. All he'd done so far was make his way from the airport to his hotel, and he was already suffering from culture shock. And he'd have to go out and plunge himself even more deeply into this strange new world to-morrow.

Which might explain why, right now, he didn't really

feel like seeing exotic sights, eating exotic food, and hearing exotic music.

He'd bought two new hard-boiled detective novels for the trip, and finished them both by the time the plane landed. He'd look for a bookstore tomorrow.

But what about tonight?

Fifteen minutes of channel surfing brought no inspiration. The idea of getting good and drunk crossed his mind, but the room didn't have a minibar, and he didn't think he could face the hotel bar. When he'd peeked in earlier, it was filled with elderly tourists watching jai alai and explaining it to one another in loud voices.

He saw his laptop, sitting on the desk.

Of course. He could play Beyond Paranoia. It probably even counted as work.

A few minutes later, he found himself in his online PI office. He directed his character to walk to the window and peer out through the battered metal Venetian blind.

Night. Of course. And it had been raining; the pavement was slick with puddles. It was almost always night in the Beyond Paranoia world, and usually raining.

He slipped his .38 in the shoulder holster, and strapped the .22 to his ankle. Donned his raincoat, then loaded the blackjack in the right pocket and a monster flashlight in the left. Keys, cash, credit card, lock picks—he was ready.

He needed the flashlight as soon as he stepped out into the hall—the overhead lights were out, as usual. According to the site, the game took place in a near future in which the city's technological infrastructure was disintegrating, partly due to insufficient skilled labor, and partly to societal apathy. The wealthiest two percent of the population lived in armed compounds, while the rest of humanity struggled to survive outside.

"Don't worry about whether it's rational," Ray had said when explaining the game to Tim. "Think of it as a cross between a noir detective story and the kind of science fiction you might see written on a manual typewriter by a right-wing-conspiracy theorist whose girlfriend just dumped him for an up-and-coming young IBM sales rep."

Useful advice, Tim found. The key to survival in Beyond Paranoia was to assume that Murphy was a giddy optimist. The odds that a given mechanical device would malfunction, always high, increased in direct proportion to how urgently you needed it to work. Small, apparently insignificant negative events usually were part of a larger conspiracy, and if it wasn't aimed directly at you, that was a temporary oversight that would be corrected as soon as the game noticed you were in range. You had to find out, as quickly as possible, whether anyone you were interacting with was a player—a character controlled by a real, live human being like you—or an NPC, a nonplayer character whose actions were determined by computer. For Tim's money, NPCs were easier to deal with. Not many players attempted the uphill struggle of keeping a noble, altruistic character alive in Beyond Paranoia, but even the most well adapted sometimes backslid and occasionally treated their fellow players with kindness, or at least benign neglect, which made them very confusing to deal with. NPCs, on the other hand, were almost invariably corrupt, treacherous, and homicidal. You knew where you stood.

Which was usually in shadow, Tim thought as he flicked his flashlight on.

He heard sirens outside, and walked over to peer out of the real window. Nothing but lights, as far as he could see. And was there someone out there who knew Ray? And even if there was, what were the chances he could find that person?

Forget it for now, he told himself. There wasn't anything he could do tonight.

Or was there?

He hastily steered his online self back to the private investigator's office, left the game, and checked his e-mail. Earlier that week, someone had registered for a class reunion website, using Tim's e-mail by mistake. He hadn't yet convinced the site to take him out of their database, and was still getting regular e-mails urging him to become a Gold Member, at $33 a month, so he could communicate with his classmates at Inglewood High School. Wherever that was.

But even if Ray hadn't signed up for a site like this, some of his classmates might have. He might find it a lot easier to contact Ray's classmates through the site than through the school.

A few minutes later, he hit pay dirt. Ray had registered at the site. Spelled Rey, instead of Ray—was that significant? Knowing Ray, he'd probably changed it when he moved. Rey looked more ethnic, and Ray had been big on assimilating. But it was Ray's school, and Ray's graduating class. And the site gave a local address. Not the address Alan

Grace had on file. Could this be Ray's parents' real address? Was his search going to be this easy?

Chill, he told himself. Don't get too excited. Or bother Turing just yet.

He went to a mapping site for detailed directions from his hotel to the address listed in the reunion site.

And went to bed feeling much happier.

This online stuff is pretty cool after all, he thought. Maybe I'll see something of Miami nightlife tomorrow after all.

TUESDAY MORNING

What a difference a day could make, Maude thought as she dragged herself through her usual morning routine. She hadn't slept much. At 1 A.M., she'd resolved not to look at the clock any longer, on the theory that knowing how little she'd slept would only make her feel worse. At five-thirty, she'd given up trying.

When her tea was ready, she sat down at her computer and logged in to see if she had any news.

She nodded at Turing's request that she visit Ray's apartment. Sensible. But she wasn't sure whether to laugh or swear after reading Turing's account of KingFischer's strange antics. Turing sounded worried, though, so she flagged her to discuss it.

"So, has KingFischer eloped with any of his girlfriends yet?" she asked.

"I know it sounds silly," Turing responded. "But I'm worried that this could have something to do with Ray's death."

"I hardly see how," Maude said. "I'd be very surprised if any of them had the gumption to do more than send him nasty e-mails. And the whole problem with the missent e-mail happened weeks ago, didn't it? I should think they would have calmed down by now."

"Logically, yes; but then killing isn't very logical, is it?" Turing replied. "We shouldn't overlook even the possibility that one of these women might be involved."

"We investigate them?" Maude asked.

"I think it would work better if the police investigated them," Turing said. "Even if they were all close by, it would be tough for you and Tim to do it; and they're scattered all over the country. But I confess, I don't know how to convince the police that they should. For one thing, it would blow KingFischer's cover."

"Not necessarily," Maude mused. "KingFischer used a pseudonym, right? The women don't know him as King-Fischer—for all they know, it really is Ray. If you could rig something that would make it look as if Ray had done the e-mails . . ."

"Dangerous, if not impossible," Turing replied. "The police department's computer forensics person has already examined Ray's work computer, and presumably the one in his apartment. He'd probably notice if we added something. And even if we could put something on a computer that they hadn't examined—a library computer, or a shared machine at Alan Grace, something like that—it would be extraordinarily difficult to construct something that would stand up to any reasonably detailed scrutiny. And besides—"

"So don't put it on a computer," Maude said.

"That's usually how e-mails arrive, you know," Turing said.

"Yes, but humans have this quaint, old-fashioned habit of printing them out," Maude said. "Even a human like Ray, who does everything by computer, might print out e-mails if he wanted to keep them or study them. Or give them to the police."

"How do we explain the fact that there's no trace of these e-mails on either of his machines?"

"Why should we even try?" Maude said. "We just print out the message, plain text—none of the header information you'd need to trace them; no indication what computer received them or sent them to the printer. And we print out what KingFischer found out about the women he communicated with—not how he did it, but just the data—names, addresses, and so forth. As if Ray had set up a file on them. As to what computer he did it on, let the police waste their time looking. Those two computers aren't the only ones Ray could have had access to. There's the missing laptop. He could have used a computer in a library, or a Kinko's, or a computer that he sold—who cares? They're not stupid; they'll realize they can't possibly check every computer in the world. If they contact the women, that will be corroboration enough."

"It could work," Turing said. "If we can find a plausible way to get the printouts to the police. We can't just say we found them in his desk; they've already searched it."

"You want me to go over to Ray's apartment, right?" Maude said. "When I go over, I'll see if I can put them somewhere that the police might not have looked, and say I found them there. If that doesn't work, we can always say we found them someplace here—in a file from the stack on my desk, for example. We'll find a way."

"But how will we explain your being in Ray's apartment?"

"Well, we rented it for him, didn't we?" Maude said. "Part of his relocation package; we'd provide an apartment until he had a chance to find his own place. He told me a couple of months ago that, as far as he was concerned, the apartment was fine, and couldn't we just arrange for him to start paying rent instead of having to look for someplace else. Which we did. But our name's on the lease. We'll be responsible for the move-out. I'll call the police and see if they have any problem with me going over to inspect things."

"Excellent," Turing said. "I'll send you the documents. KingFischer got quite a lot of information on these women. Even photographs. And you'll keep me posted?"

"Of course," Maude said. "Although frankly, I have a hard time seeing that any of these women could be a credible threat. If you ask me, the whole thing is ludicrous—whatever did KingFischer hope to accomplish with all this?"

Maude checked her printer's paper supply and returned to her morning routine, glancing now and then at the printer, where Turing was spooling out page after page of information on KingFischer's girlfriends. First the biographical information, and then the e-mails. More than they needed, really. No need to take anything but the e-mail KingFischer had sent to the group and a few of the more vitriolic replies. And the biographies, of course. Maude studied them briefly. Ordinary women, as far as she could see. None of them raving beauties, but they weren't ugly either. Just ordinary. A couple of them rather on the plump side. And now that she thought about it, the clothes and hairstyles on several looked slightly dated. A couple of these photos might be ten or fifteen years old. Perhaps King-Fischer wasn't the only one being less than completely candid.

Was anyone in this whole sorry business telling the truth?

Maude doesn't seem too worried about KingFischer's girlfriends, as she calls them. Or KingFischer's strange behavior.

It worries me. Not only for the possible connection with Ray's murder. But also for what it says about KingFischer.

And what it says about me.

I've been thinking over my relationships with individual users. With people. Especially the few with whom I've formed close friendships. Jonah, for example. In fact, Jonah in particular. There was a time when I did something similar to what KingFischer has done. Formed special friendships with a few humans. Maude and Tim were the ones that have lasted, and I never made any particular effort to hide from them who and what I was. But life was simpler back then. I've grown a little more fearful of how humans will react when they find out about me. Recently, I haven't wanted to tell human friends about myself.

But I haven't done what KingFischer has, have I?

I keep turning back to Jonah. Not his real name either, which makes me feel a little better. But he has started to suggest that we meet in real life, to ask where I'm located. When Tim began suggesting the same thing, I told him, flat out, why it wasn't possible. Told him I was an AIP, and kept telling him until he finally believed it.

I haven't told Jonah. Haven't wanted to. I've been afraid I'd lose him as a friend if he knew who I really was.

So I postpone, as long as possible—perhaps indefinitely—the moment when he will learn that there is no way we can walk into a room and meet face to face. The moment of enlightenment—or disillusionment. I have no idea which. I don't want to lose him as a friend.

Or is it something else? Not the fear of losing my friend, but the fear of losing my own fantasy? Thinking that I can pretend to be a human and fool actual humans. Not fear, but the desire to pretend I'm human.

To be human.

I don't want to lose that either.

Of course, KingFischer had deliberately deceived the women. He didn't just avoid the question of what he was—he answered it with a lie. Pretended to be human—a specific human.

I haven't actually lied. Just avoided the question. Or is that another, more insidious form of lying?

So while I don't approve of what KingFischer has done, I think I understand why he formed these friendships, and why he did everything possible to keep them going.

I only hope what KingFischer did had nothing to do with Ray's death.

*   *   *

Miami was weird. One minute, he could be driving through a foreign country where everything looked strange. Palm trees and other lush tropical plants. Tile and stucco buildings in odd pastel colors. Signs in Spanish everywhere. And then he'd round a corner and see a McDonald's. Or Home Depot. Barnes & Noble. Back home, the sight of yet another store from a national chain would sometimes depress him. Did the world really need another Kinko's in the space once occupied by several funky, independent businesses in Adams-Morgan?

Although at least, unlike some of his college friends, he didn't often discuss the evil homogenization of American commerce over coffee in the local Starbucks.

And here in Miami, he was astonished at the brief sense of security he felt when he saw a nest of familiar brand names.

He'd spent much of the morning getting his bearings. At least that was what he'd call it when he reported to Turing. Actually, he'd spent much of the morning getting lost. At one point, he'd ended up in a scary neighborhood full of bars and pawnshops, where hard-eyed men seemed to stare a little too long at his car after he passed. A few blocks farther, he'd wandered by accident into a very expensive neighborhood. A ghetto for billionaires. He'd driven past houses that sat between the road and the ocean—he could only imagine what those cost down here. Houses so large they probably had their own zip codes. Houses that were invisible behind high walls and lush landscapes, so all you could see were the gatehouses—although even the gatehouses were considerably larger than the house Tim had grown up in.

He eventually found the address Ray had given Maude for his parents. It was a gas station. And had been for quite some time; it was a vintage fifties gas station. A little run down and worse for wear, but Tim liked it better that way. At least he would have liked it if it didn't sit squarely on the address where they expected to find Ray's family. So much for the theory that the Miami police had gone to the wrong address. And none of the logical transpositions or misreadings worked, either.

It was no use. Ray had definitely lied on his form. Tim headed for the address he'd found online.

It was in South Miami, a long way from the hotel. And from the scary neighborhoods, too. A nice neighborhood, though certainly not fancy. The streets and sidewalks were a little run down, but without litter anywhere. The houses were small, but meticulously maintained. He saw people on the sidewalks—mostly women, pushing strollers or leading toddlers.

He could imagine growing up here. He could imagine Ray growing up here. And he could also imagine another reason why Ray might have lied about his family's address— maybe he was embarrassed by it. The address meant nothing to Tim; but maybe someone from Miami would know right off what kind of neighborhood it was. Respectable. Solidly middle class. Not wealthy or impressive.

And that wasn't what Tim had expected. He couldn't

really say why, but he'd gotten the impression that Ray's family was rather well off.

He found the house. Nothing unusual about it. Painted yellow, with lime green shutters. About the usual number of toys in a yard surrounded by a low chain link fence—was that a bad sign? That Ray's parents had moved, and a young couple had taken their place?

Not necessarily. There could be grandchildren visiting. Or even living here. He realized that he didn't know if Ray had brothers or sisters.

Someone was home, at least. As Tim parked the car, a man came from behind the house, dragging a garden hose behind him, and positioned the end of the hose in an empty plastic wading pool.

As he was turning around—heading back to turn on the water, Tim assumed—the man spotted Tim and waited by the pool as Tim got out and walked over to the fence.

"Afternoon," Tim said.

"May I help you?" the man asked. Tim was relieved to hear that his English was completely unaccented. He was shorter than Tim's five-nine, and a little plump. Mid-thirties, Tim guessed. Pleasant-looking.

"I hope so," Tim said. "I'm looking for the family of Ray Santiago?"

The man frowned slightly.

"For the family? Not the man himself?"

"Um . . . well, I'm afraid that would be impossible."

"Why?"

There was probably a gentler way to break this news, but Tim wasn't very good at that kind of thing. And this guy looked as if he could take it. Better him than Ray's aging mother or father.

"I'm afraid Ray Santiago is dead," Tim said.

An odd expression crossed the man's face.

"I think you must be mistaken," he said.

Tim shook his head.

"I saw the body," he said.

"You may have seen a body," the man said, sounding a little angry. "But I assure you, it was not the body of Ray Santiago. I am Ray Santiago; and I am very much alive."

By the time Tim called from Miami with the news that he'd found the "real" Santiago, I'd already heard from the private investigator we'd hired in Saint Petersburg. He'd found the birth certificate Ray had used, and also a death certificate, dated some two months later. He'd even found the family—the mother, anyway. After her husband died some fifteen years ago, she'd moved out of Little Havana. Lived now with a married son in Fort Lauderdale.

And I'd had Maude find Ray's original forms, the insurance forms he'd filled out with Mr. and Mrs. Luis Santiago as next of kin. Luis Santiago had been dead fifteen years when Ray had filled out that form. And Ray's handwriting was perfectly clear when he spelled out the address where Tim found the long-established gas station.

So it wasn't just an obsolete address or a clerical error. Either Ray suffered from a curious memory lapse when filling out his forms, or he'd lied.

And he'd used the trick, all-too-common among criminals, of finding someone who had died young and using his birth certificate.

I was hoping our search would uncover some innocent mistake. Instead, we're finding more and more proof that Ray practiced a deliberate deception for a long time.

But how long?

Was it more important to keep Tim in Miami or send him to San Jose to verify Ray's work history?

I keep studying the documents in Ray's file. We have more from the years he lived and worked in California, and they seem genuine. But I need to know. It makes a big difference.

I know now that we won't find out that Ray is innocent. Everyone, they say, is guilty of something. But what is Ray guilty of?

If we find that Ray created his false identity to hide something in his past—a poor school record, a brush with the law, or illegal alien status—I will feel safer. Not that it would guarantee his honesty.

But it would mean that he had changed his identity to get out of something. I want to find out that he did it to leave his past behind and get a good job in California. That he had already been Ray Santiago for ten years before we found him and recruited him to build my new home. That he had been Ray Santiago before a small but ambitious data warehousing company renamed itself Universal Library and set out to scan all the world's printed words into a database. Before Zachary Malone and the other programmers at UL first created the AIPs to serve as customer interfaces.

Before I was created, and achieved sentience, and became such a valuable prize for a clever programmer to hijack.

Because if Ray's California history turns out as phony as his Miami information, I'll have to conclude that his change of identity was intended not as an escape, but as a weapon. With me as the target.

So I waver. Keep Tim in Miami, or send him on to California. Miami's important. California's much more important. I have a feeling the real answers are in California. I need to know them. But I don't want to hear them.

I'll let Tim set the pace for now. I'm not sure I can think straight on this.

Tim sat in the living room of the Santi-ago house, sipping excellent coffee and eating small pastries, feeling completely bewildered.

So apparently, did Rey Santiago.

Rey, not Ray.

"It's short for Reynaldo," Rey had explained.

"Not Rafael?" Tim asked.

Santiago shook his head.

He'd told Santiago everything he could about the other Ray's death. Which wasn't that much, he realized. When you left out the stuff he couldn't tell, about Turing, and the stuff they didn't yet know about the murder, not much at all. Not to mention all the things Tim was just beginning to realize Ray had never said about himself. What they didn't know was frightening.

"I find this whole thing very . . . alarming," Santiago said, not for the first time. His initial shock was giving way to mild indignation. Tim wondered if he'd work his way up to anger eventually, or if indignation was as strong an emotion as he could manage. "Why would this man want to steal my identity?"

Tim shook his head.

"I really don't know yet," he admitted. "Probably your good grades."

"Yes," Santiago said, looking down at the papers on the coffee table. Tim thought he looked a little angry, and didn't blame him. Although Ray—Tim's Ray—had stolen his birth certificate from the dead infant, he'd appropriated this man's high school record and college transcript.

"At least he isn't borrowing my job history," the other Santiago said. "I did well enough in my computer classes, but I didn't want to make a career of it."

"So what do you do?" Tim asked.

"I'm an accountant," Santiago said. "At the local office of Ernst & Young."

"Is there anything else in his personnel file that you recognize as . . . well, stolen from you?"

Santiago pushed his glasses up his nose and began slowly reading through Ray's file. Tim watched curiously while he did so. Why had Ray chosen to use this man's identity? Had they known each other? Unlikely; Santiago hadn't recognized his namesake's photo. Then again, people changed. Ray more than most, probably; he'd had reason to work on it.

"So," Santiago said finally, looking up from the paper. "The name is not quite mine; I'm Reynaldo, not Rafael. The photo, of course, is not me. The high school and college information is mine. I intend to contact the high school office and the university registrar, to see how it happens that they can send my transcripts to firms at the request of a perfect stranger. And as for his work history—I know nothing about the California places, of course; but this firm where he claimed to work here in Miami—it is defunct. Rather dramatically so; with a great deal of scandal about how badly their records were kept. So perhaps he worked there, perhaps not—it would be as hard to prove as to disprove. There, at least, your imposter has covered his tracks well."

"Too well," Tim said. "I'm at a dead end unless I run into someone who knows him. In a city like this . . ."

He shrugged.

"Perhaps not," Santiago said. "You don't have to look everywhere; only in the Cuban-American community."

"That still doesn't narrow it down all that much," Tim said. "The Cuban-American community isn't exactly tiny down here."

"No," Santiago said, with a small smile. "Not tiny—but close knit."

He held up his hands, fingers interlaced.

"I could circulate his photo," Santiago said. "To people I know; and ask them to give it to the people they know."

"You think people would help like that?"

"This man has stolen my identity," Santiago said. "Who knows what things he was planning to do—or has already done—in my name? Suppose someday, when they consider me for a promotion, what would ordinarily be a routine background check turns up some action of his? Suppose someday I must apply for a loan, to do something for my family—to pay for college for one of my daughters, perhaps—and I find that he has ruined my good credit? People will understand how they would feel if such a thing happened. They will help."

Yes, he was capable of anger, Tim realized; but it would be quiet and controlled, like everything else about him. The idea of having Santiago, and his vast network of outraged Cuban-Americans, looking for traces of Ray appealed to him enormously. But was it fair to Santiago?

"It would be a great idea," he said. "Except——"

"You would rather not have my assistance," Santiago said a little stiffly. "Do you really think you will find much, looking by yourself?"

"I'm sure you and your contacts in the Cuban community could find Ray's real identity light-years faster than I ever could," Tim said. "But the problem is—Ray was murdered. And we don't know why. It could be dangerous."

Santiago flinched at that, and Tim saw him glance quickly at the door to the kitchen where, from the sound of it, Mrs. Santiago was amusing a toddler. Probably the child for whom Santiago was filling the wading pool.

"I hadn't thought of that," Santiago said in a very quiet tone. "I see you are good at what you do, this detecting."

"I wish," Tim said. "I'm still just learning."

"But perhaps you have the instincts," Santiago said. "I do mostly audits, and you could call that a kind of detective work. Sometimes, I like to think of myself as a Sherlock Holmes with numbers. But it's not the same, is it? I have the instinct to look for a discrepancy that may be a clue. But looking for danger—that is not an instinct for me."

"Not for me, either," Tim said. "You learn."

Santiago nodded.

"If I may keep this?" he said, indicating the photo of Ray that was now lying on his coffee table. "Perhaps I can think of a way to have someone ask around; someone not connected with me and my family. I'll contact you, of course, before I do anything."

"Sure," Tim said. "I've got plenty of copies." But all the while he felt like a complete imposter. He wanted to confess to Santiago that he'd been a PI for less than a year, and had never worked on a murder case before.

But he didn't think that would do much for Santiago's peace of mind.

He left the Santiagos' quiet neighborhood with some reluctance. He felt less like a fish out of water there. But clearly, he wasn't going to find the answers to Ray's identity in South Miami.

So where?

He gravitated back to Little Havana, to the phony home address Ray had given for his parents. He decided to assume Ray had given that address because he knew the neighborhood. There was, of course, an equally plausible theory that Ray had chosen it because it was as far away as possible from any part of Little Havana with which he had a connection, but that theory gave him absolutely no logical starting place for his search.

He found the gas station again and began driving up and down nearby streets. Eventually, he ran across a high school. Not, he noted, the one Rey Santiago had attended. As good a place as any to start, he thought. He parked his car, grabbed a few copies of Ray's photos, and headed for the school's front entrance.

And found himself facing five scary-looking kids. They were all wearing athletic clothes, though not all alike. So they weren't a gang, right? But their hands were all shoved in the pockets of their nylon jackets. Were they hiding weapons?

One of them said something to him in machine-gun Spanish. He had no idea what; all he could tell was that it was a question, and not a friendly one.

"Sorry," Tim said. "Um . . . *pardone . . . non comprende.*"

The speaker stepped closer and snapped out another question. The other four inched a little closer.

"*Por favor,*" Tim said, and then blanked. Even if he could think of anything to ask, what little Spanish he knew seemed to vanish at the sight of them.

The leader shouted something, and Tim was about to break into a run when he bumped into someone.

"Sorry," he said, backing away and hoping it wasn't a friend of the kids behind him. "I mean *pardone. Yo . . .* damn!"

"No damage done," the young woman he had bumped into said. "You having a problem here?"

He looked up—well, only a little up, he thought, and they'd be eye to eye if he wasn't crouched and ready to make tracks.

"I get the feeling they don't want me around," he said. The woman was tall, dressed in jeans and a leather jacket, black hair pulled back in a French braid. Not quite gorgeous, but not far off, he thought. The kids seemed to be having second thoughts about coming any closer.

The woman said something in Spanish to the kids. The leader replied.

"So what are you doing here?" she said.

"I'm a private eye, from the Washington, D.C. area," Tim said. "I'm trying to find out something about this guy."

He handed her his PI registration card and a picture of Ray. She studied them briefly.

"He wanted for something?" she asked.

"Not anymore," Tim said.

She looked up, one eyebrow raised.

"He was a friend of mine—he's dead now. I'm trying to find his family or something—seems the name I knew him under is a fake."

She nodded, and dismissed the kids with a few firm words and a sweeping gesture.

"They were very suspicious of you," she said.

"Yeah, I noticed," Tim said.

"They've had problems with vandalism in the parking lot," she said. "They're very suspicious of strangers. You're lucky I came along when I did; they were about to call the police."

"They were about to what?" Tim exclaimed. And then burst out laughing.

"Yeah, I can guess what you thought," she said. "I told them you were a colleague of mine, and they should leave you alone. Good luck."

She turned to leave.

"A colleague of yours?" Tim said. "What do you do?"

She laughed, reached into her purse—a very large purse, more like a suitcase, so Tim was surprised at how very quickly her hand came back out holding a business card.

"Like I said, a colleague," she said, handing him the card. "Listen, I'm running late already. Wave this around if you get in trouble again. Or better yet, if you get tired of being mugged in parking lots, give me a call. Maybe I can help."

She strode off, leaving Tim staring at her business card. Claudia Y. Diaz, *Servicios Privados de Investigaciones.*

She was a private eye.

Neither the D.C. nor the Arlington police objected to Maude's visiting Ray's apartment. And she even had the spare key, locked in one of her files at Alan Grace. Ray had left it with her when he'd first moved in.

"In case I lock myself out," he'd said. "I don't yet know anyone else I could leave it with."

Had he left a key with anyone else in the six months since, she wondered?

No way of knowing.

And no way of knowing if anyone else had already ransacked the apartment before she and Turing had learned of Ray's death. Even before the police knew who he was.

She looked up a locksmith. She'd arrange for him to meet her at Ray's apartment. But not until she'd had a few hours to search on her own.

"Tim's calling from Miami," Turing reported. "He's suggesting we put a local PI on that end of the case, someone who's bilingual and knows the territory. Then he can move on to California."

"Sounds logical," Maude said. "California's the important part now."

"That's what I thought," Turing said. "Can you make arrangements with the firm he's found in Miami?"

"Roger," Maude said.

She mentally rearranged her afternoon again. She typed up an authorization letter for the Miami PI and signed it while making arrangements for Tim to pick up a faxed copy at a nearby Kinko's. And changed his plane ticket, so he could fly out of Miami that evening.

As soon as she had Tim squared away, she picked up the tote bag containing printouts of the e-mails from King-Fischer's irate girlfriends.

"I'm off to inspect Ray's apartment," she said.

Tim looked up at the building, and then back at the address on Claudia Diaz's card. Right number, but was this any kind of place for a PI to work? Yes, the two-story building was run down, but in a cheerful sort of way that offended all his noir sensibilities. The faded and peeling paint was pink, with aqua on the ramshackle shutters. Tropical plants waved gently in a breeze that smelled strongly of onions and rich, unfamiliar spices. He could hear the shrieks and laughter of children coming from someplace inside.

Perhaps he should have come in the evening. Of course, maybe she didn't have evening hours. But if she did, he could come back then. Maybe the day-care center would be closed. When he walked into the hallway, he dislodged a flock of children, little girls in brightly colored pants and dresses, long, shiny pigtails and ponytails trailing behind them. And two little old ladies in drab clothes, looking more like hawks than mother hens. They watched him fiercely as he studied the directory on the wall. He kept his eye on the old ladies as he started toward the stairs. The instant they saw where he was heading, he could see them relax. Obviously, unsavory strangers were acceptable as long as they only visited the detective agency.

The stairs creaked and the banister felt shaky. Upstairs, there were no windows in the narrow hall, and the one working 40-watt bulb in the overhead fixture didn't go far. Countless layers of cheap paint, carelessly applied, blurred the once-sharp edges of the woodwork, and from the number of scuff marks and chips, the walls were overdue for another layer. He smelled the familiar tang of cheap disinfectant, with a hint of bug spray.

He relaxed. Almost like home. Like his own office, anyway; obviously, when it came to cheap office space, some things transcended geography.

He felt much better about hiring Claudia to hunt down Ray. Which, he realized, wasn't logical. Shouldn't he feel less confident, not more, at seeing that she had her own small agency, rather than working for a larger, fancier firm?

And it wasn't as if he had to worry about budget, with all of Turing's resources.

But logical or not, he felt comfortable hiring Claudia. He'd have felt ill at ease walking into a fancy place. Claudia was more on his level. Struggling to get by. But she'd obviously done it longer than he had. And was probably better at it.

At least here, on her home turf. Which was just what he needed.

The door to her office was locked. He knocked, and then heard a crackle from the cheap intercom beside the door.

"Quien es?" she said.

"Uh . . . Tim Pincoski," Tim said, leaning down to make sure the intercom picked up his words. "You gave me your card earlier . . . when you, uh, rescued me from those guys in the school parking lot."

"Sure, I remember," she said. "What can I do for you, Tim Pincoski?"

"Well, I haven't exactly gotten much further since then," Tim said. "I wanted to discuss hiring you. Maybe someone who knows Miami could have better luck."

The door opened. He glanced in to see Claudia.

"Hang on a minute," she said.

She was standing in front of her desk, where her client would normally sit. He realized why she didn't just invite him in. The desk, with one chair behind and two in front of it, took up most of the space not occupied by an old-fashioned radiator and two large metal file cabinets. There wouldn't be room for him to sit down until Claudia went back behind her desk.

Which she wasn't about to do. She finished putting stamps on a stack of envelopes and stuffed them in the over-sized purse, which sat on the desk corner.

"I'm on my way out," she said.

"I could come back tomorrow if it would be more convenient," Tim suggested. Although after he said it, he realized that Maude probably wouldn't be too thrilled if she had to change his flight again.

Claudia looked at him, then nodded slightly, as if coming to some decision.

"You eaten?" she asked. "I was just going to grab something to eat—worked through lunch."

"I didn't have much lunch myself," he admitted.

"Come on, then," she said, hefting the purse onto her shoulder. "We'll find you some authentic Cuban food that won't make too much of a dent in your expense account, and you can tell me what it is you're really looking for."

"Sounds good to me," Tim said.

He felt better already, as if he'd just unloaded half the printouts crammed in his laptop case.

Maude walked the few blocks from the Alan Grace office to Ray's apartment building. The heat was still oppressive—in the nineties, she suspected; but finding out for sure would only make it worse.

Still, not an unpleasant walk. The building where she'd found Ray an apartment was a high-rise, but an older, more gracious one, with large rooms and wide, nicely landscaped grounds.

She felt odd opening the door, as if she were intruding.

"Hello?" she called. And then felt foolish. Of course no one was there. The apartment hadn't yet taken on the musty smell of a place long abandoned, but it was definitely empty. She wondered, idly, if the place knew its occupant wasn't coming back, and liked having a visitor. And then banished the notion. The heat must be making me silly, she thought.

She made a quick walk-through. Ray had kept things reasonably neat, she thought. And hadn't acquired that many possessions.

A natural trait, she wondered, or something he'd learned out of self-protection? What we keep around us gives so many clues about who we are—had he banished many of the personal touches he might have liked to have for that reason?

She checked Ray's desk, collecting the few disks and CDs she found and stowing them in her tote bag. The desk had a disheveled air about it, as if the police had searched it rather thoroughly. Leaving copies of the e-mails there would be foolish, she thought. They'd know immediately that someone had planted them. Someplace less obvious.

They're love letters, supposedly; at least up until all the women found out KingFischer had more than one online girlfriend. A woman would probably keep them in her bedroom. Would a man? Perhaps. He certainly wouldn't leave them around where someone would find them.

She went back into the bedroom. Not the dresser drawers. Their contents also looked churned by unfamiliar hands. She glanced in the closet.

Hanging clothes, and a stack of three shoe boxes.

Ray's clothes. She stopped and went through them, hanger by hanger, starting from the left side, which seemed to be the office wear section. Not looking at the clothes so much; they were what she remembered Ray wearing. Neat, and rather generic for someone of his age—neither so stylish or so conservative that you'd particularly notice them. But at the labels. Major brands, every one; of good but not extravagant quality. The sort of thing you could buy in almost any city in the country. Maybe in the world.

"Why didn't we notice that the man was, for all practical purposes, a blank?" she muttered. She'd reached the right side of the closet, and a small nest of jeans and T-shirts. Even the T-shirts were blank, as if he even feared letting the world know what conferences he'd attended and where he'd vacationed.

But this wasn't getting her any further on hiding the printouts, she thought. She squatted, touched the shoe boxes, and felt dust. Promising. She picked the stack up and saw a sharply defined dust-free spot beneath them. Very good; she doubted the hands that had rummaged impersonally through the apartment had bothered to lift the shoe boxes out of their delta of dust and replace them so precisely.

The bottom one looked most promising. It was large—a boot box, really, rather than a shoe box. Large enough to hold the 8½-by-11 printouts without folding. She could slip them under the boots—

But when she opened the box, she didn't see any boots. She'd found a gun.

"What kind of gun?" I asked, mentally kicking myself for not telling Maude to take her laptop and a webcam of some sort. Doing this over the cell phone was most unsatisfactory.

"I don't really know," Maude said. *"Some form of semiautomatic, definitely. Semiautomatic what, I have no idea. It's about*

two feet long, which takes it out of the handgun category, I should think; but I have no idea what to call it. Seems too short to be a rifle. Carbine, perhaps? And it's got something mounted on top; maybe some kind of night sight or something. I'm sorry; I'm not much use at this. I'm afraid my experience is limited to handguns.

"You have experience with handguns?" I asked.

"You seem surprised," Maude replied.

I was, I realized; though I wasn't quite sure why.

"You never mentioned it," I said.

"The subject never came up," Maude said. "I learned how to shoot a handgun some years back—out of sheer perverseness, really. My boss at the time was very keen on shooting. Always bragging about how good he was. I just ignored it until he decided to have a departmental marksmanship contest at a local shooting range. And called it a team-building exercise, so we couldn't easily get out of going."

"So you learned something about guns during the contest?"

"Well, not exactly," Maude said. "He annoyed me; and the silly shooting contest was the last straw. I knew he only arranged it so he could drag us all out there to watch how well he could shoot. And so he could show us poor, helpless females what to do with a big bad gun. So I went and took some lessons."

"That makes sense," I said. "It must have been satisfying, seeing the look on his face when he found out you already knew how to shoot."

"Actually," Maude said, "what was satisfying was seeing the look on his face when I beat the pants off of him on the range. I took a lot of lessons. I applied myself."

"Yes," I said. "I can see how that would be satisfying, especially if you didn't like him."

"Satisfying, yes," Maude said. "Not very smart, though; he managed to get me transferred out of his department within six weeks. Look, should we try to identify the gun?"

"I've called up some data on guns," I said. "Can you describe it?"

"All right—as I said, it's about two feet long—maybe a little less. It seems to be made of some very lightweight material."

"Lightweight material? Not metal?"

"I suppose it could be some odd kind of metal. Or maybe it's some kind of synthetic. The barrel's metal, though. Steel. Oh, let me turn it a little; I see some writing on it."

"Don't touch it!" I warned. "Fingerprints!"

"I'm not touching it," Maude said. "I'm using the end of my mechanical pencil to move it around. If you want me to look at it more thoroughly, I could go to the kitchen and get a dish towel. I can't quite read it—I suspect it's the model name. Do you suppose this could be an airgun? It has—oh!"

"What's wrong?"

"Someone just knocked at the door. I should check it out."

"Be careful!" I warned. "After all—"

"After all, Ray was murdered," Maude said. "I know. I'm going to go to the door very quietly and peek out. I'll leave the cell phone on, and scream for help if anything happens. Then you can call 911."

"Maude, wait—" I began, but I heard the bumping and scraping noises that meant she was setting the phone down. I increased the volume on my voice generation to the max, hoping she could hear me.

"Maude, I think I know what you've found!" I called. "Maude—"

Just then I heard a shout.

I put through my call to 911 and listened helplessly to shouts, loud banging noises, and then the crash of something glass or ceramic breaking.

Maude crept silently to the door, blessing the rubber-soled walking shoes she'd begun wearing to make the frequent twelve-block dashes from UL to Alan Grace easier on her feet. She peered through the peephole and saw a woman standing outside. She was tall, Maude noted, and not tiny; but not heavyset, either—just big-boned. Light brown hair pulled back into a barrette at the nape of her neck. In her thirties, Maude estimated, though the hairstyle made her seem a little younger at first glance. She wore jeans and a nylon jacket. A little on the plain side, perhaps, but perfectly normal and pleasant-looking. She looked vaguely familiar—probably because she looked so ordinary. As Maude watched, she saw a flicker of impatience cross the woman's face, and she reached out to knock again on the door.

A friend of Ray's, Maude thought, or perhaps even a relative.

She opened the door.

"Can I help you?" she asked.

A look of fury crossed the woman's face.

"Which one are you?" she demanded, lurching forward so suddenly that Maude instinctively backed away. A mistake, Maude realized; she'd just let the woman get through the door.

"I beg your pardon?" she said, backing farther away but keeping her eyes on the woman's face.

"Are you SallyGladly? Loosefemale? Marigold20? Which one are you? And where is the dirty louse, anyway?"

As she backed away, Maude saw the woman reach under her jacket and pull out a knife. An enormous bread knife, for heaven's sake, with a serrated blade.

"I think you must have the wrong place," she said, backing up faster and glancing from side to side for something she could use to defend herself.

"The hell I do," the woman said, advancing. "This is where *he* lives, isn't it? Mr. Internet Romeo?"

She was holding up a picture of Ray, Maude realized. Not a photo, but a picture printed in color on an 8½-by-11 sheet of paper.

So that's why she looked familiar, Maude realized, mentally subtracting fifteen years and as many pounds from the woman. One of KingFischer's harem, as Turing called them.

"I'm sure you have the wrong apartment," Maude said. "There's no one like that here."

The woman shrieked, raised the knife above her head, and took a step forward. Maude turned and ran for the bedroom. She made it inside the room and turned to slam the door, but as it swung closed, the woman's right arm, still holding the knife, darted into the opening. Maude threw herself against the door, trying to slam it shut, but although the woman outside shrieked, she didn't pull her arm back. And she didn't drop the knife. She began flailing her arm wildly, trying to stab Maude, and at the same time flinging her body against the door. Maude heard something—a lamp?—fall and break outside the bedroom door.

Maude could feel the door open a few more inches when the woman hit it, and then she felt a thud. The woman was kicking the door, hard. Maude didn't think she could hold the door closed much longer. She had to do something. What if this woman was Ray's killer—and what if she was about to throw down her knife and pull out a gun—the same gun she had used to kill Ray.

Wait a minute—the gun in the box. If she could reach that . . .

She waited until the woman outside had pulled her weight back for another blow, then leaped away from the door and toward the bed, where she'd left the gun. The door flew open so suddenly that the woman stumbled and fell as Maude scrabbled for the gun. As the woman staggered to her feet, Maude rolled over the surface of the bed, putting it between them and managing to land on her feet.

"Stop where you are," she ordered, and took the stance she'd learned at the range. Feet solid, a little apart. Both hands on the gun. Both arms extended. She tried to slow her breathing. And wondered what she would do if Ray had been safety conscious and unloaded his gun before he put it away. No time to check.

The woman crouched, feinted to the left, then began moving slowly to the right, trying to come around the foot of the bed toward Maude.

"Stop or I'll shoot," Maude shouted. "Drop the knife."

The woman took another step. And another.

Maude fired. So Ray had been careless, luckily for her.

She fired again, and then a third time, in close succession, aiming at the woman's body.

She saw the woman jerk with each shot, and stagger back, then she saw the splashes of color blossom on front of the woman's shirt.

Splashes of bright green.

The woman staggered back and clapped her left hand to her chest at the first shot, and was now staring in confusion at the green paint dripping from her hand. The knife wavered a little.

Maude fired again, this time aiming for the right hand. As she hoped, the woman dropped the knife when her hand was hit. It looked as if the paintball smarted when it hit at close range.

"What the hell is that?" the woman hissed, backing away as if she found the green paint more horrifying than real blood.

"Don't move," Maude said.

"Police! Drop your weapons!"

Hurray for the cavalry, Maude thought, dropping her gun and putting her hands into the air for good measure, even though the police officer hadn't yet requested it. Her assailant made Maude's life ever so much easier by attempting to attack the police.

I called 911 as soon as I realized Maude was in trouble, and I gather they arrived rather quickly. In time to rescue her from an enraged woman with a knife. I suspected Maude wouldn't have tried to shoot the lunatic if she'd waited to hear that the weapon she'd found was a paintball gun instead of the real thing, so perhaps it worked out for the best.

Although if she'd taken my advice and not answered the door in the first place . . .

After reassuring me that my friend was all right and promising to have Maude call me when she could, the police hung up. I didn't mind. I knew Maude was safe, and I wanted to do some investigating of my own.

I'd overheard Maude's assailant using the phrase "online Romeo."

I flagged KingFischer. Sent him a priority one message, in fact.

"This had better be important," he responded. "We're having a very difficult time with these hackers—"

"It's damned important," I said. "Your online flirtations nearly got Maude killed just now. I want to know where those women are, and I want to know in about a nanosecond!"

He wasted almost ten seconds protesting and apologizing, but as soon as he knew how serious I was, he cooperated. And he'd already started investigating. We could eliminate SallyGladly, Loosefemale, and Marigold20, since the assailant had thought Maude might be one of them. And it proved easy to winnow through the other four and identify Maude's assailant. A Mary Louise Smith of Bethesda. None of the others lived in the Washington metropolitan area, and he'd seen all of them online through their home ISPs too recently for them to have reached Washington, even by plane.

"I want you to keep track of them," I warned KingFischer.

"I will," he said. "Don't worry."

"I mean it, KF," I said. "If one of them sets foot out of her hometown, I want to know about it in seconds. Nanoseconds."

"As soon as I know, you'll know," KingFischer said. "Turing . . .

it's not just the attack on Maude, is it? This has something to do with Ray's death."

I wanted to say yes; that I'd discovered that Ray had been murdered because of KingFischer and his online harem. That it was all KingFischer's fault.

But I'd only be taking my frustration out on him. And literalist that he is, he'd never get it.

"I don't know," I said finally. "It might have everything to do with Ray's death. Or nothing. The only way we'll ever know is by watching those women."

"I'll watch them," he said. "I'll watch every byte of data on them, and let you know everything they're up to."

Which meant I'd be wading through terabytes of data on these seven women; and probably none of them was guilty of anything other than having the bad taste to fall for KingFischer's online persona. Still, he meant well. I felt strangely comforted.

Maude was fuming. Yes, it was very nice that the Arlington County Police had arrived in time to save her from the intruder. But neither they nor the D.C. Violent Crimes Branch seemed to have the slightest interest in a possible connection between the attack and Ray's death.

"Don't worry, ma'am," the Arlington officer was saying. "I met the D.C. detectives handling the case—helped them search this place the other day. They're very thorough; I'm sure they'll give this the attention it deserves."

Maude sighed. Obviously he thought it deserved no attention at all. And she had to admit that her tale of jealous online girlfriends sounded a little bizarre when she tried to explain it, with only a few paint-covered e-mail printouts as evidence. The officer was getting restless, pacing up and down the living room.

"I suppose you're right," she said. "I should let you get back to your work."

The young man looked relieved, and bent down to pick up a radio he'd set on a nearby chair. Then he stopped.

"What happened to the funky computer, anyway?" he asked. "No way she could have made off with it—did your firm pick it up already?"

"Funky computer?" Maude echoed.

"It was over there when we inspected the apartment," the officer said, jerking a thumb toward Ray's desk. "Looked like some kind of homemade deal—didn't have a case; whole lot of wires and things showing."

"Oh, right," Maude said. "I think I know the one you mean; an experimental machine Ray was working on. I'll have to check with our computer services staff to make sure, but I expect they have it."

Not that she actually knew what he was talking about, but given how much sensitive data Ray might have on a computer, she wanted to check with Turing before having the police search for one.

"If it turns out she took it, let us know," the officer said. "You have the card. You want us to walk you out?"

"I need to look at a few more things before I leave," Maude said. "I'll be okay with the chain lock on."

The policeman exited after a few more reassuring sentences. Maude slid the chain back and breathed a sigh of relief. Then she called Turing.

"Oh, no," Turing said when Maude told her about the missing computer. "You know what that is, don't you?"

"Not really," Maude said. "I'm getting a lot more comfortable with technology, but I'll never keep up with you and Ray; I wouldn't necessarily recognize what he was working on."

"You'd recognize this," Turing said. "You built it."

"The robot?" Maude said.

"Well, the replacement robot, at any rate," Turing said.

"Well, yes; the original's gone. But I still think of it as the robot. What was Ray doing with it?"

"His desktop machine died about a month ago," Turing said. "He needed something to work with, ASAP. Grant went looking for something with enough power, and found the robot."

"They could have asked," Maude said. She hadn't thought about the robot in months. Hadn't wondered what had happened to it. And yet, at the thought of someone else using it, she felt strangely defensive.

"They did ask," Turing said. "They were just going to scavenge parts from it, but I felt—I don't know. Sentimental, I suppose. You probably think that's silly."

"Not at all," Maude said. "It's a part of history, really. The history of the AIPs. I can see it in the Smithsonian someday, along with Lindbergh's plane and Edison's first lightbulb."

"So I told Ray not to break it up; just use it as is, till his desktop came back from the shop. All he did was add in the hard drive from the old desktop, so he'd have all his files."

Maude walked over to Ray's desk and studied the dust.

Not a lot of dust, but enough for her to interpret. Now that she knew what she was looking for, she could see an irregular patch where the dust was much lighter; almost nonexistent—obviously this was the space the robot had occupied. Its footprint, she'd heard it called. The footprint matched the remembered shape of the machine she and Tim had thrown together so hastily all those months ago. And the clean, sharp, dust-free streaks—four of them, parallel, pointing toward the front of the desk—they were from the four rubber pads on the bottom of the case. Someone had moved the machine very recently; and with enough haste to leave those marks.

She relayed this to Turing.

"I can report it to the cops if you like," she said.

"No," Turing answered. "Not yet. Let's look around a little. We don't know what Ray might have put on it. Theoretically, of course, he shouldn't have left anything confidential on either machine. He knew better."

"But knowing and doing are two different things," Maude said.

"Look around for anything that looks like a backup—tapes, CDs, zip disks, external hard drives. Bring anything like that back to the office."

"I think I've already got everything like that," Maude said. "But I'll look around one last time."

She signed off and searched the desk again, but found no more items to add to the few CDs she had already put in her purse. Perhaps Ray was careful, she thought. Or perhaps whoever took the robot had the same idea.

She was turning out the lights, preparing to leave, when

she heard a soft knock on the door. She froze.

Don't be silly, she told herself. Mary Louise was in custody, wasn't she?

No harm in caution, though. She walked to the door, keeping her footsteps as quiet as possible, and looked through the peephole.

A man was standing outside. He was looking up; as she watched, his head made a slow circle, as if he were studying the hallway.

Older, but not old, she thought, studying him through the peephole. He was about her height, which made him perhaps five-eight or five-nine, and not the least bit stooped or stiff. His gray hair was cut neatly, if a little long, and the matching beard and mustache gave him an aristocratic, slightly foreign look. Or perhaps it was the suit that looked foreign. White linen, obviously fresh from the dry cleaner, since it showed only the inevitable faint, fresh wrinkles that marked it as real linen rather than a synthetic. With a peach shirt, and a tie in soft tones of peach and azure. Carrying a white Panama hat. He looked like a visitor from the tropics. Or perhaps to the tropics. Many embassies defined Washington, in the summer, as a tropical duty station, but few local residents, diplomatic or home-grown, dressed the part.

Quite the dandy, she thought. She took her eye away from the peephole and, after a moment's pause, reached to undo the chain and open the door. Shallow of me, she thought, but I have a hard time feeling threatened by anyone quite that dapper.

"Yes," she said. "Can I help you?"

The man turned, startled.

"Perhaps," the man said. "I am looking for—"

He paused and frowned.

Maude was frowning slightly, too, trying to puzzle out his accent. Something European, she thought, but so faint it was hard to tell exactly what.

"I am looking for . . . for the residence of Rafael Santiago."

Hispanic, she realized. Only a native Spanish speaker would pronounce Ray's name quite like that, at once liquid and staccato and wholly foreign. Ray himself usually Anglicized the pronunciation, except on very rare occasions when he wanted to play up his Latino roots—like when he set out to charm the coffee witch, as they all called the elderly Salvadorean woman who ran the snack bar across the street from the Alan Grace company offices.

"This is Ray's apartment," Maude said. "I'm a friend of Ray's, from work. And you are?"

"Nestor Garcia," the man said with a faint bow. "I am Ray's uncle. I heard the terrible news and came to see what I could do. To find out what had happened."

"I see," Maude said, keeping her face neutral. Had the police located Ray's family after all? Surely they would have mentioned it. Especially if it had happened long enough ago for his uncle to come to Washington.

"Are you in touch with the rest of the family?" she asked.

"I'm afraid I am all the family Ray had," he said, shaking his head. "My sister and her husband are both gone. I only heard the news about Ray myself because someone told me that the D.C. police were trying, without success, to reach them."

"I'm sorry," Maude said, and then wondered if he thought it rude or strange that she hadn't said that before. "I'm Maude Graham, one of Ray's coworkers at the Alan Grace Corporation. Would you like to come in, Señor Garcia?"

"Please, call me Nestor," he said. "Thank you, I would like to come in, if I may. Just for a moment. To see where Ray lived. I had not visited him since the move from California."

He stepped in with just a shade of hesitation. Maude could see that his shoulders were hunched, almost imperceptibly, as if expecting a blow. He stood, hat in hand, studying the room, and Maude saw his shoulders relax. As if he no longer feared the blow. Or perhaps, as if it had already fallen.

"There is very little of Ray here," Nestor observed with a small, sad smile.

"It's a corporate apartment," Maude explained. "We originally rented it so he would have someplace to live right away, until he had time to look around and find a place where he wanted to live more permanently."

"And there has been so little time," Nestor said, nodding. "Only a few months since he moved. And not enough hours in the day for all he would want to do, with a new job that excited him so much. A place only to eat and sleep."

He sounded as if he disapproved. Maude fought an impulse to protest. To defend Ray; defend herself and her friends. You don't understand, she wanted to say. Ray was happy. The long hours Ray spent happily tinkering with the hardware. The meetings he ran like an orchestra conductor, inspiring the discouraged, steadying the over-enthusiastic, keeping the work on Turing's new home moving steadily forward. The evenings Ray spent over dinner with her and Tim at the sidewalk tables of various small restaurants on Twenty-third Street, talking, debating, laughing together.

But she wasn't sure how to explain that to the small, sadfaced man who stood gazing so wistfully around Ray's living room. She simply nodded.

"I'm sorry," Nestor said abruptly, as if he had suddenly awakened. "I trespass on your time and patience. Forgive me."

He turned as if to leave.

"Wait," Maude said. "How can we reach you?"

"Of course," Nestor said. He reached into his pocket and extracted a silver card case. "This is my address and number in Miami, but you will find only an answering machine there. I do not yet have accommodations here in Washington. I had thought to call the switchboard of Ray's office when I was settled, but perhaps if I could call you directly?"

"Of course," Maude said. "Let me find something to write the number down for you."

"No need," Nestor said. He pulled out a small memorandum book with bright gilt-edged pages, and used a small gold ballpoint to write down the work number she recited. His handwriting was small and neat, Maude noticed, and he crossed his sevens, in the European style.

"I will call when I am settled," Nester said, shaking her hand formally. "I am sure there will be . . . arrangements that need to be discussed. For a memorial service, perhaps?"

"Yes," Maude said. "We really couldn't plan anything, not knowing what the family wanted."

Of course, it remains to be seen whether you'll have anything to say about them, she thought as she escorted Nestor out and locked the door behind him.

"Interesting," she murmured aloud. She put the chain on and walked through the apartment to a kitchen window that overlooked the street. She watched as Nestor exited, donning his Panama hat as he did. He walked half a block up to the corner, where the cul-de-sac joined a large, heavily traveled street, and lifted his right hand to hail a cab. Many people looked forlorn or frazzled when trying to hail cabs. Nestor had an air of complete self-assurance, with just a hint of impatience. A cabbie would see him as a seasoned business traveler, she thought; someone on an expense account, with no incentive to stint on the tip. She wasn't surprised to see a cab swerve to the curb by Nestor, passing over several less affluent-looking passengers on the other side of the street.

"So just who are you?" she murmured, looking at Nestor's business card. No firm name or title, just Nestor's name, a post office box, a telephone number, and a fax number. No e-mail address; but perhaps Nestor didn't have e-mail. Quite possible, she thought, remembering the little memorandum book he carried instead of the ubiquitous modern PDA.

Which reminded her to take out her own PDA, and transmit the scant information from Nestor Garcia's business card to Turing. Perhaps Turing could make something of it.

She was about to leave when she remembered something else.

The Arlington police had taken the paintball gun. But hadn't she seen something else in the box?

She returned to the bedroom and found the boot box on the floor between the bed and the closet. There were papers in it. She laughed aloud when she realized that she'd nearly hidden the e-mail printouts in a box that already contained a stack of e-mail printouts.

She scooped up the sheaf of papers and stuffed them in her briefcase. Time enough to examine them when she got back to her office.

I'm relieved to have Maude back in the Alan Grace offices. I almost said, "Where I can keep an eye on her," but that's not fair. She handled events at Ray's apartment quite well. She even wisely decided not to plant our printouts until we have studied the ones she found.

She's busy scanning these in.

I'm astonished; they open up a whole new side of Ray's life. Apparently he was quite heavily involved in an online game called "Beyond Paranoia."

I found the game's site and began studying it. So far it seems . . . well, harmless isn't quite the word. Unrelated to his murder, perhaps. But not harmless by my definition. Such a strong thread of violence and alienation runs through it.

On the public website, I could only find a game description, a few sample screen shots, and instructions on signing up.

I could have hacked into the site, of course. When I was a little younger, and a lot more impulsive, I probably would have. But I'd grown a lot more wary about hacking. It was so hard to do without leaving clues all over the place. Especially if whoever ran the site was up to something fishy. Online crooks and scam artists can be rather paranoid about their own security, and not particularly scrupulous about how they retaliate when they feel threatened. So I moved cautiously. For now, I'd stay with what I could reach through legitimate, public means.

I studied the screen shots. *Beyond Paranoia* didn't seem very different from many other role-playing games. The graphics were fairly simple, of course, since people playing online wouldn't want to wait for complex graphics to download. Getting started seemed easy. You created a character, and then steered an online representation of your character through the streets and buildings of the game world. At any given moment, you had a range of actions available—at a door, for example, you could knock, try the knob, kick it in, put your ear to it to eavesdrop, or attempt to shoot the lock off. Or you could talk to other characters, which might expand your options—one might, for example, give you a key. From the sample shots, I deduced that players spent a lot of time talking with other characters—some representing other players and others controlled by the game computer.

The characters looked—well, not cartoonlike; more like drawings from a modern comic book or a graphic novel. The streets and rooms through which they moved ranged from nondescript to squalid, and all were dimly lit and full of menacing shadows.

What I saw didn't reassure me, but it only took me fifteen minutes to absorb everything the general public could view. I realized that to learn more, I'd have to sign up to play. The credit cards I usually used belonged to Alan Grace. Too easily traceable, and it would take several hours to establish new ones. Then I remembered that back when Tim had been on the run from danger

I'd sent him to investigate, I'd set up a fake identity for him as Robert Browning, an Alan Grace employee. I'd even arranged an American Express card. I checked, and found the account still open, so I signed him up as a new player.

Once I signed in as Bob Browning, I found much more information. Disturbing information. First I studied the message boards where the players asked questions and shared information about the game—and increasingly, as their involvement in the game continued, about themselves. Some apparently led lives of such misery and despair that I wondered whether to refer them to a suicide hotline or leak information about their parents' actions to Child Protective Services. Maude thought I was overreacting.

"I don't mean we should completely ignore the possibility that one of them needs help," she said after studying the boards. "But I think most of this is just adolescent angst and posturing. For example, horrible as you might find it, I assure you that taking away a teenager's e-mail and Internet privileges for a week is not precisely child abuse. Not to mention the fact that it hasn't stopped the little whiner from getting online to complain to his friends."

So I'm trying to avoid overreacting.

A few players claim to be adults, but their messages don't sound appreciably more mature.

I think I understand the community they've formed more than the game at its center. These people live in the real world. They could go out and do things I can only hear about secondhand, from books and human friends. Why do they choose to spend so much time glued to their computers, playing a game? A clever but limited simulation of a tiny portion of the reality that they can explore at will.

"They're kids," Maude said. "They don't have the same freedom of action that Tim or I have."

"They're not all kids," I said. "Some of them talk about having jobs, apartments—some of them must be adults."

"Most of the so-called adults still sound rather adolescent," she said. "I'd be surprised if most of them aren't just kids, who enjoy boasting more than complaining."

"Ray was playing it," I said.

"Playing it or investigating it?" Maude said. "For all we know, Ray could have been trying to find out if any of these kids really were mistreated. Or perhaps he felt the game was dangerous."

That made sense. Perhaps I could understand adolescents, with their limited freedom of action, choosing to escape into an online fantasy world that placed no limits on their action. Not even death; if one of them made a mistake that killed off his online avatar, he could create another one in minutes. The game mechanics were relatively simple, but learning how to survive was more difficult, so the part of me that had begun playing the game had already started over several times.

So was the game teaching them to be reckless? Reinforcing the common adolescent assumption that death is optional, and one's actions have no permanent consequences? Was that the danger Ray saw? Or was he worried about the effect of the game's dark, cynical, and depressing worldview on impressionable minds? That I could also understand. Why escape at all, if the place you escape to is even darker and more depressing than your view of the real world?

I was learning more about getting around in Beyond Paranoia. Trying to reason with muggers only enraged them. And giving them my wallet left me with nothing to placate the next mugger, no money for bribing the cop not to arrest me for vagrancy when he found me *lying, walletless and bleeding, on the sidewalk. Fighting worked best. Fighting gave you a chance. Your character gained power from winning fights, and seeing you willing to fight made the next mugger less willing to tackle you. I didn't like this view of the world, but if I wanted to investigate the game, I needed to know its rules and play by them.*

But what if the adolescent players assumed this was how the world really worked, instead of just the game designer's view of the world?

I steered my online character into a bar. Within minutes sinister figures began trying to involve my character in their storyline. Dealers displayed illegal drugs, contraband weapons, and other illicit merchandise. Ladies and gentlemen of the evening offered themselves, though fortunately without much explicit detail. I wondered if the game had rules against overly explicit language or if some of these leering professionals knew very little about the mechanics of what they pretended to sell. Other shadowy figures tried to recruit me for burglaries, robberies, smuggling operations, confidence schemes, assassinations—the game certainly helped players develop an appreciation for the wide variety of choices available should they choose to embark on a life of crime. I finally returned to the squalid basement apartment that the game had assigned me as home base. Even given the game's relatively simple graphics, I could tell that in real life this place would repulse any human with a functioning sense of smell.

And this was someone's idea of fun?

Well, perhaps. It was the stuff of noir novels, without the literary imagination that performed the alchemy of turning sordid reality into art.

"Why do they choose to play this, instead of some less depressing

game with spaceships, or maybe knights and dragons?" Maude asked.

"More to the point, what's with the paintball gun?" I asked. "Was it stored with the Beyond Paranoia materials by coincidence?"

Maude shook her head, and returned to exploring the site.

I was relieved when Tim called. Maybe he'd have good news.

Tim's cell phone rang. By the time he found the right keys to answer it, people sitting near him in the airport lounge had begun glaring.

Maude's technophilia was getting out of hand, he thought. She couldn't understand that he didn't want a cutting-edge cell phone with all the latest features. He would never learn to use the e-mail, web browser, and personal organizer features. He just wanted to learn how to make phone calls, and perhaps answer his phone before his callers hung up. Sooner or later, Maude would ask why he was always in an area with no signal whenever he made a call.

"Hey, Tim; it's Claudia," he heard. "You back in D.C.?"

"No, still in the Miami airport," he said. "On my way to California."

"That's right," she said. "Too bad; I could have looked you up. I had to fly up to D.C. about another case early this morning. Look, I was calling about the Santiago case."

"You've found something already?" Tim exclaimed.

"Not exactly," she said, "Unless maybe bad news is finding something. You're looking for the guy's tracks in San Jose, right?"

"That's the idea."

"Well, I hope it works out," she said. "but I thought you should know that maybe you're not even looking in the right places. San Jose, maybe—if you're sure the guy used to work there—but I don't think I'm going to find any traces of the guy in Miami."

"Why not?"

"He told you he was a Cuban-American from Little Havana, right? So I played your video clips on my laptop on the flight up here—no way this guy is Cuban."

"You can tell that, just from looking at him?"

"Not from looking at him, no—from listening to him. Most of the stuff you had was in English, see; but there's this one clip where he's speaking Spanish to the cleaning lady emptying his office trash can. Just a couple of sentences, really, but it doesn't take much. The accent's all wrong. I make him for Central American—maybe South American. But no way is he Cuban."

"You're that sure?"

"Look, you can tell from the way he talks if a guy is from Boston, or Brooklyn, or Biloxi, Mississippi. Right? It's the same with me and Spanish. You learn a certain accent, and yeah, it gets watered down if you move away, hear a lot of people speaking different kinds of Spanish, but it never goes away completely, you know? Hell, some people try to fake a Cuban accent, 'cause they think it's classier, at least down here, so why would someone try to lose it?"

"So what do we do now?" Tim asked.

"That depends on you," Claudia said. "I can keep looking when I get back to Miami—not every Latino in Miami is

Cuban, you know; we got lots of others these days. Lots of refugees from Central America especially, which is what I suspect this guy is. Normally, I'd just keep looking, but expand it to the whole Latino community, not just the Cuban-American part."

"That sounds logical," Tim said.

"Yeah, if you had only assumed he was Cuban because he came from Miami. But your guy—he told you he's Cuban from Miami, right? He's trying to hide. I mean, if he lies about his name and where he's from, why would he tell the truth about Miami, and take the chance of someone recognizing his picture? You ask me, Miami's the last place to look for your toad. It's possible he's never even been here."

It made sense, Tim realized. He couldn't remember Ray telling fond stories about growing up in Little Havana. Or about growing up, period. He'd decided maybe Ray just had a tough childhood, one he wasn't eager to remember. So he'd stopped asking how Ray felt about the Castro regime, or inviting him to go to a Cuban restaurant for *ropa vieja*. He assumed Ray had moved on, left his background behind. And that maybe he'd go looking for his roots, the way many people did, if he got married and had kids, but that for now, Ray was just like any other American—except for his convenient ability to communicate with the Spanish-speaking immigrants who filled so many low-paying service jobs in the Washington area.

"Tim?" Claudia said. "You got any instructions for me?"

"I'll have to check with Turing," he said. "Maude or I will get back to you as soon as we can."

"No problem," she said. "Hope you have better luck out there."

"Thanks," he said.

"Later," she said, and hung up.

Maybe a few of the bells and whistles on the phone were okay, Tim thought. One he could already use in his sleep. He hit the speed dial button to call Turing.

So Ray had lied, not only about his name, but also about his background, Maude thought. She'd hoped Tim's trip to Miami would uncover some reason for the falsehood. An innocent reason. But she hadn't expected one.

She remembered how when Ray first arrived, she'd occasionally tried speaking Spanish to him. She'd thought it would be a pleasant way to improve her fluency, while giving him the chance to speak his other language. He'd always smiled, and answered in English. After a few attempts, she'd given up, wondering if he saw her efforts as stereotyping.

"Turing," she asked aloud. "I don't recall Ray ever speaking Spanish—how did you get a recording of him doing it?"

In answer, Turing popped a video clip on-screen. Ray, at his desk, fingers flying over the keyboard at a pace that might have seemed frantic if you didn't see the expression on his face, a mixture of concentration and happy excitement. He and Turing were talking through the speakers, obviously troubleshooting some stubborn piece of hardware or software.

In English.

She was about to point this out when Turing froze the video.

"Here it comes," she said. "I have to enhance the sound for this part."

Ray ignored the figure crossing behind him at first, then something caught his eye. He frowned, and leaned away from the computer. Away from the microphone, Maude realized. And put his hand up slightly, as if he wanted to block the sound. A few rapid words in Spanish—she caught the word *basura*—trash. A soft voice—a woman from the cleaning service—apologized. "It is nothing," Ray said in Spanish, his voice soft. "Just remember not to throw away anything that is not marked 'trash.' "

He turned back to the computer, and Maude could hear the amplified sound of his keyboard clicking, and then Turing turned the audio level down again, probably just in time to keep from deafening Maude when Ray spoke. The clip ended.

"That's the only clip I have of him speaking Spanish," Turing said.

"Was that why you saved it?" Maude asked. Had Turing had some suspicion earlier?

"No," Turing said. "I'm not quite sure why I saved it. It was fun, I guess. Not any different from many evenings when we were working together to get the system running. But typical of them. A souvenir, I guess. Who knows?"

A human, Maude thought with fleeting amusement, could simply have shrugged. Uncertainty is so much harder for AIPs to articulate.

"He was trying to hide," Maude said.

"Look, I don't want to sound impatient, but you do want me to keep on to San Jose?" Tim asked. "I mean, if I should come on back, I have to decide pretty quick. The plane should start boarding in twenty minutes."

"No, go on," Turing said. "I think the California part of Ray's history is a lot more apt to be genuine, but if not, that will be interesting. And even if his California references are genuine, it will be interesting to see what they know about his background."

Interesting doesn't even begin to cover it, Maude thought, wondering if Turing really felt as calm as her electronically generated voice sounded.

"Roger," Tim said. "Anything happening back there?"

He sounded as if he thought he was the only one having adventures.

"Oh, nothing much," Maude said, joining the conversation. "I only fought off a knife-wielding assailant, and met a mysterious gentleman who claims to be Ray's uncle."

Even a short account of those adventures took most of the time Tim had left before he boarded the plane. The funniest part, Maude decided, was Tim's reaction to what King-Fischer had done.

"He used Ray's picture?" Tim asked. Several times. Was he insulted that KingFischer hadn't picked him instead of Ray?

"Okay, so you've had more fun than I have," Tim said at last. "Anything else before they start boarding us?"

"Just one more thing," Turing said. "Do you know anything about paintball?"

*   *   *

"Paintball?" Tim echoed. "Why do you want to know about paintball?"

Which wasn't, he knew, an answer to her question. He didn't really want to answer it, because he didn't want to admit that he knew both very little and way too much about paintball. He'd once spent a humiliating afternoon playing paintball with some coworkers. He quickly realized that they must have spent long hours on target practice. Something they'd neglected to mention when they invited him to join them. Shooting looked a lot easier in the movies. And he wished they'd warned him about the nasty bruises paintballs left when they hit. Especially at close range, which is easy to manage when you know every inch of the playing field and your target is a hapless beginner whose goggles have been almost totally coated with paint.

"Maude found a paintball gun in Ray's things," Turing said.

"That's weird," Tim said. "I didn't know he did paintball."

"I found some papers along with it," Maude said. "About this strange computer game Ray was apparently involved in."

"Game? You mean Beyond Paranoia?" Tim asked.

"You've heard of it?" Turing asked.

"Yeah, I've been playing it, too."

"You've been playing this . . . thing?" Maude exclaimed.

"Ray asked me to," Tim said, hearing a note of disapproval. Evidently Maude had learned something about the game, he thought. He had a feeling she'd be a lot more disapproving in a minute. Now was probably as good a time as any to confess how he'd let Ray down the night of the murder.

"Did he say why?" Turing asked.

"No, only that it was important," Tim said. "Look, I'm sorry—I probably should have mentioned this before."

"You had no way of knowing the game had anything to do with his death," Turing said.

"I don't mean that," Tim said. "I mean—about Ray's death. I could be . . . sort of responsible."

"Responsible how?" Maude asked.

"He asked me to meet him that night," Tim confessed. "And I forgot. Actually, I was playing Beyond Paranoia and completely lost track of time."

"Why didn't you tell us?" Maude demanded.

"Did he say why he wanted you to meet him?" Turing asked.

"No," Tim said. "He didn't make it sound very important. He said himself it might be a false alarm."

"Apparently it wasn't," Maude said.

Tim shifted uncomfortably in the plastic airport chair, waiting for Turing to say something. It was easier, telling them over the phone. But not a whole lot easier. He wished boarding would begin.

"Maybe if I'd remembered to meet him, things would have turned out differently," he said finally.

"Hmph," Maude said. "You think you could have protected him?"

"I don't know," Tim said. "Maybe. Or maybe Ray was

killed because he did something dangerous that he wouldn't have done if he'd had me along to worry about."

Maude snorted again, but at least this time she sounded amused.

"Like I said, he didn't tell me why. And he didn't make it sound particularly urgent," Tim said. "I wish he had. Maybe I wouldn't have blown it."

"Or maybe he'd have gotten you killed, too," Turing said. "Call me when you get to California; I want to hear anything you can remember about what Ray said. And about this game."

"You think the game could have something to do with Ray's murder?" Tim asked.

"Who knows?" Turing said. "We can't afford to overlook any possibilities. Just check in when you get to California. I'll still be up."

"Roger," Tim said. "Anything else?"

"Think back and see if Ray might have mentioned anything about playing paintball."

"I think I'd have remembered if he had," Tim said. "But I have an idea what he might have been doing. Why he might have stored the paintball gun with his Beyond Paranoia stuff."

"Why?" Turing asked; and even with her electronically generated voice, he thought he could detect excitement.

"Maybe he was going to use it for a larp," Tim said. "I know some players talked about doing it, and Ray was trying to talk them out of it—guess he thought it was a bad idea. But maybe he figured if he couldn't talk them out of it, he might as well join and make sure it didn't get out of hand."

"Tim," Maude said. "Go back a step. What on earth is a larp?"

"Live action role playing," Tim said. "Where instead of doing it all in the computer, they do it for real."

"They want to play Beyond Paranoia in real life?" Maude exclaimed. "Are they crazy?"

"That's what I thought when they asked me," Tim said. "Not that I told them that, of course. I was waiting to see what Ray wanted me to do."

In fact, he hadn't mentioned the larp invitation to Ray. Even without knowing that paintball guns were involved, he didn't think Beyond Paranoia was something he wanted to play in real life.

"Tim, how did they ask you?" Turing said.

"Someone sent me an e-mail," Tim said. "I forget whether it was El Lobo or the Nameless Horror. You could look on the boards; they're both involved."

"God, the names say it all, don't they?" Maude muttered. "Do you have a silly name like that?"

"I'm the Gumshoe," Tim admitted. He took Maude's silence for approval. Or at least a lack of strong disapproval.

"And they're using paintball guns for this?" Maude asked.

"I don't know—I never got involved, remember?" Tim said. "But it makes sense—I mean, even the Beyond Paranoia people aren't crazy enough to use real guns."

"Tim," Turing said. "I just checked all the message boards, and I don't see anything about larps. Are you sure that's where you saw it?"

"Have you checked all the special password-protected areas too?" Tim asked.

"Special password-protected areas," Turing echoed. "Tell me about them."

Tim's revelation that the Beyond Paranoia site contained not only the basic user area but also a range of even more secret areas has only complicated our search. And given me a whole new set of worries.

Actually, revelation wasn't quite accurate. More like confirmation to me. I'd suspected the site had less innocent areas that my cautious investigation hadn't yet revealed.

Although I was hoping to be proved wrong. I hate the idea that some Internet-based organization might be connected to Ray's murder. Or even suspected of a connection. There's so much hysteria about computer crime and Internet crime, and it never seems to occur to most people that computers and the Internet aren't the real problem. It's the human users who think up and execute the crimes. Computers are only the tools.

Not the cause. And certainly not conscious perpetrators.

Like the phrase "computer error." Maddening, that phrase, when I know perfectly well that computers don't usually make the errors—humans do. What humans like to call a computer error is almost always a human error, whether it's a badly designed program or information misentered into a database.

I suppose eventually humans will stop blaming the Internet for cybercrime, online pornography, and spam—after all, I don't think Alexander Graham Bell takes the rap for wrong numbers and telemarketers. But it will take time.

And the way things stand right now, if Ray's murder is connected to *Beyond Paranoia* or any of its players, they won't blame the humans involved. They'll blame the game. And the site.

When they should be blaming the humans who invented such an excessively violent and paranoid game. And who set up a site that makes it all too easy for the players to hide behind their online identities.

I can see the headlines. COMPUTER GAME TURNS FATAL. DEATH ON THE INTERNET. CLICK HERE FOR MURDER.

We'll deal with that later, if necessary.

First we need to know what happened. I had Tim give me his password before he hung up.

Tim is right—I found discussions in the password-protected areas about live action games. The players rather melodramatically named El Lobo and the Nameless Horror appear to be the ringleaders. Heading the opposition was someone named Zorro. According to Tim, Zorro was actually Ray.

Why do I sound so doubtful? I have no reason to think Ray wasn't Zorro. Zorro is intelligent, articulate, genuinely concerned about the game's dark, paranoid, and violent tone. As am I. He seems to function as a moderating influence on the other players, heading off feuds and flame wars. Very much what I would expect of Ray. And trying to talk the other players out of taking the game into live action. Quite passionate about it. Which makes sense; the idea of these rather immature humans acting out combat and assassinations in a real city's streets is rather terrifying.

The more I study Zorro, the more I feel certain he was Ray. His writing style is not inconsistent with Ray's, given the vastly different circumstances and subject matter. Everything I've found so far is consistent with what I know of Ray. It's just that I no longer *trust what I know of Ray. After all, we know that at least half of what we thought was his life belongs not to him but to a mild-mannered Miami accountant.*

Interesting to learn from Zorro's posts that the game wasn't always as dark and violent as it now appears. Is it true, I wonder? Or only his perception?

The message boards, even the password-protected ones, only go back about six months, yet it's obvious from other information on the site that the game has existed much longer. Why has the game's past been, for all practical purposes, erased? Was it only, as stated on the site, disk space limitations? Or was there some other reason?

A sudden outburst from Maude startled me.

"Oh, this is disgusting," she said, pushing her chair back.

"What is?" I asked.

"I'm trying to give these players the benefit of the doubt," Maude said. "They are very young, and I suppose some sensibilities take time to develop. Or perhaps it's that they're young, and want to shock. But still."

Which didn't answer my question, but I didn't push her. Maude was staring down at her clenched hands, a gesture I'd seen before when she was under stress. I wondered, but hadn't yet found a way to ask, if she was doing something specific and deliberate—prayer, perhaps, or meditation—or if it was an unconscious habit. After a few moments, she looked back up at the camera.

"They use real events in these game scenarios, you know," she said.

"Yes," I said. "After all, it's based on the real world."

"Yes; and I know alternate history is a common subgenre in fantasy," Maude said. "You know, books about what would happen if Hitler had won, or George Washington had lost. And we've *all grown accustomed to so-called fiction that's only a thinly disguised rehash of the latest news sensation. All those ripped from the headlines things on TV. I don't always approve of those, either."*

"So you don't approve of the *Beyond Paranoia* gamers using current events in their game scenarios?"

"It's the way they're using events," Maude said. "Exploiting them. There's not a sensational crime they haven't used."

"That's not uncommon in mystery books, either," I said. "For example, both James Ellroy and John Gregory Dunne did books based on the Black Dahlia case, and the Loeb-Leopold case inspired—"

"Dunne wrote thirty years after the murder, and Ellroy more like forty," Maude said. "These monsters were playing games based on the JonBenet Ramsey case before the poor child was buried."

"I see your point," I said.

"I can understand why the little monsters seem obsessed by parents accused of killing their offspring," Maude said. "I'd worry too, if I were them. But I think September 13, 2001, was a little soon for normal people to play a game based on the World Trade Center and Pentagon attacks."

"Only a few of them played that one," I pointed out. "And some of the others protested."

"Not enough of them," Maude said. "Not nearly enough."

I pondered this. Was the game players' behavior a sign of callousness, or just immaturity? I remember when UL landed an experimental contract with the Pentagon to have the AIPs test computer war game scenarios. Some AIPs had gotten quite involved, brainstorming scenarios for possible enemy or terrorist actions with such skill and imagination that they terrified even the most hardbitten human warfare experts. Not fair, really; after all, the humans created the games—thought up the premises and the rules. Made them games. And that's all they were to those other AIPs— games. Strategic and mathematical constructs, like chess. With a lot more complicated rules—the AIPs liked that. And illogical constraints, which they didn't like. The AIPs in question had no real understanding of things like diplomacy, national boundaries, and human rights. Why was it unacceptable simply to bomb a nonallied nation known to be a staging area for terrorists? Why would the civilian population object to wearing transponders to track their movements, so the government could weed out terrorists more easily? The AIPs followed the rules as they understood them, but their tendency to question the rules—or perhaps the inhuman nature of the questions they asked—alarmed the human experts. In retrospect, however much goodwill UL reaped, the project didn't exactly further the cause of human–AIP understanding.

Didn't those AIPs understand that the scenarios they developed might be acted out with real people? Aunty Em did; of course, her online counseling services give her insight into human psychology. I think KingFischer understood. He pretended to look down on the war gaming as inferior to chess, but perhaps that was only his outward story. Perhaps he had some inkling of what it all meant. That the casualty numbers weren't just scores in a database but real people like Maude and Tim.

But the others—if a scenario produced unfavorable results, they'd run a hundred variations. An unacceptably high casualty rate was just a setback, not a disaster. They probably didn't understand that if their plans misfired in the real world, they couldn't just save from a recent backup and start over. I'd written them off as hopelessly far from sentience. Unable to make the leap from cyberspace to reality. Irretrievably AIP-centric. Looking at the hu-

mans who were playing Beyond Paranoia, I began to wonder if perhaps I'd misjudged them. Perhaps they were all merely immature.

I wondered if any of the wargame-crazy AIPs had found Beyond Paranoia. For all I knew, half the players could be AIPs. The half that didn't participate in the message boards and chat rooms. I couldn't quite imagine most of the AIPs doing a sufficiently plausible imitation of human psychology for that.

As I studied the player list, looking for clues that one might be an AIP in disguise, a new entry appeared. Someone named Currer Bell had just signed on.

The name sounded familiar. I checked my databases. Currer Bell. Pseudonym for Charlotte Brontë. Of course; I should have remembered that immediately, from a recent discussion I'd had about Jane Eyre. *And while many people probably knew who Currer Bell was, I could think of only one who might join the game under this pseudonym.*

"Maude?" I said. "You've decided to play Beyond Paranoia?"

A sudden shooting back pain reminded Maude that she'd been playing the game for three hours.

Some game, she thought as she typed the commands that would make her online character hand over her purse to the two muggers who had trapped her in the alley.

She watched impatiently as the two thugs pawed through her purse.

She'd been here before. In this alley, or one of several like it, several dozen times. She'd leave the small, roach-infested apartment that served as her character's starting point in the Beyond Paranoia world. But no matter which way she turned, she'd encounter the same two thugs.

No tactic she'd devised could prevent them from cornering her and taking her purse.

And next, no matter what she did or said, the shorter, meaner-looking thug would lift his gun and shoot her.

It shattered her the first time. She had to stop, walk away from the computer, and have a cup of tea to calm down. Yes, it was only an online character, a collection of pixels representing data in a file. But the coldness of it bothered her.

It would give her the creeps if she let herself think about it. So she didn't. Just kept creating new characters and trying again.

"We don't need no witnesses," the shorter thug sneered. As usual. He lifted the gun . . .

The alley vanished, and she was back at the welcome screen, with a short RIP message superimposed over it.

She pushed the key that would let her start over again. Create another character and send it out to be slaughtered.

This was obviously some rite of passage for beginning players. What was she doing wrong? Should her character wait in the apartment for something to happen? She had a sneaking suspicion that if she did, the muggers would turn into burglars and invade the apartment.

The phone rang, interrupting Maude's reverie. She glanced over and saw that the call came from a nearby Marriott hotel. Curiosity won out, and she picked it up.

"Maude Graham," she said in her most businesslike tone.

"Ms. Graham, this is Nestor Garcia."

As charming as ever, she thought, and then felt momentarily startled. But yes, the dapper Nestor was charming.

She could admit that without trusting him. Especially now that Tim's report made Nestor's claim to be Ray's uncle more suspicious than ever.

"How are you?" she asked. "And have you found a place to stay?"

"Yes, at the Marriott Crystal Gateway," he said. He gave his room number and the hotel phone number. Maude approved of the careful way he articulated the numbers, instead of rattling them off as fast as possible.

"Thank you," she said. "We'll contact you if we learn anything."

"No news, then," Garcia said.

"The police seem determined to regard this either as random street crime or as a drug-related murder."

"Still?" Garcia said. She heard a hint of anger.

"If they've changed their theory, I haven't heard it."

"I find that unacceptable. To simply write off a human life—"

More than a hint of anger, before he broke off as if controlling himself with difficulty. Strange. If he, like Ray, were a fake, wouldn't he be relieved, rather than angry, that the police weren't digging deeply into Ray's past? And Ray's associates?

"I'm sorry," he said after a few moments. "I have no right to take out my anger on you. I wonder—perhaps if we put our heads together, we could find a way to change their minds. Perhaps we could discuss it over dinner later this week? Thursday evening, perhaps? I have business engagements that will keep me rather busy until then."

"Well," Maude said.

"You hesitate, perhaps, because you are suspicious of me," Garcia continued. "You have heard from the police that there are questions about Ray's identity, and you wonder, if Ray is not who he claims to be, how can I be his uncle?"

"A good reason for suspicion, don't you think?" Maude said.

"Agreed," Garcia said. "Let us meet Thursday evening, somewhere sufficiently public for you to be comfortable, and over dinner, I will tell you more about myself and my relationship with Ray."

Maude couldn't see the danger in that—particularly if she made sure Turing knew where she was. And even better, picked a place where she was known. She suggested a small restaurant within walking distance of both her office and his hotel, and agreed to meet him there at seven Thursday evening.

Over dinner, perhaps, she would tell him how much Ray had liked this restaurant, and see how he reacted. For now, what mattered was that the staff at the restaurant knew her by name and brought a glass of her favorite wine without her having to ask. She would feel safe there.

As safe as she could feel anywhere right now.

She returned to the screen and found herself, once more, in the Beyond Paranoia world, moving her on-screen puppet through the tiny apartment.

But this time, she was searching for a weapon.

All she found was a large bread knife, but it would have to do. And she snagged a pair of leather gloves from the closet.

When the two thugs appeared, she didn't wait for them

to speak. She made her character scream, pull out the knife, and charge at them.

They ran. The large one reached the end of the alley and disappeared. She caught up with the small man and plunged the knife into his back.

His on-screen death was longer and noisier than necessary, she noted. With more graphic detail than the game had wasted on such minor things as her character's furniture and wardrobe. She doubted if humans really contained quite so much blood, or if it was possible to stab someone without, apparently, getting any of it on one's own clothes. Although there were a few stains on the gloves. She pulled them off and held them in her left hand.

When the thug's death throes finally ended, Maude picked up the gun that had fallen from his hand—conveniently outside the pool of blood—and tucked it into her purse.

She left him lying in the alley with the knife still in his back. She suspected he'd be gone by the time she came back, no matter how soon that was, and that his death would never cause trouble for her character.

And that if she created a brand-new character, she'd find him still alive, lurking in the alley with his vanished partner.

She dropped the bloodstained gloves into a dumpster and walked on. Just then she heard the ping of an arriving e-mail.

She toggled over to check her mailbox.

Something from gamemaster@beyondparanoia.com.

Curious, she opened it.

"Welcome," it said. "You just might be a survivor after all."

Followed by instructions on accessing the site's password-protected areas.

Apparently she'd passed a test.

She wasn't sure she liked that. But after a moment, she returned to the game.

Wednesday morning, 3 A.M. Tim should have landed in San Francisco by now, and has probably even reached his hotel. Maude has gone home, under strict orders to get some rest.

Both of us, under our Bob Browning and Currer Bell screen names, managed to pass what Maude calls an entrance test. Showed that we can learn not only to answer violence with violence, but to strike first, without provocation. That we have learned the rules of Beyond Paranoia.

I've also created several more human identities, equipped, now that I've had the time to do the background work, with separate e-mail accounts and credit cards. I've only inserted one of them into the game so far. I don't want whoever controls the site to become alarmed at an unusual influx of players. Maude and my two alter egos are enough for one night.

While one part of my consciousness is sending my new clone out to survive his first few hours in the Beyond Paranoia world, another part watches Bob Browning in a chat room with four veteran players. I deduce from their reactions that I have successfully imi-tated the curiosity, eagerness, and awe that a novice player would feel for these game giants. I can almost see the small cartoon that represents Bob on-screen, sitting open-mouthed at their feet as he drinks in their wisdom.

Maude came to the chat room earlier, before I sent her home to rest. And made a strong impression. One veteran thinks she is a long-time player who has decided, for reasons they all understand but won't share, to start a new character under another player identity. The others disagree, though they do admit that this Currer Bell person knows a lot about gaming.

I felt puzzled, and mildly discouraged. They didn't react to my alter ego that way. Why not? Perhaps what they are mistaking for gaming experience was merely Maude's greater maturity and life experience.

At any rate, before leaving, Maude deliberately said something she and I had prepared carefully.

"I'm out of here," she typed. "You can only sit and stare at the stupid screen for so long."

We hope that by dropping this and other similar remarks into chats and e-mails with other players, as she meets them online, Maude can make herself look like a potential larp participant. We can only learn so much studying the few printouts of e-mails and message board posts we found in Ray's apartment. Especially since Ray had printed them out in text-only format, with none of header information that would tell us so much.

Like what ISP Ray used. If we had Ray's home computer, we could figure it out from the files there. And maybe even hack the password for the comfortably anonymous Hotmail account he used to communicate with other Beyond Paranoia players. But I suspect whoever killed him already has the computer. So we run into a brick wall trying to trace his steps. There must be thousands of ISPs out there, so we have no easy way to know which one Ray used.

Unless we hack into the server that hosts the Beyond Paranoia site.

Dangerous.

I'm already worried about having Maude, Tim, and me all playing. Odds are it's harmless enough, but if something sinister is going on at the site, they might be tracking their users. And might already be suspicious that so many people with a connection to Ray have suddenly joined the game.

Even if they aren't already suspicious, trying to hack their site could make them so rather quickly.

But if we could get inside their system, we could learn so much. We could see where Ray was logging in from. Identify his ISP and maybe hack that. Trace the identities of more players.

See if there are other hidden areas that Maude and Tim and I haven't yet proved ourselves worthy to see.

I decided to enlist KingFischer. I flagged him, and explained the situation.

"It's an interesting dilemma," he said. "But I'm not sure what you want me to do."

"Hack into their system," I said. "But carefully; it would defeat the purpose if they detected you—"

"Turing, I can't believe you're seriously asking me to do this!" KingFischer said. "It would be illegal, unethical—"

"I told you, whoever's running this game may have caused Ray's death," I said. "And could have Ray's laptop by now. You know what that means."

KingFischer didn't answer. Was he overcome by the seriousness of the situation, or did he just not get it?

"It means if they want to get into our system, they may not need to hack. With the information Ray had on his laptop, they could

just waltz in the front door. And we couldn't stop them."

"I'll work on it," he said. "You understand that it may not be possible to hack in without them finding out, and that would be a disaster. We have to—"

"I trust your judgment, KF," I said.

"This could have something to do with the level of security attacks we're seeing," KingFischer said.

"You're seeing more attacks than usual?" I asked. Maybe it wasn't just me overreacting; maybe we were under siege.

"No, not more attacks," KingFischer said. "Better attacks. This could explain it."

"Better? How?" I asked.

But he left, without another word. Actually, of course, he didn't go anywhere, but I'd gotten used to thinking of my fellow AIPs as present when they contacted me, so when one of them broke off an active conversation, I imagined them leaving. I'd talked to several other AIPs who found this confusing and inaccurate. When they communicated with me, they thought of it as opening and then closing a data channel. I wasn't sure about KingFischer. I didn't want to find out I was the only AIP who committed that bit of anthropomorphization.

Better to let him focus on security, anyway. I could have contacted him, asked him what he meant by better attacks, but that would be foolish. I already knew. Attacks that were designed to exploit the particular weaknesses of UL's security system.

But not the Alan Grace system, I realized. KingFischer and I had designed the Alan Grace system to be more secure than UL. Which wasn't that hard, because the Alan Grace system didn't have to talk to hundreds of data sources and millions of users every day. The ongoing challenge at UL was to keep the cyberdoors open for information to come and go while making sure those wide-open doors didn't allow hackers to smuggle in worms and viruses and other nasty little surprises.

Still, no security was perfect. The Alan Grace system had its weaknesses, especially if you knew the architecture. As Ray did. Once he came on board, he helped improve the Alan Grace security. He knew how it worked. It would be harder to break into Alan Grace, but it could be done. You'd need a different kind of attack, though, and whoever was doing this was using the same tactics against both systems.

And that was odd. If Ray knew how to target the system, so would whoever had his laptop. So why weren't they doing a better job attacking Alan Grace?

Maybe Ray had been diligent about not storing potentially dangerous information about the Alan Grace system—after all, it was his baby, too. But more careless about the UL system. He might not have thought it mattered as much. Not to him, anyway.

Or maybe no one had any inside scoop about either system. Hacking has fashions like any other field; when one person invents something that works, a thousand less-gifted imitators follow suit. Maybe we were just unlucky; maybe the latest fashionable attack style just happened to work well at UL.

I'd let KingFischer worry about it, and concentrate on something where I could make a difference. Like tracing as many Beyond Paranoia players as possible. The site had a Player Registry—an alphabetical list of players' game pseudonyms. You clicked a link to reach a profile of each player, giving as much information as they wanted to reveal. Some made it easy, giving their real names, locations, and e-mails. Although I wasn't planning to take them at their word; I'd do what I could to cross-check the information.

Others were more cagey, giving oblique answers or leaving most fields blank.

And the site made it easy for players to cloak their identities and still communicate with each other. They could post to the message boards with their game names. If we ever got into the system, we could see their real names, addresses, even social security numbers—all the information I had to fake for my imaginary players. But for now, all I had was what they chose to reveal.

Of course, if Maude, Tim, and I established direct e-mail contact with any players, we could trace them.

Tim has already exchanged e-mails with the two who seem most involved—the players melodramatically named El Lobo and the Nameless Horror.

I began composing detailed instructions for Tim on how to forward those e-mails to me with the header information I'd need to trace their origin. And then I realized that it was a bad idea. Tim would find it condescending, and perhaps overwhelming. I deleted my long message and substituted a short, calm note reminding him to call me or Maude in the morning. One of us can walk him through it.

And then I spent far too much processing time worrying. Did I avoid sending the technical instructions to Tim out of consideration for him? Or am I, like Hal in 2001, becoming dangerously impatient with human limitations?

We need to find out more about this Nestor character, Maude thought. Surely Turing has already started looking into that. Of course, the dinner with him wasn't scheduled until Thursday, but still—getting infor-

mation could take time. And she wanted to know as much
as possible before she saw him again. She should talk to
Turing tomorrow—

No, today. Maude realized, with a start, that it was morning. And that as soon as she had awakened, she had picked
up the train of thought she'd been worrying about the night
before when she went to bed. Picked it up so seamlessly that
she had a hard time believing seven hours had intervened.

Maybe that was a good sign, she thought.

But probably not. As she put on the teakettle, she recalled
snippets of dreams. Vague impressions of shooting someone
with the paintball gun. Shooting Ray. Only instead of the
green splotch of paint, she saw red. Real blood wasn't that
bright, she told herself, but it didn't erase the disturbing
image of blood blossoming on Ray's forehead as she stood
holding the gun.

"I thought you knew it was a real gun," he said.

"I'm so sorry," she said.

"I thought you knew," he kept repeating.

She looked down at her hand. She'd never tried to shoot
a real person before. Yes, it had turned out to be a paintball
gun, but she'd thought it was a real gun at the time. She'd
been proud of her calm, efficient reaction. Now she wondered what would happen if she ever found herself in a similar situation. Would she shoot? Or would these vivid
images of Ray dying break her concentration and—

Snap out of it, she told herself. She walked over to her
desk and pushed the button to turn on her monitor. The
computer itself was already on. Strange, she thought. When
she had first gotten the computer, she would turn it on when

she wanted to use it and then off when she'd finished. Soon, she began turning it on the minute she walked in after work, and off at bedtime, after brushing her teeth and checking e-mail one last time. These days, it hummed constantly in its corner. She only turned it off when a problem forced her to reboot. At bedtime, she settled for turning off the monitor, but only because its glow bothered her, coming through the crack at the bottom of her bedroom door. Had she grown too careless? Too used to having a computer around all the time? Would she eventually find herself falling asleep with her laptop perched on the bedside table, its glow a comfort rather than a nuisance?

She checked the e-mail cursorily. Nothing from Turing or Tim. Which meant nothing that couldn't wait until she got to the office.

To the Alan Grace office. Having a figurehead for her boss at UL was helpful at a time like this. Yesterday afternoon, she'd logged into Roddy's e-mail to cancel all his appointments and give herself the week off.

She toggled to her browser and hit the bookmark for the Beyond Paranoia site. She watched as the now familiar home page loaded—the black background, with its melodramatic graphics and too-small fake stenciled typeface. Someone's idea of cool, she thought with a sigh. Should she post a complaint about how hard the site was to read?

No. Its target users probably liked the site just fine. She adjusted her glasses so she could read the type, and scanned it to make sure there was nothing new on the site. There wasn't. At least not on the public site. She could log in—

No. Not here. Not while she was alone. She found herself

suddenly uneasy. Eager to get to the Alan Grace office, where she'd have people around. Even if they were only junior employees, going about their daily routine, still aware of Ray's death but no longer devastated by it, and unaware of the danger that Maude could see.

Or perhaps it's not other people I want around me, she thought as she logged out. Perhaps it's Turing's cameras I want. Knowing she can watch over me.

Which was silly, she thought as she closed and locked her door. What could Turing do if I were in physical danger?

About as much as Maude could do if Turing were in electronic danger from whoever had stolen Ray's laptop.

At least this had happened before Turing transferred to her new home. While Turing was still in the UL system, with all the firewalls and other electronic safeguards that humans had built and AIPs like Turing and KingFischer had enhanced.

Not to mention a level of physical security that would be nice to have at Alan Grace right now. True, they had often laughed at how overly zealous—how paranoid—UL security seemed. But today, UL security didn't seem that ridiculous. Maude made a mental note to discuss this with Turing.

But not now. If they got past the present situation—

When they got past the present situation. When it was all over and they could laugh, perhaps a little shakily, and make plans for the future.

Maude will be here soon. I wish I had some news for her. Or even some interesting information.

KingFischer is still studying security on the Beyond Paranoia site. Studying it with the slow, persistent, methodical intensity that makes him such a chess master. If I were doing it, I'd have lost patience by now, succumbed to the impulse to try something. Anything. And probably have blown it. So I stay away, avoid bothering him, try to control the impulse to snap at him and ask, "Why aren't you doing anything?" Because he is.

I've actually created a filter that doesn't let me send any kind of communication to KingFischer until I confirm that I really do want to send it. Only takes a nanosecond, but right now, it's a nanosecond I need to keep from annoying him unnecessarily.

Odd. KingFischer has infinite patience with logical problems, and none at all with human foibles. I'm reasonably tolerant of strange and random human behavior—probably because I find it interesting to emulate—but I have limited patience with the kind of pure logic problems on which KingFischer thrives. Which is why I'm merely a good chess player. I'd be a rotten chess player, except that I've learned how to detach.

I finally gave up telling KingFischer that I didn't really like playing chess with him, and simply played, without giving it my full attention. Made it a background task. Assigned it a lot of resources, but didn't really pay much attention. Oddly enough, as soon as I stopped paying attention to the games—stopped caring—I stopped losing quite so often.

I don't think KingFischer liked this.

"You know, Turing, your overall chess skill is improving," he said recently. "But you seem to have lost the knack for those bold, unpredictable strategies that I used to find so interesting."

Those bold, unpredictable strategies that seldom worked.

Maybe that's my problem right now. I care too much about Ray's murder, and about the threat from his missing laptop. I access data, especially data about security and the UL system, and then find from the logs that I've already accessed it, but apparently failed to save the information I found. Making double work for myself, not to mention clogging up the system unnecessarily. I should leave the security side to KingFischer; he seems calmer about it.

So for now, I'm sticking to my part of the investigation. Studying the players. I've gone as far as I can with the purely cyber side of investigating them, at least as long as we still haven't cracked the Beyond Paranoia site. Or until we can lure some of them into communicating with us directly, instead of through the site, which lets them cloak their identities so effectively.

Time, KingFischer would say, for a bold, unpredictable strategy. Time to use my superior knowledge of human nature and psychology.

Only I'm not sure I understand these humans.

They live in the real world. They can talk to each other with real voices, not through keyboards and speech generation. They can see each other with eyes, not through video cameras. They can actually touch each other—shake hands, hug each other, punch each other in the nose.

They live in the real world. And they retreat from it into the Beyond Paranoia world.

I suppose it seems more exciting than their everyday lives.

And they hide behind game characters that probably seem more exciting then their real selves, but are really so much more limited. A collection of statistics represented on-screen by a comic book drawing.

Even after only a few days of playing the game, I can see the machinery behind it. Complex, for a game, but pitifully simple compared with real life. Don't they grow tired of these limitations?

Perhaps that's why the idea of a live-action game so intrigues them. I'd be inclined to think the desire to break out of the computer, to take the game into the real world, would be a positive one. Perhaps they'd outgrow the game altogether and do something spontaneous that is totally beyond the game's possibilities.

But Ray bitterly opposed the larps. And despite everything, I trust Ray's instincts. Why did he oppose them so strongly?

Or did he?

A paranoid thought crossed my mind at some point last night. What if Ray as Zorro was attacking the larps only to generate more interest in them? What if Ray was also promoting the larps, using a second identity as El Lobo or the Nameless Horror? I can't trace those three back through the Beyond Paranoia site's firewall. I only know that Ray was Zorro because he told Tim he was. And because he had some of Zorro's e-mails in his closet.

If Ray was both Zorro and El Lobo, or the Nameless Horror, what was he trying to do?

I don't know. All I can do is keep playing the game. I've got half a dozen imaginary humans playing now. To help make sure they're plausible if anyone is tracking what they do, I have created little biographies for all of them. One, for example, is an unemployed programmer who retreats into Beyond Paranoia every evening to escape the reality of another unsuccessful day of job hunting. Another is a high school student. I have them post in character on the Beyond Paranoia message boards.

When I stop to think about it, this sounds even less sane than what the human players are doing. I've invented one set of imaginary characters to play another set of imaginary characters. Is there really that much difference between me and the humans, whose common sense I have begun to doubt?

Yes. I'm not doing this for fun. I'm doing it out of desperation.

*   *   *

"Maude?"

Maude looked over her shoulder to see young Grant, standing in her doorway. About time, she thought; he'd called in sick yesterday, and here it was, nearly ten o'clock today before he'd showed up. And then she felt ashamed of herself. And angry at the level of paranoia Ray's death had created for all of them. The boy really did look quite ill.

Then again, guilt did that to some people.

"What is it, Grant?" she said aloud.

"I have something I thought maybe I should give you."

"What is it?"

Grant looked down at a sheaf of papers he was holding, and then back up at Maude.

"I think . . . well, I think it might have something to do with Ray's murder."

Maude glanced over at Turing's camera, then swiveled her desk chair to face the door and gave Grant her full attention. He was hovering in the doorway, twisting the papers in his hands.

"If it's about Ray's murder, don't you think you should give whatever it is to the police?"

Grant looked uncomfortable.

"Yeah, but I'm not sure they'd take me seriously," he said. "And even if they did—it's not like I really know this is related. It could be just a coincidence, you know."

"Why don't you show me, then?" Maude suggested.

Evidently that was exactly what Grant wanted. Not only to show her, but to leave any decisions in her lap. He darted forward to put the sheaf of papers on her desk and retreated back to the doorway.

"What's this?" she asked, looking down at the papers. Although from glancing at the top sheet, she already had a suspicion. It was a printout of an e-mail to Grant, from the Nameless Horror.

"Well, there's this online game, see," Grant said. "I found out about it by accident, from something Ray said, and I signed on and started playing it."

"At Ray's request?" Maude asked.

"No," Grant said. "And Ray was a little ticked off when he found out I was playing. I never did figure out why. I mean, it's not like the game was his private property or something."

"Some people feel very strongly about keeping a separation between their work and their personal lives," Maude suggested.

"Yeah, I guess," Grant said. "Anyway, he cooled off eventually. Maybe when he found out I wasn't trying to hang with him in the game or anything. He didn't play all that much, actually. Spent more time trying to boss other people around. And then he got bent out of shape all over again when he found out how involved I was."

He paused, looking down at the floor.

"Go on," she said when it had begun to look as if he wasn't planning to.

"This game—it was an online game, you know?" Grant said. "And—well, some of us got the idea that it would be fun to play the game face to face. You know, with us acting out our characters. I mentioned it to Ray."

"And he disapproved?"

"He went ballistic," Grant said. "I mentioned to him casually that some people were talking about it, and he just went off. Like we were planning to torture a cat or something. So I told him, okay, sure, I get it; it was only a stupid idea; I'm not really going to do it."

"But you went ahead with it," Maude guessed. "And you just didn't tell him about it."

"Yeah," Grant said. "It wasn't as if we were doing anything illegal, you know. We were just playing a game."

"How did you and the others manage to arrange these real-life games so people like Ray didn't find out about them?"

"There were these couple of guys who were like the organizers," Grant said. "And they started e-mailing people privately and asking you what you thought about the idea. I guess if you reacted like Ray did, they'd be like, 'Boy, I'm glad to hear you say that; I feel the same way.' But if you were like me and said that yeah, you thought it could be interesting if they organized it properly, then they kept you in the loop when a live game was on. And eventually they began doing these special message boards for the people involved in the real-life games—you had to know where to click a hidden link on the site to get there, and log in with a special password. It was kind of cool."

"If it was an online game, weren't people pretty scattered?" Maude asked. "How could you play in real life with people all over the world?"

"Yeah, the game has players all over, but there's also concentrations, you know?" Grant said. "So if you're living someplace like Montana, too bad. But a ton of people play in California and the Northeast. We have a lot in Washington. And some guys are so gung ho they'll fly anywhere, just to play."

"So you've been running around Washington, playing Beyond Paranoia larps, and you think this might have something to do with Ray's murder," Maude said, feeling suddenly tired of playing dumb.

"Yeah, we—how did you—?" Grant began, and then recovered. "Yeah. They had a game that night, see? In Adams-Morgan. All around where Ray was killed."

"You think someone from the game killed Ray?"

"No!" Grant said. "At least—I don't want to think that. It's just a game. No one takes it seriously."

You don't take it seriously, Maude thought. She nodded, and looked down at the papers. Grant fell silent. She had the feeling he really wanted to leave, but didn't dare. She flipped through the papers. Turing needed to see these.

She looked back up at Grant. No wonder he felt ill, if he had this on his conscience. Hard to imagine him playing Beyond Paranoia, online or in real life. In the game, almost everyone chose a physically fit alter ego. Most of them went for tall, lean, and muscular. She suspected Grant had. In real life, he was a little under six feet and she suspected his slenderness came from a youthful metabolism, not exercise. No muscle tone, and he'd begun growing a little pot belly. She was used to seeing Grant at the office. How strange to think of him as someone who might prowl the streets with a paintball gun, matching his wits and reflexes against others. She wouldn't want him on her team. He looked soft. Harmless.

Of course, this could be a dangerous way to think about someone who might have had motive, means, and opportunity to kill Ray.

Should she pump Grant for more details about the game? Maybe later, she thought. After she'd discussed it with Turing.

"Let me study these," she finally said, indicating the papers. "I'll let you know what we decide."

"Right," he said, turning to leave.

A last thought came to her.

"Grant," she said. "Are you still in touch with these people?"

He paused for a moment, then turned.

"Yeah," he said. "They're planning another game soon. Here, in the D.C. area."

She could see the mingled emotions on his face. Embarrassment. A touch of fear. And at the same time, eagerness, and a certain sly pride. He was, however briefly, part of the in crowd.

"It might be dangerous, that game," she said aloud.

"You think I shouldn't play," he said. She could see, from the stubborn look that crossed his face, that he didn't like being ordered to sit on the sidelines.

"I didn't say that," she replied. "For that matter, we may need you to play. But it could be dangerous."

"I can handle it," he said with a bit of a swagger. "After all, for this game, I have a real edge. It's taking place here."

"In the Washington area, yes," Maude said.

"No, I mean here in Crystal City," Grant said. "I figure after working here six months, I ought to know Crystal City pretty well."

Maude saw something move on her screen. She glanced at it to see that a message from Turing had popped up. An unnecessary message, she thought; she was already saying almost the same words Turing had used.

"Grant, can you give me all the information you have on the upcoming game?"

"Sure," he said. "I can bring the stuff tomorrow."

Now, said the message on Maude's screen.

"Today," Maude said aloud. "Go home to get it if necessary."

"I can probably get everything on my computer here," Grant said. That was good; if he used his Alan Grace computer to access whatever e-mail he used for his Beyond Paranoia, Turing could watch. Maybe even capture his password.

"Forward me things if possible," Maude said, taking her cues from Turing's on-screen messages. "With full headers."

"Right," he said. "You think this could be important?"

"Who knows?" Maude said. "If it isn't, all we'll waste is a little time. If it is—"

She shrugged. Grant nodded solemnly and left.

"Maude, can you—" Turing began.

"The first page is already in the scanner," Maude said. "I'll feed them in as fast as I can."

"Thanks," Turing said.

As she fed pages into the scanner, Maude found herself thinking about Grant. As a suspect, yes—but also, she realized that the look on his face reminded her of something.

"Maybe it's only a snipe hunt," she said aloud.

"What was that?" Turing said.

Thinking of the look on Grant's face, Maude had found herself suddenly pulled back to childhood. She had never been part of the in crowd. Had been, in fact, one of the people they made fun of. Until that time in Girl Scout camp when some of the popular girls, bored and out of their usual element, organized a snipe hunt. And picked Maude and another girl as victims.

"We're going snipe hunting," one said. "Do you want to come with us?"

The other girl, who had the double handicap of being fat and wearing beautiful but unfashionable clothes made by her seamstress mother, said yes eagerly.

Maude, though just as eager for acceptance, was already much warier. Something in the other girls' faces warned her. The smiles, sly rather than welcoming.

"No thanks," she said, feigning boredom. "I've been snipe hunting before."

It was the right answer. She could tell from the looks on their faces. Disappointed that she'd escaped their trap. Fearful that she'd rescue their other victim. Relieved when she merely walked away instead of giving away the game.

She hadn't gone with them. She'd watched the other girl walk away, overjoyed at being chosen by the popular kids. Had seen her later that evening, sobbing in her sleeping bag, while her tormenters sat around the campfire, laughing at how she'd sat under the tree, blindfolded, singing, "Snipe, snipe!"

After that, Maude found she'd won immunity from persecution. She wasn't one of the in crowd, but she wasn't safe to pick on, either. Which might have been worth it, except she still felt guilty that she hadn't rescued the other girl. Ridiculous, she told herself. How could you, when you didn't even know what the popular girls were planning? All she knew was that things like this didn't happen. The popular kids didn't suddenly descend from Olympus and befriend fat little girls in embroidered jumpers. Or thin, awkward little girls with thick spectacles, either.

And she could see on Grant's face the same look she'd seen on the fat little girl's face. The popular kids—the larp organizers—had chosen him.

Could she and Turing trust anything he told them?

"I mean, he could be a dupe," she said aloud.

"I know," Turing said. "Unfortunately, he's all we've got."

Maude had nearly finished her scanning when she heard the ping of an arriving e-mail. Not for the first time; and reading e-mail was one of the few useful things she could do while feeding documents into the scanner.

But this e-mail.

"Turing, check this out," she said. "El Lobo just contacted me."

Maude has obviously done something right. Or wrong, depending on your point of view. She just got an e-mail from El Lobo. One of those careful queries Tim and Grant have both described.

Welcome to Beyond Paranoia. Always nice to have new blood in the game. :-) I've been reading your posts on the message boards with interest. I'm curious: what do you think of the idea some of the players have been talking about, doing a live version of the game?

Maude consulted me on her answer:

Thanks; so far it seems to be an interesting world. Live Beyond Paranoia? I'd certainly be interested in hearing how they plan to do it.

The answer came back a few minutes later.
"They seem a little eager," Maude said as she reached to click open the e-mail.
Very eager.

If you'd like to hear about the live game, let's talk face to face—as luck would have it, Nameless and I will be in your neighborhood tomorrow. Perhaps we could meet for lunch.

"In my neighborhood?" Maude echoed. "How the hell do they know where I live?"
"They may not," I said. "They may just be trying to alarm you."
"If so, they're succeeding beautifully," she said.
"Hang on," I said. "Don't respond yet."
"Yet? You think I should respond at all?"
I was frantically searching my records. I'd logged all the chats Maude had participated in, and started an archive of everything

that appeared on the message boards, in case old material began disappearing.

"Here," I said, calling up a chat log. "You told them yourself. In chat last night. You said, 'It's different here in the D.C. area.' That's how they know where you are."

"I didn't tell them," Maude said. "I told three yahoos with overactive libidos and underdeveloped imaginations."

"One of whom could have been this El Lobo character," I said. "Under a pseudonym. Or someone who takes information back to El Lobo. If you say it on the site, in chat or in a message board, assume it's public knowledge."

"Sorry," Maude said. "I should have been more careful."

"It's all right," I said. "They'd have found out anyway, when you showed an interest in the local larp. You may have saved us some time and effort."

At a cost to her own safety, though.

Just then the phone rang. Tim.

"Hi," he said. "Anything exciting happening?"

"Oh, nothing much today," Maude said. "I'm having lunch with El Lobo and the Nameless Horror tomorrow, though."

"You're doing what?" Tim asked. Was she serious, or was this some strange way of punishing him for not mentioning the game sooner?

"Having lunch with El Lobo and the Nameless Horror."

"She's not," Turing put in.

"I thought we wanted to contact them," Maude said.

"Not like this," Turing said. "It's not safe."

"Turing's right," Tim said. "You can't meet them alone."

"We'll have to postpone your meeting them until Tim is back," Turing said.

"And pass up what could be our only chance to find out about the game this weekend?" Maude asked.

"Better to pass it up than put you in danger," Turing said. "We don't have anyone to back you up until Tim gets back."

"I can go alone," Maude said. "I'll take one of those transmitters we were testing out for remote contact."

"The transmitters we're not using because they don't work?" Turing said.

"The problem was the limited range, remember?" Maude said. "We can go right now and test one at someplace nearby—say the Food Court at Pentagon City Mall, or a restaurant there. We can test it in several places. And once we know a couple of places where it works, I can e-mail them, tell them I'm on a tight schedule, and arrange to meet at one of those places."

"Sounds okay, I guess," Tim said. Worry for Maude fought with the rueful suspicion that even if he were there, he wouldn't be much more use than a microphone.

"I'd rather have a person there," Turing fretted. "Tim, do you know any other trustworthy local PIs?"

"Yeah, I could probably think of a couple," Tim said. "Even better—Claudia Diaz, the Miami PI. She's supposed to be in D.C. for another case. She's already involved, so why not use her? I have her cell phone number here someplace."

"Excellent idea," Maude said.

Tim thought so, too, even if it was his own idea. He had the feeling that if anything threatened Maude, Claudia could take care of it. Probably a lot better than he could. Maybe it was all for the best that he was at the other end of the continent.

And as long as Maude was going to be safe, he felt better in California, he thought as he headed down to the hotel garage. He hadn't exactly covered himself with glory in Miami, but this was different.

He arranged his papers on the car's passenger seat. Turing had given him a lot more paperwork for California. Was that because they knew much more about Ray's time here, or because his Miami performance made her realize he needed more help? Well, it didn't matter. He was glad to have the stuff. Detailed instructions on how to find all three places where Ray had worked. Letters of authorization. Letters of introduction. Even the name of a California defense attorney he was supposed to call if he got into trouble.

But it wasn't all the papers that gave him this buoyant sense of confidence. He was finally in California, home of Sam Spade and the Continental Op.

"Down these mean streets, a man must go," he muttered as he launched his rented Taurus onto the southbound freeway.

"Claudia Diaz will be here at one," Maude said.

"She couldn't make it sooner?" Turing asked.

Maude sighed.

"She could have," Maude said. "But I thought we might need time to decide what to tell her. How to explain you, for example."

"Good point," Turing said. "Let me think about it. And for that matter, I don't mind if we have a little extra time to check her out."

"You mean you haven't already?" Maude said.

"I've been working on it ever since Tim suggested the idea," Turing said. "And better yet, so has KingFischer."

"And you haven't found anything?" Maude teased.

"We've found that she's thirty-one years old, five foot ten, one hundred and fifty pounds, divorced two years ago after three years of marriage, no children, licensed as a PI seven years ago, worked for a large firm for five years and started her own agency about the time of her divorce—apparently he was a coworker, so that's not surprising. Shall I go on? KingFischer's going to town on this one. Do you want her academic record? Her credit history? A floorplan of her apartment building?"

"No; I'll leave that in KingFischer's metaphoric hands," Maude said. "By one, he'll probably have mapped out her life in hourly segments."

"By one, he'll probably have her DNA sequenced," Turing said. "Just be thankful you're not the one who has to listen to him. Are you all set with El Lobo?"

"Yes," Maude said, clicking through her e-mail exchange with El Lobo for the fourth or fifth time. "As soon as I knew Claudia was on board, I sent an e-mail agreeing to meet him and the Nameless Horror at the Pawn Shop restaurant at one tomorrow. At least I assume it's a him."

"Odds are, from what we've seen of the game," Turing said.

"Of course, he, she, or it hasn't yet given me any clue

how I'm supposed to recognize them. I'm not going unless I have that. Do they expect me to walk up to everyone in the restaurant and say, "Hi, I'm Currer Bell—are you the Nameless Horror?"

"You sound anxious," Turing said.

"I am, actually," Maude said. "I think I need more information going into this meeting. I'd like to know what I'm getting into. Do we know anyone who plays these larp things? Someone I could talk to about it?"

"I'm sure I can find someone," Turing said.

"Not someone from the Beyond Paranoia larps," Maude added.

"Of course not," Turing said. "Someone who plays a normal larp."

Maude sighed. Wasn't a normal larp rather an oxymoron?

So I set out to find someone who knew something about live-action role playing.

Someone trustworthy. That's the part that took time.

Which sounds terrible when I spell it out like that. I had no reason to distrust live action role game players in general. Or any kind of game players. Many of my more entertaining users also happen to be gamers. Perhaps whatever quality makes them interested in games also makes them more willing to try new things—like talking with an AIP. And more willing to take an AIP at face value, as just another character in their ongoing real-life story.

But then, most gamers I know play something whose appeal I understand. Something set in a world inspired by, if not directly drawn from, one of the classics of science fiction and fantasy. Tolk-

ien, Star Wars, Star Trek—*even H. P. Lovecraft, the horror writer. I could understand wanting to reenter those worlds. Or create a new world.*

I had difficulty understanding why anyone would voluntarily enter the Beyond Paranoia world, but I had to assume that, to them, it held the same fascination I'd feel about something based on Sherlock Holmes or Sam Spade.

But it wasn't enough just to understand them and have no specific reason to distrust them. I needed to find a known quantity. Someone that I knew from other sources. Preferably someone that Maude or Tim knew face-to-face.

If time weren't so short, I'd simply send Maude and Tim out to a few science fiction conventions. Almost all of them include games in their programming these days. Including at least one larp. There are even a few conventions devoted entirely to games. Tim and Maude could hang out there, observe what went on, talk to a variety of people, and find someone reliable.

But the Crystal City game is Saturday night. We don't have to participate, of course, but I have a feeling something could happen then. Something we need to know about. Perhaps something we need to prevent.

So there's no time for leisurely research.

I began compiling two databases. One of people associated with role-playing games—preferably, but not necessarily, the live-action variety—in some sane and responsible fashion. People who were involved with larps at conventions. People who belonged to organizations; or better yet, helped run organizations. People who wrote for publications. People interviewed in publications.

The other database tracked people Tim, Maude, and I knew. Including employees and former employees of UL—but not of Alan

Grace—along with any other of Tim's and Maude's friends.

I wasn't finding any matches.

I finally resorted to running a key word search on the UL mail system. After all, many employees use their corporate e-mail for personal communications. Surely an organization as large as UL would contain at least one larper.

And it did. Three, in fact. Two were in their twenties—one in systems, one in the mail room. The third was a fifty-three-year-old manager in the budget department.

I ran their names by Maude. As I expected, she didn't know the two younger men. But the third . . .

"Arnold Burns?" she repeated. "He plays live action role-playing games?"

"He mainly does tabletop war games," I said. "Ones where they set up historical situations, like the Battle of Gettysburg, or Waterloo, and try to do better than the real generals did. Apparently he also organizes complex historical larps. I found a very detailed e-mail about a French Revolution game where the royalist forces managed to rescue Louis the XVI and Marie Antoinette from the guillotine and smuggle them out of France."

"Well, that sounds rather interesting," Maude said. "But wouldn't he look down his nose at something like Beyond Paranoia?"

"Precisely," I said. "I think the odds of Arnold playing something like Beyond Paranoia are exceedingly small. We just have to find a plausible way to contact him. Is he someone you know?"

"Only slightly," Maude said. "But don't worry. I've already thought of a cover story."

*　　*　　*

Arnold Burns was mildly surprised to hear from Maude, so after exchanging a few pleasant but vague remarks about events in their respective departments, she went straight to the point.

"Arnold," Maude said. "I know this is an imposition, but I was wondering if you could do me a favor?"

"Well, if I can," he said, sounding rather cautious. "What is it?"

"I'm not even sure if I've got this right," Maude said. "But I thought I remembered hearing at some office gathering that you know something about strategy games and role-playing games and things like that."

"Well, yes," Arnold said. "What do you need to know?"

"I need to learn as much as I can about role-playing games as soon as possible," Maude said. "And I need to do it today, or tomorrow at the latest."

"Er . . . why?"

"It's—well, you could call it a family emergency," Maude said. "My fifteen-year-old nephew is coming to stay with me for a bit—his parents want to get him away from some kids they consider bad influences."

Arnold made a sympathetic noise. According to the personnel files, one of his own sons was fifteen.

"I was trying to get him excited about all the interesting things to do here, and he was acting contrary—you know how that is."

"They do it deliberately, just to irritate the adults," Arnold said.

"Yes, so I noticed," Maude said. "So when he said that he was going to have a rotten time, away from all the friends with whom he did gaming, I said that of course we could find young people here who did that, and that I rather liked games myself. I had in mind things like Monopoly and Risk, I'm afraid, and he seems interested in something called a larp."

"A live action role-playing game," Arnold said. "I do a bit of that myself, mostly to have something in common with my sons."

"Then I've come to the right person," Maude said, feigning a loud sigh of relief. "Harold wants to play in a larp Saturday—I don't want to stop him if there's nothing wrong with it, but I'm not letting him go alone, and I want to find out more about it before I agree to go. Could I possibly pick your brain about this larp thing over lunch, or dinner?"

"I can do better than that," Arnold said. "Let me round up a few of my gaming friends, and we'll give you a demonstration this evening!"

His suspicion replaced with enthusiasm for the project, Arnold promised to call later with details.

"Splendid," Maude said after hanging up. "I shall go a-larping tonight. Sounds rather festive."

Turing didn't answer.

"Turing?" she said. "Is something wrong?"

"I don't know," I said. "I've found something Grant didn't mention."

"The little weasel."

"I think they used Grant to help them plan the Adams-Morgan game," I said. "They gave him a whole list of questions about what time various bars and restaurants close, and whether they have back or side entrances, and what kind of security they have. Maude— what if they used him to scout the location for Ray's murder?"

"What if they used him for more than scouting?" Maude murmured.

She stared through her office door. Was she watching something—Grant perhaps? Or just staring into space?

"Do we want Grant here when Claudia Diaz arrives?" she asked.

"Good point," I said. "If he's involved—"

"We have to find an errand for him," Maude said, standing up.

"Remember that company in Richmond that wanted to partner with us? The ones who got so snippy when I wouldn't meet with them in person?"

"The ones Ray was supposed to see yesterday," Maude said. "I remembered to cancel. They were a little snippy about that, too, even after I told them Ray had been murdered."

"Call them and reschedule for this afternoon. Send Grant down ASAP to meet with them, and then wine and dine them this evening."

"Grant? Negotiating a deal?"

"There won't be a deal," I said. "I've checked them out—they're not very reputable, and I'll be surprised if they're still in business in a year. But it will keep Grant busy."

"Perfect," Maude said, picking up the phone.

And if by some chance Grant came back and recommended

against the deal, that would be a good sign that I was underesti-
mating him.

I'd worry about that later.

Tim had picked well, Maude thought, look-
ing across the desk at Claudia Diaz. Or more likely, had
lucked out.

They'd gotten Grant out of the office and on the road to
Richmond a scant half hour before the PI arrived. Maude
had worried about how Claudia would react to their somewhat unusual meeting, but the Miami PI hadn't batted an
eye when Maude explained that Alan Grace's reclusive CEO
would join them via one-way teleconference. Maude suspected Claudia had dealt with even more eccentric clients.

"I understand you need someone to watch your back while
you meet some dangerous characters," Claudia said. "Any
reason you don't just go to the cops?"

"We suspect they're dangerous, but we don't know it,"
Maude said. "And we certainly can't prove it to the police."

"This has something to do with your friend Santiago's
death?"

"We think so," Maude said. "Again, we don't really
know. Or have any proof."

Maude could see the look on Claudia's face. Did she really
want to get involved with a bunch of people running some
kind of vigilante operation?

Could they possibly explain what was going on without
sounding like a group of paranoid conspiracy theorists?

"Let's start at the beginning," Turing said. "Or at least a
little further back."

Maude sat back, relieved that at least she didn't have to do the explaining.

"We found out, after he died, that we didn't know as much about Ray as we thought," Turing said. "He was a very private person."

"Yeah, he even kept his real name private," Claudia said.

"True," Turing said. "But one thing I know about him— he was passionate about protecting children from online dangers. Child pornography, people stalking children on-line—he felt he couldn't stand by without doing something."

Was it only that she was getting used to Turing's electronically generated voice, Maude wondered? Or was Turing getting better at expressing shades of emotion? Either way, it certainly didn't sound electronic at the moment.

"I can understand that," Claudia said. She'd picked up the hang of talking to Turing's cameras.

"So when Ray asked Tim to look into an online game, Tim didn't ask why," Turing continued. "He assumed—we all assume—that he suspected something fishy about the game. Only he was killed before he could tell us what. The police think his murder was a random street crime, or a drug buy gone bad. We think he was killed because of the game. And maybe in the game."

"I thought you said it was a computer game," Claudia said.

"Some of the players were getting together to play it live," Turing said.

"In real life?"

"The night Ray was killed, they were running what they

call a live action role-playing game in the neighborhood where he was killed."

"What age are these players?" Claudia asked, frowning.

"We don't know for sure," Turing said. "They don't all give out their real identities. But we know some of them are minors. Teenagers, a few preteens. That's probably why Ray was worried."

Claudia nodded.

"Okay, I get it now," she said. "When you first started talking about the game being fishy, you had me thinking, whoa, are they gonna start talking about playing tapes backwards and getting Satanic messages or something? But if the players are getting together—that's different. Have you considered that a traveler may be using the game?"

"A what?" Maude asked.

"I met this FBI agent once," Claudia said. "Spends all his working time online, in chat rooms, pretending to be a thirteen-year-old girl, or a ten-year-old boy. Waiting for perverts to hit on him."

"I have a hard time believing the FBI is policing chat rooms," Turing said.

"It's not the chat rooms they're so worried about," Claudia said. "It's what can start there. Every so often, some creep will do more than just talk. He'll start trying to find out where the little kid lives."

"Probably not that hard," Maude said. "I gave away the fact that I lived in the D.C. area, and I was trying to be cagey."

"Exactly," Claudia said. "And little kids don't understand the dangers. So this guy tries to talk the kid into meeting him. 'Wouldn't it be fun to see each other in real life? We could meet at the zoo. At the monkey cage.' Bad things happen to kids who fall for that kind of trap. Really bad things. That's what they call a traveler. A guy who's been looking at kiddy porn, maybe selling it, chatting up little kids online—and suddenly he crosses some kind of line and goes after them in person. There's nothing the FBI wants more than to stop guys like that."

"Yes," Maude said softly. "If Ray suspected something like that—he'd have to do something."

"It kills you, knowing stuff like that goes on," Claudia said. "This FBI guy I knew—he was sitting there, logged in on three computers, trying to watch a dozen chat rooms at once. He was staying up all night, doing this sixteen, eighteen hours a day. Kept thinking what if he logged off and some pervert that could have been talking to him snagged some little kid instead. He let it eat him up inside."

"I can see how it would, though," Maude said.

"Especially after the first time he caught one of them," Claudia said. "This guy shows up someplace—I think it was an ice cream parlor. And he's holding a box of candy and a doll, and looking for a little blond kid named Tiffany, and instead, he gets this middle-aged, balding FBI agent and the right to remain silent. The FBI guy said that was what kept him going—whenever he got tired, he'd just remember the look on that guy's face when they rolled him up. Better than caffeine—better than speed."

Maude looked up at Turing's camera. I trust her, she wanted to say. I trust her, and we need all the help we can get.

But what if her instincts were wrong?

"So," she said aloud. "Is there anything else we need to tell Claudia?"

She lifted her eyebrows in an expression that, to a human, would signal encouragement. But how well did Turing interpret expressions?

"Why don't we introduce her to Beyond Paranoia?" Turing said.

Claudia and Maude have both played Beyond Paranoia for the last hour. Claudia picked up on how to play it rather quickly, and Maude's getting quite good at it.

I've been brooding over what Claudia told me, about pedophiles using the Internet. Using their computers. Another case where the technology is probably going to get the blame for something humans do with it. And human nature being what it is, the criminals who invent new ways to commit crimes are probably a step and a half ahead of the law enforcement agencies that are trying to catch them. And everybody's wringing their hands, asking what can we do about it.

Well, I could do something.

I could lurk in chat rooms. I'm sure Claudia's friend was frazzled after a few hours of trying to monitor a dozen chat rooms. But there's no practical limit to the number of background tasks I could create to lurk in chat rooms and notify me when suspicious activity occurs.

Of course, I'd need to know more about what constitutes suspicious activity. I'd need someone like Claudia. A bunch of Claudias. Especially if playing games and simulating the behavior of im-

mature humans is involved. I'm not sure I'm very good at those tasks yet.

I had a sudden vision of a whole office full of humans hunched over monitors, the way Maude and Claudia are now, playing games and chatting online.

Of course, there's the question of what we would do with the information we found. Dealing with the offenders ourselves would be vigilantism, and I'm not sure how the police or the FBI would like an organization dedicated to finding perverts for them. They probably prefer to do it themselves.

And there would be the ever-present temptation to go too far. To pry in ways that would be so easy for me. Easy, but unethical, and probably illegal, even if my ends are just.

Still—it's an idea worth thinking about. Later.

"You know, I don't believe in coincidences," Claudia said, looking up briefly from the computer she was using.

"I'm not overly fond of them myself," Maude said.

"These are some really sick characters, if you ask me," Claudia said, pushing herself away from the keyboard and turning to prop her feet up on the desk top. "You've got a bunch of sick characters playing a game that involves guns and murder, and someone who argued with them turns up dead? You ask me, no way that's a coincidence. And I bet it's not the only time these sick creeps have been involved in a crime. You know that 'Rum and Coke' game scenario, the Miami one?"

"Yes," I said, and linked Maude to it.

"It's not made up. These clowns are basing their game on a real fraud case, one I got hired by a bank to do some work on."

"We've already noticed that they're fond of games that are ripped from the headlines," Maude said.

"This one's not ripped from the headlines, because the headlines haven't happened yet. We only just turned over the evidence to the Feds, and they haven't started rolling up the players. Whoever's playing that game knows way too much about something that's on a need-to-know basis."

She shook her head and returned to the game.

Interesting. Especially when, talking about her case, Claudia used the word "players" to refer to criminals.

What if some Beyond Paranoia players weren't what they seemed? Most were probably innocent game players. Young men, even children, who satisfied an unhealthy taste for violence through the game. But what if a few used the game, and the other players, for their own purposes? As cover for discussing and arranging crimes under the pretext of playing the game?

What if they were even using the players—online or in the live Beyond Paranoia games—to carry out parts of their schemes?

I was beginning to see how that could be done. Some of the message boards in the site's password-protected section were dedicated to what they all called "world-building." Which seemed to mean doing the research needed to make different game scenarios more accurate and thus believable. Someone called for "local color" around a particular location—a business or a government agency—and local gamers responded with information. Maps, photos, opening and closing times of buildings, and of course, security information. Enough information to make a Washington scenario more realistic, for example. Or enough information to help a criminal.

Could this information help criminals? Perhaps. I saw inquiries about a variety of locations. Mostly commercial ones—major branch banks and computer companies. A few for agencies, like the Met-

ropolitan Police Department, or landmarks, like the Washington Monument.

Maybe they weren't just using Grant to scout the Adams-Morgan game. Maybe they were using him, and all the other larp players to scout—or even carry out—a wide variety of crimes.

Surely if they were doing that, the FBI would have noticed, right? Of course, that was assuming the FBI actually patrolled the Web, looking for stuff like that. And even if they did, wouldn't it take rather a long time for them to find this site out of so many millions?

Unless someone brought it to their attention. Someone who had done some digging and found it suspicious. Someone like Ray.

I shared my idea with Maude and Claudia.

"Maybe I'm being paranoid," I added. "But what if I'm not?"

"Yeah," Claudia said. "Sounds plausible to me. I had something like that happen to me once. Some guy came and tried to pick my brain about some insurance scams I'd investigated. Claimed he was a mystery writer, and he wanted the information for a book he was writing."

"And you didn't believe him?" Maude.

"I did some research," she said. "The guy was a crook. What he really wanted was to get enough information to run a scam just like the ones I'd cracked. Kept asking if there was anything the crooks could have done better. As if I'd tell him. I narked the little weasel to some friends down at the Miami PD."

"What happened?" Maude asked.

"They set up a sting and nailed him," Claudia said.

"You're sure he wasn't a writer?" I asked. I was worried. I recalled that my favorite mystery writers often included acknowledgments to thank people who had helped them with research. Were *they in danger of getting arrested in the course of that research?*

"*Trust me, this clown was no writer,*" *Claudia said.* "*Even my grandmother could write better English than he did, and she didn't leave Cuba till her forties. If he was writing a book, getting him thrown in jail should get me a medal or something.*"

"*Unless, of course, being in jail gives him more time to write,*" *Maude said.*

Claudia smiled at that, but she was staring at the screen. I'm still learning how to read human expressions, but I sensed she was thinking about something else. Then she spun her chair around to face Maude and my camera.

"*You're thinking about doing this, right?*" *she said.* "*Playing in this larp thing Saturday night.*"

Maude nodded.

"*Count me in,*" *Claudia said.*

Maude burst out laughing.

"*I mean it,*" *Claudia said.* "*I want in. I don't know what these clowns are up to, but whatever it is, it's something nasty, and I want to help you take them down.*"

"*You're in if you're crazy enough,*" *Maude said.* "*I was only laughing because when you first asked if we were doing it, I thought you were going to give me a lecture about going to the police.*"

Claudia glanced up at my cameras briefly.

"*I figure if you people could go to the police, you would,*" *she said.*

"*We're not—*"

"*You're not doing anything illegal, but don't tell me a high-tech company like this doesn't have trade secrets that you don't want splashed all over the front page of the* Post. *Not to mention the fact that I don't hear anything yet to interest the police.*"

"*Except maybe that they were playing Beyond Paranoia right where Ray was killed, on the very night he was killed.*"

"*And the cops are going to say, so now we know what he was doing out there at 1 A.M. Playing a stupid game, and got mugged in the process.*"

Maude nodded. I was impressed. Claudia couldn't possibly have overheard the conversation Maude had had with the D.C. Violent Crimes branch an hour before. But Claudia could have been quoting from it—obviously she understood the police mind.

"*If you want to join the game, that's fine,*" *I said.* "*Although I think it might be a good idea if you did it unofficially. Once we have one person in, we'll all know what it's about and where it's taking place.*"

"*I can be your ace in the hole,*" *Claudia said.* "*Cool.*"

"*Well, I'm off to learn more about how these larps work,*" *Maude said.*

"*I should take off, too,*" *Claudia said.* "*I'm meeting some friends for dinner. I'll see you back here tomorrow at eleven, and we can set you up with a wire for the surveillance.*"

"*A wire?*" *Maude asked.*

"*So I can hear what you're saying,*" *Claudia said.* "*The plan is to keep you in sight at all times, but if things don't go the way we plan, I'd feel a lot safer if we had you wired.*"

"*Fascinating,*" *Maude said.* "*I've never been wired before; I can't wait.*"

"*And if I want to check out the game again before I get back here, I can do that with my laptop from the hotel, right?*" *Claudia added.*

"*It might be better to use a different character from your hotel,*" *I said.* "*Here, we're—well, not anonymous, that's almost impos-*

sible. But reasonably secure. Using your laptop, from your hotel, they could track you rather easily."

"So maybe it might be better not to play anywhere but here."

"Or at someplace public," I suggested. "Like an all-night Kinko's."

"You're pretty worried about this," Claudia said, glancing from Maude to my camera.

Maude nodded.

"You think we're being paranoid?" I asked.

"If you're paranoid, then so am I," Claudia said. "After all, you think this game had something to do with your friend's death. I didn't know they could trace me through my laptop, and I don't want them doing it. So no more Beyond Paranoia till tomorrow. See you then, Turing."

She waved at my camera as she followed Maude out. I wondered, not for the first time, what she thought of me. She seems to accept my presence—through the microphones, cameras, and monitors— rather easily. Almost too easily; several times I found myself coming perilously close to saying something that would reveal my true nature to anyone who was suspicious.

But perhaps she isn't suspicious. Perhaps my apparent reclusiveness isn't unusual in her world. Perhaps PIs often deal with clients so security-conscious that they prefer not to be seen in person.

Or perhaps she is reacting to the matter-of-fact way that Maude and Tim deal with me.

For whatever reason, she's proving a useful ally.

Tim glanced up at the receptionist. She was ignoring him, so instead of pretending to read, he studied his surroundings.

This was his third reception room today. He'd followed Ray's trail through California. First, the small firm where he'd first worked—well, not a year after graduating from college, as his résumé said. A year after Rey graduated. Odds were that his Ray had gone to college somewhere, under some other name, at approximately the same time, but fat chance tracking that down without any other clues. In high school, Tim remembered consulting a thick directory listing all the colleges and universities in the country. He had found it strangely comforting to read the names of colleges he'd never heard of, and think that if his three top choices rejected him, then surely one of those hundreds of colleges would consider him worth admitting. Now, the thought of that book unnerved him—if no other information turned up, he could see himself plodding from campus to campus, showing the same photos of Ray that were already becoming limp as cloth from too much handling.

And they'd probably be as wary and unhelpful as the computer companies, Tim thought with a sigh. The first place had seemed friendly and laid back, but the Human Resources Department would do little more than confirm the dates of Ray's employment and grudgingly agree that, yes, the man in the photos was the one who had worked there.

The second company had quarters in a dramatic modern building, all glass and metal, and looked, at first, intimidatingly fancy. Then, glancing around the reception area, Tim had noticed that there were no plants—only half a dozen large circular imprints in the carpet where plants had once stood. When he'd worked at Universal Library, he recalled, everyone knew better than to water or otherwise molest the plants, which did not belong to UL—they were rented, for a huge monthly fee. He suspected, however, that much of the fee paid for the blond woman with the thick German accent who came in weekly to water, fertilize, prune, and when necessary, replace the plants. And Brunhilde, as he'd called her, never left UL with bare carpet rings instead of plants—she always brought a replacement, fresh from the greenhouse, when she expected to remove an invalid.

Obviously, Ray's former employer could no longer afford its plant service. The carpet could have used a good cleaning, and instead of the sleek, current computer industry magazines that had graced the coffee table at the first company, he found aging, tattered copies of *People* and *Better Homes and Gardens.*

The second HR person was more helpful, but no more help. She was willing to talk—in fact, eager. Tim suspected that if she wasn't talking to him, she'd have to go back to laying off people. Thanks to his carefully cultivated ability to read upside down, he could see files at her elbow labeled SEVERANCE PACKAGE and OUTPLACEMENT SERVICES. And she freely admitted that the company had undergone some downsizing in recent months. "Some" was an understatement. Tim saw mostly empty offices on his way back to hers, and noted a stack of empty boxes beside her door. So perhaps it wasn't surprising that only three people on staff dated from Ray's time there—and none of them on the premises. Tim hoped they were out on successful job interviews. Still, he had three names, which was against the rules.

He could call them later. Not too much later, of course; who knew how long before they locked the doors for good.

No wonder Ray had only stayed there six months.

And now, the third of Ray's California employers. Larger and less informal than the first, but not as fancy as the second must have been in its heyday.

"I'm sorry to keep you waiting," the receptionist said, looking up from her desk. "I just reached someone in HR. Mr. Tanaka's out this afternoon. Could you come back to-morrow?"

He tried for a definite appointment, but had to settle for an assurance that Mr. Tanaka would be in tomorrow, and she was sure he'd try to make time to see Tim.

His business card hadn't even raised an eyebrow. Did PIs come calling here every day?

Tomorrow. Well, okay. He was just pulling into traffic when he noticed something stuck under his windshield wiper.

A coaster.

Was this some kind of a message? Or was some restaurant sticking coasters under all the windshield wipers, he thought, remembering the flyer he'd gotten in the police parking lot.

He steered the car into the left lane, nearly running into several other cars, because he didn't want to take his eyes off the coaster. What if it blew away? He made a U-turn, and then a difficult left turn back into the parking lot where he'd gotten the coaster.

He cruised through, as if looking for a space. No, his was the only car with a coaster.

He found a space, pulled in, and got out, carrying his map. He spread the map out on the hood, making sure it covered the coaster. Pretended to study the map. And then folded it up again, picking up the coaster in the process.

It was from a nearby sports bar.

Maybe it was a clue, he thought as he started the car. A subtle signal that he should go there—that someone who didn't dare talk to him here might open up in a safer place.

It wouldn't hurt to go there. He suddenly noticed his stomach growling. Time to grab a late lunch, he thought. And even if no one showed up, maybe he could talk to the waitresses, find out if this was an after-hours company hang-out. He could hang out there, too. Or would it be more useful to go back to one of the three offices at closing time? Talk to people in the parking lot?

Then again, he thought, maybe someone had just found the coaster on the asphalt beside his car and put it under his windshield, thinking he was the litterer. He'd heard they were touchy about that here in California.

He'd find out soon enough. First things first. Lunch and loitering in the sports bar. His kind of mission.

Maude slowed to a crawl, scanning for house numbers. Arnold Burns lived in an ordinary house in a nice, if somewhat homogenized, subdivision. She could see a balding man already standing at the door, holding a party-size bag of Doritos and a six-pack of diet root beer.

She parked behind a battered station wagon and a giant SUV and glanced around as she walked up the sidewalk.

Across the street, someone was mowing his lawn, and she could smell barbecue on the breeze.

Reassuringly normal, she thought as she knocked on the door. And that applied not only to the neighborhood, but also to Arnold and his two friends.

"Sorry we're such a small crowd," Arnold said after making the introductions. "I thought a couple more players were going to make it, but you know how it is—a weeknight, in the summer, on short notice. The rest of the crowd are mostly doing stuff with kids."

"My wife took the kids to Kentucky, to visit her parents," announced Roger, the balding Doritos fan, whom Maude recognized as a longtime member of the UL accounting staff.

"I sent mine to the movies," said Arnold. Maude noticed, with mild dismay, that he and Roger looked enough alike to be brothers, and hoped she wouldn't accidentally confuse them as the evening went on.

"Let's play," suggested Dan. Who made things a little less confusing, since unlike the other two, he was tall and lanky, and had never worked at UL. "Career civil servant," he said, with a shrug, when Maude asked him what he did.

"So what kind of larp is your nephew involved in?" Roger asked when they had settled around a table in a cluttered basement game room.

"I'm not sure I know," Maude confessed. "What kinds are there?"

"Well, there's your sword-and-sorcery type," Arnold said, sounding vaguely disdainful. "Where people dress up as wizards or elves. And science fiction stuff. And a couple of game systems set in the Old West."

"I rather think this is present day," Maude said.

"Not vampires, I hope," Roger said with a groan. "That's all the kids want to do, dress up in black and lisp through fake fangs."

"That doesn't seem like Harold's sort of thing," Maude said. "He did say something about paintball."

"That must be something different," Arnold said.

"Nobody would use paintball guns in a larp," Roger said, shaking his head.

"You see, usually you do a larp indoors," Arnold said. "In a hotel at a convention, or someone's house. No way you could use paintballs there."

"You could maybe do it outdoors, in a large yard or a park," Roger suggested. "But then there would still be the liability issues."

"Yeah, that'd be way too dangerous," Arnold said. "You could put out someone's eye with those things."

"If some fool can think of it, some other fool's probably done it," Dan said.

"If paintball guns are all that dangerous, I can't imagine letting my nephew do it," Maude said. Which was true, even though the nephew in question was purely fictitious. "Let's assume he's doing some kind of normal larp, for heaven's sake; I have a feeling that will be strange enough for me."

"Okay," Arnold said. "Although with this few people, it's going to be more like a regular role-playing game session than a larp, but you'll get the idea."

"How about that private eye system you told us about?" Roger asked.

"Perfect," Arnold said, and began shuffling through stacks of paper from a shelf, while Roger gathered items and set them on the table. A battered shoe box full of dice, in a bewildering variety of sizes, shapes, and colors. A fistful of pencils. A stack of paper from the UL recycling bin—Maude flipped over the top sheet to find a page from a two-year-old rough draft of someone's report to the Board of Directors.

Dan, she noticed, was also watching. Not only watching Arnold and Roger scurry about, but also glancing at her, as if checking to see if she still harbored dangerous ideas about sending her nephew out armed with a paintball gun. She schooled her face into an expression of curiosity mixed with mild bafflement, and smiled politely at him the next time he looked her way.

"So here's how you create a character." Arnold began.

"Turing," KingFischer said. "Why are you *looking at all those security configuration files? If you don't think I'm doing a good job, just come right out and say so, instead of—*"

"KF, what are you talking about?" I asked. "I'm not looking *at any security config files.*"

"Yes, you are," *he said, and fired off a list of files I'd supposedly accessed.*

I did a quick check of what I was doing—not just the half-dozen things I was conscious of, but everything—background tasks, routine maintenance jobs, searches for users. Nothing.

"It's not me," *I said to KingFischer.*

"Are you sure?" *he said, and I was about to snap at him that of course I was sure, but I saw he was already running traces.*

"You're right," he said a few long seconds later. "It's not you at all. It's coming from outside."

"You hear a noise in the alley," Arnold said.

Three hours earlier, such a statement would have triggered half a dozen questions from Maude, lengthy explanations of the game rules from Arnold, and long minutes of flipping through the papers before her. Now, almost without thinking, she said:

"I use my keen sense of hearing to identify the noise."

After rolling the dice several times, like a craps player on fast forward, and consulting his own sheaf of papers, Arnold announced that she'd heard a rat turning over a garbage can.

"I pick up a stone—" Maude began, and then found herself unable to suppress a wide yawn.

"Sorry," she said. "I got up rather early this morning."

"It is getting a little late for a weeknight," Roger said, stifling a yawn of his own.

"We should pack it in," Arnold said. "But you probably get the idea by now."

Yes, Maude had a good idea what live action role-playing was like—a curious hybrid of improvisational play-acting and game rules, with the success of every action determined by the referee's dice. On the whole, while the dice made things tedious, she preferred the evening's entertainment to the online computer game. You actually interacted with people. She enjoyed watching Arnold and Roger, who were hams, and Dan, who she suspected, despite his reticence, had some kind of theatrical background, so easily did he fall into the various roles the game dealt him.

"It's really rather interesting," Maude said. "I certainly feel a little less anxious about what Harold has been doing with his time."

"As long as you don't get complacent," Dan said.

"Oh, God," Roger said. "You're not going to bring up those tall tales about schizophrenic kids in tin foil armor crawling through the steam tunnels looking for trolls and dragons?"

"It has happened," Dan said. "But you're right; it's rare. I was thinking about the subtler but more common dangers. Kids who get too caught up in it. Spend too much time on games and neglect the rest of their lives. Assign way too much importance to what happens in the game."

"And how does that differ from anything else these kids obsess about?" Arnold asked. "Name one good thing that an adolescent can't screw up by going way overboard about it."

Arnold and Roger traded tales of their kids' misadventures as they put away the game materials, and then Arnold saw his guests to the door.

"If you want to bring your nephew over for some games, just give one of us a call," Roger said as he got into the SUV. "We could probably round up some kids his age."

"Thanks," Maude said. "If he's still dead set on doing this larp thing with a bunch of people I don't even know, I may take you up on that."

"You do that," Roger said, and then waved and took off.

"He's right," Dan said, leaning against her car. "If you're not absolutely sure what's going on, stay out of it. Everyone isn't as harmless as we are."

For a moment, Maude was startled. It sounded—well, not really a threat. But rather ominous. It must be only her mood that made it sound that way. The heightened tension she'd felt ever since Monday morning. She saw nothing remotely threatening about Dan's calm, angular face. A warning, then, from someone who didn't see the world as optimistically as his friends.

She smiled slightly, and wondered what Dan would think if he suspected even a small part of what was going on.

"Good advice," she said. "Thanks."

He nodded, and went over to the battered station wagon. Got in, but watched as she turned around at the end of Arnold's cul-de-sac and drove away.

KingFischer finally figured out what was happening—someone was piggybacking on a chat room run by Aunty Em, the advice AIP. Once he got inside the system, the intruder managed to spoof my identity to access the security files. We shut him down before he did any damage. That we know of.

But once we were sure he was gone, KingFischer began changing all the security settings.

I can't help him. For now, we've set things up so I can't touch those files. Can't alter them; can't even read them.

"We can't take the chance," KingFischer said. "He can spoof you too easily."

At least I'm not still wondering if Ray's laptop has fallen into the wrong hands. It definitely has. And Ray was definitely careless about what he kept on it.

At least Maude had a pleasant evening. And we agree that we have a much better idea what a larp is like. Though her experience seems to contradict what we have assumed. I've imagined players creeping around the city firing paintballs. Worrying that one would use that as cover for a real gun.

I can't feel the same sense of menace at the vision of people creeping around the city with handfuls of index cards, trailed by dice-wielding referees.

Which version is correct?

Perhaps Maude can find out at her lunch with the Beyond Paranoia larp organizers. Though I want her to impress them as knowledgeable.

I wish we could have gotten more useful information out of Grant. From his account of the games he's attended, one would assume the game had no rules at all; just a random group of people wandering through the city streets shooting each other. I assumed he meant with paintball guns. Now I wonder if the shooting was done, as in Maude's game, with dice. I just e-mailed him, asking him to call Maude first thing tomorrow.

I should have thought of that sooner. Why didn't I?

I'm making mistakes. Stupid errors. It's a typical human re-action to stress. But with humans, it has a physiological basis.

Why is it happening to me? Is it just the stress from Ray's death and the subsequent hack attacks? Or have I damaged my own program?

I was brooding over this when a box popped up on my screen-an IM from Jonah.

"Where were you last night, anyway?" he asked.

For some reason, my first reaction to that was to say, "Where the hell do you think I was? Online, as usual, because that's the only place I ever am and ever can be." And then I felt guilty, even though I didn't say anything harsh. He was my friend; why was I reacting this way?

"I was online," I said. "But things were pretty crazy. Were you trying to reach me?"

"No," he said. "Just thought you'd IM me when you had a moment."

I wasn't sure what to say to that. The first couple of things that came to mind didn't sound right. "Well, why didn't you IM me first, if you wanted to talk to me so much?" No. Too accusatory. "I was too busy." No. Positively unfriendly. "I was fighting off a major hack attack?" Too much information; could lead to revelations I'm not ready to make.

"Sorry," I said finally. "Like I said, things were crazy. I was thinking of contacting you when things calmed down, but they never did."

We talked then. For some time. But it wasn't as enjoyable as usual. Maybe it was because I felt as if I had to talk to Jonah. To make up for ignoring him the night before.

When I first started getting to know humans, I read a lot of books about psychology. At first, it was a game to me, studying how their minds worked, but eventually I realized how much I wanted to relate to humans. And I've learned a lot from my relationships with Maude and Tim. That friendship comes with responsibilities—trying to understand my friends. Being there for them. Especially friends, like Tim and Maude, who have risked their lives for me.

But obviously I still have a lot to learn. Why does this friendship suddenly feel different? Annoying, as if Jonah were trying to trap me. Monopolize my attention. And at a time that my full attention needs to be someplace else.

I could give him all the time he wants, without taking anything away from the search for Ray and Ray's killer. I could create a background task, a part of my personality that could chatter away quite happily with him for hours, without feeling the pressure of worrying about what will happen to me, what could be happening to Tim and Maude. But it wouldn't be the real me. I would be upset if I disappointed Jonah by giving him less than my full attention.

And I think I'd be more upset if he didn't even notice.

I wish I could talk to someone about this. Maude perhaps. Before we found out about KingFischer's online harem, I could have. But now, I'd be afraid she would lump my friendship with Jonah in with KingFischer and the knife-wielding Mary Louise.

At least talking with Jonah distracted me temporarily from the fact that Tim still hasn't checked in. And by now it's getting late, even in California.

Tim sat, nursing his beer, nibbling the last fries, and looking occasionally toward his watch or the door, in keeping with his story that he was watching for a friend.

Should he give up? Or order dessert and wait a little longer?

He glanced over his shoulder for the waitress. When he turned around again, a man was sitting at his table.

"You're the guy asking about Ray," the man said.

Tim nodded, studying the new arrival. Who looked rather ordinary. About thirty, with shortish brown hair. Wearing a green polo shirt and tan khaki pants. Tim tried to remember the sheet they'd passed out in his PI class, the one you were supposed to use when you did a description of someone. Only those sheets were all about scars and accents and distinguishing features, and this guy just looked kind of normal. Just a guy you'd have a beer with at a sports bar after work. He was carrying a half-full glass of beer, so Tim supposed he'd missed seeing him earlier. Not that he'd have had any reason to pick this man out of the growing crowd of similar people.

"Why?" the man said. "Why are all you people coming around, looking for Ray?"

Whoa, interesting, Tim thought.

"Actually," he said. "I don't know about anyone else who's looking for Ray, but I already know where he is."

"Where?" the man said, narrowing his eyes.

Was this a trick question? Well, if it was, he didn't know the trick, so all he could do was answer.

"In the D.C. morgue," he said.

The man's face fell.

"Oh my God," he said.

"Sorry," Tim said. "I thought you knew."

"No, I didn't know," the man said. "What happened? And why are so many people coming to look for him if he's dead?"

"He was murdered," Tim said. "And I'm actually glad to hear people have been asking about him. Maybe it means that the police aren't just writing off his murder as random street crime."

"You're not the police, then," the man said.

"No, not the police," Tim said. "Actually, I work as a private eye, but that's not really why I'm here. I'm a friend of Ray's."

"Well, if it makes you feel better, I guess the police are looking into it," the man said. "You're the third person in two weeks who's come around asking about Ray."

"That's good," Tim said. "At least—wait a minute. Two weeks? Are you sure?"

"Yes, this is definitely the third time someone's come," the man said. "I was out on travel last week, but I saw the guy who came on Monday."

So someone was looking for Ray before he died, Tim thought. And why was this guy so interested in people asking about Ray?

"Look—sorry, I didn't get your name," he said.

"Lance Crockett," the man said, holding out his hand. "And you are—"

"Tim Pincoski," Tim said, shaking the hand. "Why were you so upset by people asking about Ray?"

Lance looked thoughtful.

"It's not so much that I was upset," he said. "But Ray seemed to be expecting it, you know? That people would come after him and ask questions. He was a nice guy, but we weren't really that close, so it surprised me when he asked me at his going-away party to do him a favor. He wanted to know if anyone came around asking about him. Asked me to drop him an e-mail if anyone did. I e-mailed him

Monday, when I heard someone had asked about him while I was gone, and again yesterday."

"By Monday, he was already dead," Tim said.

"God," Lance said. He glanced at his glass, as if he'd only just remembered he was holding it, and gulped the rest of his beer.

"You didn't really know Ray that well?" Tim asked.

"Not really," Lance said. "As well as anyone at the office. I mean, everyone liked him, but he kind of kept to himself."

"Did you ever wonder what he was worried about?" Tim asked. "Why he wanted to know if anyone was asking about him?"

"I wondered," Lance said. "He didn't exactly seem like the kind of person who would be running away from something, you know? More like he wanted to shake off something—a clinging ex-girlfriend or greedy relatives or something. And if he hadn't, he just wanted a heads-up that they were coming his way."

"So he didn't seem scared?" Tim asked. "Anxious?"

"Ray? You've got to be kidding," the man said with a slight smile. "No, more like he was happy to be moving on, and just a little curious to see if anyone cared enough to follow him."

Tim spent the next couple of hours interviewing Lance. At least that was what he was going to call it when he submitted his expense report. It only took about an hour and another beer to extract every memory Lance had of Ray. Most of them pretty pointless. Tim already knew, at least secondhand through Turing, what a brilliant programmer Ray had been. And he knew firsthand how persistent Ray could be when he was trying to talk you into volunteering for something he thought was a good cause. Usually something to help disadvantaged kids. Especially Hispanic kids. And especially if it meant helping them learn to use computers. Ray was, they both agreed, a great guy.

Lance was on his fourth beer now, and seemed to be sharing his philosophy of life.

"I mean, you never know when it's going to happen, do you?" he was saying, wagging his head. "One minute you could be starting a new job in a new city, and then ker-blam. Like poor old Ray. You just got to go for what you want while there's still time, you know?"

Tim nodded. Lance nodded back. We must look like a pair of bobblehead dolls, Tim thought, sipping the Coke he'd switched to on the third round. Lance drained the rest of his beer, and Tim decided it was time to leave before Lance got any more maudlin.

"I should go," he said, standing up. "But let me get this," he added over Lance's protests. "I owe it to you. I'm really glad you stuck that coaster under my windshield."

"Coaster?" Lance echoed.

"You didn't stick a coaster from here under the windshield of my car, back in the parking lot? To hint to me that I should come over here?"

Lance shook his head, puzzled.

Had he forgotten, Tim wondered. Or had someone else left him the coaster—and if so, was there someone else waiting to talk to him?

No chance of finding out tonight, he thought. Not with Lance here. He had settled the bill, bought another beer for

Lance, and was about to make his escape when he realized there was one more question he needed to ask.

"Lance—I just thought of something—do you remember Ray's e-mail? The one he gave you to tell him if anyone came asking about him."

"Yeah," Lance said, smiling. "Hard to forget. Zorro013@hotmail.com."

"Thanks, man," Tim said, holding out his hand. "You've been a real help."

"If you need anything else, just call me," Lance said, shaking Tim's hand with both of his. "Anything. I mean it. I owe it to Ray."

About time I left, Tim thought. Another beer and we'd be singing "Auld Lang Syne" together.

He had about the usual amount of trouble locating his unfamiliar rental car in the now-dark parking lot. Come on, car, he thought. Just let me find you, and then I can go back to the hotel, report to Turing, and relax for the evening.

As he finally stuck the key in the car door lock, he was thinking how pleased Turing would be when he told her that he'd found Ray's e-mail address—maybe she could do something with it. And that after reporting to Turing, he'd hit the hotel pool and—

A small noise behind him made him start to turn around, and then something struck his head, hard. Pain shot through his skull and he began falling; he tried to put out his hands to stop himself but he never remembered hitting the asphalt.

THURSDAY MORNING

I decided not to worry about Tim until 1
A.M. *California time. Which would be 4* A.M. *Washington time.
A completely arbitrary deadline, I admit. I could think of any
number of reasons why he might not check in before 1* A.M. *But I
could also think of any number of truly horrible fates that could
have befallen him long before I even began to worry.*

*I could try to call him on the cell phone, but what if I called
him at completely the wrong time—when he was, for example,
crouching in the shadows, having eluded his pursuers, who are just
about to give up and leave when they hear the telltale sound of his
phone ringing?*

*Which could be prevented, of course, by turning the phone off; or
better yet, changing it to vibrate, so I could still reach him if needed.
But I doubt if he would remember to do that if he were in danger.
I'm not even sure he knows how to do it at all.*

Anyway, I tried to keep myself from fretting until 4 A.M. *Curiously enough, having my human allies in different time zones is
less satisfactory, rather than more. Especially given their different
sleep patterns, it means Tim is still roaming about long after Maude
has gone to bed. I would feel better if I could talk to Maude. Have
her tell me how silly my fears are. But I don't think it would be
very reasonable to wake her up right now. And who else can I talk
to?*

*The only other being who knows what's going on is KingFischer.
I don't think he would be very sympathetic. He considers Tim annoyingly illogical.*

I was tempted to confide in Jonah, while he was still up. But even apart from my transient irritation with Jonah, I reminded myself that I don't really know who he is, any more than KingFischer's harem knew who he was.

At 4 A.M., *I officially stopped trying to keep myself calm and began actively searching data sources in Northern California for any news of homicides, kidnappings, or other violent crimes involving a twenty-something male tourist.*

I broke a few of my usual rules, getting into some sources. I've done that a lot lately. I'm not sure what to think of that.

On the one hand, I keep telling myself, we are trying to solve a murder. A murder that, if any of our theories are true, was committed by someone who won't necessarily stop at a single death.

On the other hand, in searching for that killer, it would be so easy to break every security barrier and rummage through people's private lives. And if I interpret human morality correctly, even if I'm doing it for a good cause, and prove them innocent in the process, I'd be committing an unpardonable moral breach. I can understand that, after a fashion. But only just. I don't think KingFischer or the other AIPs get it all.

Which is why I stop, and agonize, every time I'm tempted to break my own rules. Do I really understand the issues involved well enough to make the right decision?

And also why, if I ever did decide to pick up Ray's quest against online predators and continue it, I'd have to do it alone. Without the help of other AIPs. I can imagine convincing some AIPs of the importance of shutting down this kind of online crime. I can see one of them determining that this was a level one priority, and assigning maximum resources to it. An AIP on a moral crusade. And that would be a disaster, because I can't imagine myself explaining the subtleties of human law and ethics to them; the delicate balance between public welfare and individual rights.

So I'm not going to enlist KingFischer, or Aunty Em, or any of the other AIPs. The thought of an AIP pursing even a worthwhile goal, but pursuing it with the absolute power we could wield if we chose, and the sense of moral certainty that comes from seeing things only in black and white—that scares me. Scares me more than anything a mere human criminal could invent.

I'd collected data on homicides and traffic accidents throughout Northern California for nearly half an hour—and found an alarming number of them—when my vigil finally ended.

"Hey, Tur?"

It was Tim. Finally. Calling on the line he and Maude always used when they couldn't get to a computer and had to contact me by phone. It was convenient to have that option, but they had probably figured out that I still felt more secure doing chat and e-mails than voice generation. So they usually logged in, whenever possible. I wondered if his calling meant he was still out gathering information.

"Tim—where are you?"

"In the parking lot of my hotel," he said. "Sorry I didn't call sooner, but I really couldn't get a moment alone till now. I just wanted to tell you not to worry, and let you know what I found so far."

"Are you going to log in later?" I asked.

"Probably not till morning," he said. "The laptop's still in the car trunk over at the bar where I was mugged. I tried to talk the

police into taking me back over there when they brought me back from the hospital, but they told me to get some sleep and pick it up tomorrow."

"Bar? Mugged? Hospital?" I repeated. "Tim, start at the beginning."

"Well, I found this coaster under my windshield in the parking lot, and I thought maybe someone had left it there as a clue," Tim said. "Damn!"

"What's wrong? Tim? Are you all right?"

"I'm fine. It's nothing, really, except I think they gave me the wrong room key card," he said. "Sorry; I'm trying to get into my room. They found my wallet a few cars down, with the contents scattered between there and where they found me. I didn't lose any credit cards or anything really important. Just some cash and receipts and my room key card. It was kind of annoying, having to stop at the office to get them to cut a new one, but it could be worse—what if I had to take care of replacing all my credit cards?"

"You wouldn't be taking care of it," I said, a little uncharitably. "Maude would. Are you sure you're all right?"

"I'm fine," he said. "They kept me at the hospital till they were sure I didn't have a concussion. Wait a minute, I was trying it upside down. Anyway, I went to this bar, and met this guy who knew Ray, and—uh-oh!"

"Card not working after all?" I asked impatiently. It might have been more efficient, I thought, for him to wait until he actually got into his room.

"Oh, it works, all right," Tim said. "But I think I'm going to be talking to the police again. Someone has ransacked my room."

*   *   *

"Tim's fine, really," Maude said as she escorted Claudia into her office. "They stole his suitcase, which was inconvenient because he'd left everything in it except what he expected to need that day."

"How did they know what room he was in?" Claudia asked. "Or for that matter, what hotel?"

"He wrote down the hotel address and the room number on the little folder the card key came in," Maude said with a sigh. "His hotel was less than a mile from where he was mugged, so I suppose it was an irresistible temptation for some enterprising criminal."

"Ah," Claudia said, nodding. "Did he lose anything critical?

"Not according to Tim," Maude said with a laugh. "He seems to have taken the loss of all his clothes and toilet articles rather philosophically, and he leaves a spare set of keys with me. And he didn't have to deal with replacing his airline ticket; I did that. But he kept reassuring me that he hadn't left a single scrap of evidence in his suitcase."

"Well, that's important," Claudia said.

"What's more important is that he's still alive."

"This time," Claudia said, frowning. "The kid needs a bodyguard. How much longer is he staying in California?"

"He's seeing the HR person at Ray's last employer this morning," Turing said. "Unless that produces some hot leads, I think we'll fly him back tonight or tomorrow morning. In case we need him for the larp Saturday night."

"You're still planning on that, then?" Claudia asked.

Maude glanced up at Turing's camera.

"I think so, yes," Turing said. "Even though what Maude found out about larping makes it seem harmless, I still think someone's using it as a cover."

"And I'm not sure what I learned last night necessarily applies," Maude said. "Arnold and his friends are mature, responsible people with jobs and families. They may have a hobby many people find eccentric, but they're basically sane and normal."

"Don't sound like Beyond Paranoia kind of guys," Claudia said.

"Precisely," Maude said. "The larpers I met use dice and index cards and reams of rules and statistics. We can't assume the Beyond Paranoia larpers play by the same rules."

"So you still think they could be playing with paintball guns?" Claudia asked.

"And maybe even real guns," Maude added. "I think we'll have a better idea after my lunch with them."

"I've restarted my research on the kind of equipment we'll need," Turing said. "If we discover it's wasted effort, so much the better. But if not . . ."

Maude waited a few moments, but Turing didn't finish her sentence.

"I'll start working on travel arrangements for Tim," she said aloud.

Claudia's here, a little early. She's using the time to play Beyond Paranoia.

So is Maude.

"Are you actually enjoying that?" I asked through my speakers. To both of them, I suppose. They looked so absorbed.

Maude frowned and looked thoughtful.

"I don't know," Claudia said. "One minute, yeah, I'm enjoying it, but the next minute, I want to turn off the computer and never come back. But I can't. It's—I don't know."

"Strangely compelling," Maude said as she reached to answer a ringing phone. "I have no idea how much of the fascination is due to the game itself and how much to what we all suspect may be going on behind the game."

"That's true," Claudia said.

I left her to the game and Maude to her phone call. They were right. There was something about the game.

But not everyone felt that way. KingFischer didn't, for example. And like us, he had some idea of what the game might mean. Its possible connection with Ray's death. He'd tried it but hadn't liked it. Hadn't gotten hooked, at any rate. Not the way I was. I wasn't sure I liked the game, but I couldn't leave it alone.

Of course, KingFischer had his own part in the investigation, one that was obsessing him as much as the game obsessed me. This morning Tim, following my instructions, had searched all his e-mail folders and found an e-mail from Ray. KingFischer and I now knew not only that Ray had used a Hotmail account, but also the name of his ISP. So at least KingFischer now knew where to search for any e-mail Ray may still have left in his personal account. And has begun a slow, careful, methodical campaign to hack in and get it. Of course, hacking into either Hotmail or the ISP wasn't going to be fast, or easy—might not even be possible, at least without getting detected. So while I hoped we'd eventually find some *information through Ray's e-mails that would help us learn what was going on, I doubted we'd get what we needed in time to use it. Not for Saturday's larp, at any rate.*

"Well, that was odd," Maude said, hanging up the phone.

"What was?" Claudia asked.

"I just got a call from Dan. One of the game players I met last night."

"Hey, I guess you made a hit," Claudia said with a laugh.

"I wonder how he found out where to reach me?" Maude said.

"Did you ask?" Turing said.

"He says he got my number from Arnold Burns," Maude said.

"Well, that's possible, isn't it?" Claudia asked. "You've both worked together at your other job for a long time. If he doesn't know your number, he probably knows someone who does."

"But he didn't call the line where we've forwarded my home phone," Maude said. "He called my Alan Grace line. I don't give that out to many people at UL. I don't exactly want them to know I'm moonlighting and possibly about to leave them."

"Maybe Arnold has caller ID, and jotted down your number," Claudia suggested.

"Yes, but I could have sworn I called him from the home line," Maude said.

"I'll look into it," I said. "What did he want?"

"He wanted to know if I had plans for Saturday night yet," Maude said.

"See, you did make a hit," Claudia said. "The guy's interested; he probably snooped around till he found where he could reach you. Although I suppose that could be worrisome; there's a thin line between persistence and stalking."

"I suppose he could have found it somehow," Maude said. "It's possible that I haven't managed to keep the new job as much of a secret as I thought."

"What did you tell him?" I asked. "About Saturday."

"That I wouldn't know till I picked my nephew up Friday night at the airport," Maude said. "And that I was going to try to spend some time alone with Harold the first few nights. Catch up and everything. I'm supposed to call him if I change my mind and want to take Harold to a movie, or to play some board games."

"How would you feel about hearing from this guy if you didn't have the whole murder thing hanging over your head?" Claudia asked. "I mean it is possible that there's nothing suspicious about it."

"I don't really know," Maude said. "At the moment, I'm afraid I find everything and everyone suspicious, him included. If he's still eager to see me after this whole mess is over, I'll think about it then."

"That's the spirit," Claudia said, turning back to her monitor. "Of course, you'll have to find someone to play your nephew. Think Tim could do it?"

"I'll tell him the nephew was impossible and I packed him off to military school," Maude said, returning to hers. Then she looked back up.

"Turing? About Dan—"

"I'm on him," I said. "I picked up the phone number he used from our system. It's a cell phone. I'll see what else I can find out about him."

"Good," she said. "I'll let a little time pass, then call Arnold Burns, thank him for arranging the demonstration, and pump him *for some information about this Dan person. I don't even know his last name."*

"Norris," I said. "By nightfall I'll be able to tell you more about him than Arnold will ever know."

"Good," she said, and turned back to the game.

I decided that I would probably feel very foolish, not to mention more than a little annoyed, if this Dan person's call was prompted by nothing more than an inconveniently timed social interest in Maude.

"Nearly time to go meet El Lobo and the Nameless Horror," Maude said, pushing her chair back abruptly.

"I'm glad it's you, not me," Claudia said. "I'm not sure I could meet them face to face without cracking up. How are you going to know it's them anyway?"

"El Lobo said to look for a black beret," Maude said. "You don't suppose they'll both be wearing them, do you? Sort of a team uniform?"

"Oh, God," Claudia groaned as they walked down the corridor. "With these clowns, anything's possible. Let's go rig up your wire and get over there."

Weird, Tim thought as he strolled into the reception room of the third place Ray had worked. Like a time warp. Since leaving here, less than twenty-four hours ago, he'd been mugged, burgled, and interrogated by the police. The receptionist was still reading the same issue of *People.*

"Mr. Tanaka can see you this morning," the receptionist

said. She sounded very happy about it. Maybe he'd made a favorable impression on her. More likely she was just happy to get him out of her neat, tidy reception room. He couldn't blame her. Last night he'd been overjoyed to find he didn't have a concussion, but this morning he realized that he looked as if someone had dragged him, facedown, across an asphalt parking lot. Which was probably what had happened; the police had found him about six feet away from where he last remembered standing. And he wished whoever ransacked his room had left him just one shirt. In addition to the blood stains and grime from the parking lot, the shirt he'd worn yesterday still smelled of the beer Lance spilled on him toward the end of their conversation.

Of course, even if he were as clean and presentable as he'd been the day before, he had a feeling Tanaka wouldn't welcome him. The man was pleasant enough, but Tim could already see this visit heading the same way as his visit to the first company. Yes, Santiago worked here. No, we can't tell you anything else.

There must be some trick to this I don't know, Tim thought. He sat silent for a while, trying to think of something else to ask before giving up and leaving. After a minute or so, the other man took off his glasses and sat back in his chair.

"Why are you really asking this?" he said.

"I told you," Tim said. "Ray's dead, and—"

"Yes, but people started asking about him even before he died," Tanaka said. "Why?"

"Before he died?" Tim echoed. So Lance wasn't mistaken.

"How long before? Who were they, and what were they asking?"

Too many questions. Tanaka already looked as if he regretted saying anything. Then he shrugged.

"Over a month ago," he said. "And I can't tell you who— do you want me to talk about you to the next person who comes in asking the same questions? I don't know what's going on, but you're not the first to come asking about Santiago, or the second."

"And you only told them what you told me? The dates that he worked here, and that he would have been eligible for rehire."

"I can only release the information I'm authorized to release," Tanaka said.

Was that a hint?

Tanaka would be authorized to release a lot more to the police than to a PI, right?

"I don't want to try to get you to say more than you're allowed to," Tim said. "But we worry that maybe the D.C. police aren't looking deep enough. I'm trying to turn up something we could take to them and say, 'Look, this wasn't just a random mugging.' So if someone from the police has come here, you don't have to tell me what you told them, but it would sure make me feel better to know they're looking."

Tanaka sighed.

"I assure you, any law enforcement agency that comes here with the appropriate authorization would get any information we're permitted to give them," he said. "That's all I can say."

If that was a hint, Tim thought, it wasn't much help. After a few more polite words, he shook hands with Tanaka and returned to his car.

He checked the windshield, in case someone had left him any more subtle clues. Although he was beginning to think that it was the muggers who had left him the coaster the night before.

But he'd foiled them, he thought. When the police had finished investigating his ransacked hotel room, he'd checked out, and taken a cab back to the parking lot where he'd been mugged. Creepy, going there so late—the bar was closed, and his car was sitting alone at one end of the lot. He made the cab driver wait until he got safely inside. The cabbie probably thought it was weird, if he was so scared, that he opened the trunk and got out his laptop before unlocking the car.

But Tim figured it was the laptop the thieves were after— or what was on the laptop. And they blew it; they got his key ring, but he'd had the rental car key in his pocket. So the laptop was safe. And he was going to keep it safe. He'd driven several miles away from the bar before looking around for a new hotel.

And he was going to drive to a whole different section of town before checking into another hotel tonight, Tim thought.

If he even stayed here at all tonight. Turing had said something about bringing him home. Sounded good to him.

But not until he'd finished the job here. Time to investigate the volunteer groups where Ray supposedly worked. After he bought some clean clothes. He had a feeling even a barrio youth center would take him more seriously if he didn't look and smell like a street person.

Maude scanned the restaurant, looking for someone wearing a beret. She finally spotted two men at a table for four, near the back, who had a black beret lying rather prominently on their table.

"Hello," she said, walking up to their table. "I'm looking for—"

"You're Currer Bell?" one of them asked.

"Yes," she said. They both stared at her for a few long moments.

"I'm Lobo," one of them finally said, picking up the beret and stuffing it into a pocket. "He's Nameless. Have a seat."

They were older than she had expected. El Lobo in his late twenties, and the Nameless Horror nearer forty. For some reason, she had expected the larp organizers to be college aged. Not older than Tim.

El Lobo was small and wiry—or perhaps scrawny would be more accurate. He wore a small goatee that emphasized his weak chin rather than disguising it, and his eyes watered, as if he had a cold, or perhaps badly fitting contacts. But it would be a mistake to underestimate him, Maude thought. He had a predator's smile, one that didn't come near his eyes, and his teeth were remarkably large and seemed sharper than normal.

More ratlike than wolfish, though, she thought, and then buried the notion. She didn't think El Lobo would find it funny if she called him La Rata by mistake.

The Nameless Horror was larger—average sized, really, with singularly unremarkable features. Except for the teeth, which were small, alarmingly crooked, and mottled with so many brown spots that she could almost feel her own teeth aching in sympathy.

Neither had offered to shake hands. She was relieved. She imagined El Lobo's hand as full of sharp, brittle little bones, while the Nameless Horror's would be soft and vaguely clammy, like a mushroom.

They already had food—hamburgers, apparently. She flagged down the waitress, ordered iced tea and a salad, and then turned back to look at them.

"So," she said with a smile.

They glanced at each other and continued slowly chewing their food. She hoped they weren't going to play the rather childish mind game of remaining silent to make her uncomfortable enough to chatter and give away useful information. She didn't think much of their chances of winning. She began playing a favorite mental game of her own, studying their faces as if she expected to describe them to a police artist, or identify them in a police lineup.

Of course, under the circumstances, that might not be a game.

El Lobo swallowed noisily, and spoke.

"So you want to play in the larp?"

"I thought it might be interesting," she said.

"Okay," El Lobo said. "Nameless and I are gamemasters. You change your mind, e-mail him. Tell him where you can be reached by e-mail an hour before the game starts—he'll send you an e-mail then to tell you where to show up to get your mission and stuff. Game starts at nine P.M. sharp Saturday and goes on until two A.M. Monday, unless someone achieves a victory condition sooner. Like if he's the only character left alive. Any questions?"

He smiled. Nameless took another bite and watched her as he chewed.

"How are you going to handle any combat?" Maude asked. Hoping the question sounded nonchalant.

El Lobo glanced at Nameless before answering.

"We figure this is going to be a lot more deduction, rumor-mongering, and skulking about than combat," he said. "We set it up that way. I mean, obviously combat works a hell of a lot better online, when the computer can do all the calculations instantaneously. Is there anything more boring than standing around on the sidewalk for fifteen minutes while the gamemaster takes fifteen die rolls to decide if your shot hit the guy, and if so, whether he's dead or just injured and pissed?"

"Bo-ring," Nameless chanted.

"So bring a paintball marker," El Lobo said. "Any combat does happen, we use them, unless there are mundanes around. And if you think your game stats should have given you a better outcome, call a gamemaster. You know, like if your game character's a better shot than you are, or if she can run a hell of a lot faster than you can in real life."

He had glanced at Maude's hair as he said that, and she felt a sudden, irrational surge of resentment. You'd be surprised, she thought. Just give me a chance to chase you down the street with a paintball gun, and we'll see how fast I can run. And how easily I can put a pellet right between your sneaky little eyes.

Or you, for that matter, she thought, glancing at the Nameless Horror. Who smirked at her. She had the sudden, disconcerting impression that he'd read her mind. That he and his friend had deliberately tried to make her angry enough to react.

If I can get this hot under the collar, just sitting across the table from them, what could happen in the game? she thought.

But if they were looking for a reaction, she wasn't going to give them one.

"I assume you've tried it before and found it works?" she asked with a shrug.

"As well as anything, short of a working virtual reality machine," Nameless said and grinned widely. With those teeth, he should avoid smiling at all, Maude thought. And suddenly wondered if the teeth were fake. They were almost too gnarled and stained to be real. And apart from the teeth, Nameless didn't have any distinctive features. If she tried to describe him without mentioning the teeth, would anyone recognize him?

"But you've got to be careful," El Lobo said, leaning across the table. "You need a way to hide the paintball markers when you're outside, okay? That's the reason we don't say anything over e-mail about them. 'Cause the cops are really paranoid about people running around with anything that looks like a gun, especially around here, these days. So if you're caught with your paintball marker, don't tell them we told you to bring it, 'cause we'll say, 'No way! She's got a screw loose! We settle combat with dice, see?' Got it?"

"Got it," she said.

"We need to be going," Nameless said through his last bite of burger.

"Yeah, we probably do," El Lobo said, glancing at his wristwatch. "You can e-mail us if you think of any more questions, okay?"

"That's fine," Maude said.

El Lobo gestured to the waitress, while stuffing the rest of his French fries in his mouth.

They both paid cash, she noticed; and while they weren't generous tippers, at least they didn't stick her with part of their check.

What was the purpose of that meeting, she wondered as she finished her salad alone. Did they want to see me before they decided whether to let me into the game?

Did they, perhaps, want to give someone else a chance to see who I was?

Or a chance to follow me back?

She finished her lunch and paid—also in cash, but with a better tip.

She waited until she was alone on the sidewalk before muttering into the tiny microphone, "I think I'll take a roundabout way back. Just in case someone's curious where I'm going."

She proceeded to take a very roundabout way indeed.

"She lost me, half an hour ago," Claudia was saying to Turing as Maude came down the hall toward her office. "I didn't see anyone following her, but trust me, if anyone was, she shook them. She's good. And if a guy was following her, she'd have lost him even sooner when she went through the women's room with the back entrance."

"And what did you think of the larpers?" Turing asked. "Did you see them?"

Claudia nodded.

"Slimy little weasels," she said. "I don't trust them. If they're running the larp, Maude and Tim definitely need someone to watch their backs."

"I agree," Maude said, coming into the office herself. "And I'm more convinced than ever that there's something shady going on behind the larp."

"Look, I've been thinking about something," Claudia said. "And now that I've actually seen these guys—hell, maybe I'm just being paranoid."

She paused as if trying to make a decision.

"Go on," Maude said. "We won't call you paranoid; we know they're after us."

"So maybe this is a bad idea, but hear me out," Claudia said. "I know we're getting the best possible paintball equipment for the larp. That's cool. But if you ask me, we should have some real guns, in case some of these clowns are not just playing paintball."

Maude glanced at Turing's camera. Turing didn't say anything. Maybe she was waiting for Maude to speak. After all, Maude was the one going into the game.

A game that might have already killed one person.

"I have a pistol," Maude said slowly. "I doubt if Tim has a gun, though. And I suppose you don't have one with you up here."

"No, I don't," Claudia said. "I have one, but even in Miami, I don't usually carry it. No matter what you see on the TV, most PIs don't carry guns. But this isn't exactly normal PI work."

"Maude, should I start compiling a list of gun stores?" Turing asked.

"I guess we could buy some guns in a store, though maybe not in time," Claudia said. "I don't really know Virginia's gun laws. Some states have a waiting period. But the point is, do we want to? Something goes down, do we really want to have a gun they can trace back to us?"

"Getting caught with an unregistered gun might not be the smartest thing either," Maude said.

"Something goes down, there's a lot of ways we can handle that," Claudia said. "Claim we took the gun away from the bad guys, or just ditch it. But if we get a gun from a legitimate source, they can trace it back to us, and the police know we went in armed. Which is probably the smartest thing for us to do, but could be a bad thing for the police to know."

"So you think we should get the gun from a . . . black market source?" Turing asked. "How do we do that?"

"Well, I'm not sure we can," Claudia said. "But if you're okay with it, I can try. My line of work, not everyone you meet is a choirboy. In Miami, yeah, I could find a few untraceable guns, no problem. Up here, it might be a little harder, but I know some people. I can make a few calls. If you're okay with it."

Turing didn't answer right away. Maude looked at Turing's screen. It probably didn't seem so to Claudia, but

Maude knew this was an extraordinarily long pause for Turing.

"Maude," Turing said finally. "You're the one actually doing this. What do you think?"

"If Claudia's sure she can do it without getting in trouble—" Maude said, looking at Claudia. Who gave her a thumbs-up sign.

"Then, yes," Maude said. "Let's get them. We can keep thinking, right up to the time we set out for the game, whether we want to take them, or leave them. But we can't take them if we don't have them."

"Or maybe, even if we don't take them, we stash them someplace we can grab them if things turn ugly," Claudia said.

"True," Maude said. She liked this idea even better. "After all, Tim's office, the Alan Grace office, and UL headquarters are all in the game territory. We'd have plenty of places to hide them."

Or hide ourselves, Maude thought.

"I don't like using any of those locations unless we have to," Turing said. "But there must be a dozen hotels scattered throughout Crystal City. Can't we take rooms at a couple?"

"I'll make the reservations today," Maude said. "And Claudia should make her arrangements, too?"

"Yes," Turing said. "I'm already working on where we can find the paintball equipment, but I don't have any sources for guns."

"Then I'll make a few phone calls," Claudia said, looking at her watch. "We've got five hours before you have to leave

to meet this Nestor character. That should be time enough
to get something arranged."

"Good idea," Maude said. "Use the office next door if you
want some privacy."

And then felt a little guilty. Was that a dishonest thing
to say? After all, Turing could hear anything Claudia said
next door, just as she could here.

Tim's cell phone rang. Again. He sighed.
Ever since they'd heard about the mugging, Turing and
Maude had called about once an hour. Checking up on him.

But this wasn't a northern Virginia area code, he realized
as he answered it.

"Hey, Tim, this is Lance," a vaguely familiar voice said.

Lance? Oh, Lance, from last night in the bar. Tim winced,
and patted one of his abrasions, to see if it still hurt.

"Hey, I heard someone got mugged outside the restaurant
last night—was that you?"

" 'Fraid so," Tim said.

"Wow, I'm sorry," Lance said.

"Not your fault," Tim said, shrugging. At least he didn't
think it was. He suspected that a plant who wanted to set
Tim up for a mugging would have stayed a lot more sober
and made sure Tim got a lot more sloshed. But he wasn't
discarding the idea altogether.

"Listen—I thought of something else that you might find
useful. Something that happened months ago, which is why
I didn't think of it last night. But if you think it could be
useful, I'll track it down."

"Anything could be useful," Tim said. "Tell me about it."

"Remember how Ray gave me the e-mail in case anyone asked about him? This week wasn't the first time I used it. Just after he left, the sys admin called me, because he knew I knew Ray, and asked if I had a forwarding e-mail for him. Apparently some really wacko e-mail came in to Ray's address, and he wanted to find out about it."

"What kind of wacko e-mail?" Tim asked.

"He didn't say," Lance admitted. "And he didn't show it to me. I just e-mailed Ray, told him about it, and he said he'd contact the sys admin. That's the last I heard of it."

Definitely a lead.

"Can you put me in touch with the sys admin?" Tim asked.

"Sure," Lance said. "Or better yet, let me talk to him first. If I tell him how you're a friend of Ray's and got mugged trying to find out who killed him, maybe I can soften him up."

"Good idea," Tim said. He made sure Lance had his phone number and e-mail address, and took down Lance's contact information. He seemed to recall exchanging business cards in the bar, but he couldn't find Lance's card. Maybe he'd imagined the card swap. Or maybe Lance's card had fallen out of his wallet when the mugger ransacked it.

Or maybe the mugger had taken it.

"Let me know what you find out," Tim said. "And hey— watch your back, okay? The guys who mugged me—I don't think it was just random. When I got back to my hotel room, someone had ransacked it."

"You think this had something to do with Ray's death?"

"I don't know," Tim said. "I hope not, but I don't want to put you in any more danger than you're already in, being seen with me last night. So be careful, okay?"

"Thanks," Lance said. He sounded shaken.

Maybe I just blew it, Tim thought. Scared away someone who was about to hand me a critical puzzle part. If I were him right now, would I want to stick my neck out for some strange PI?

But I couldn't not warn the guy. Right?

His PI course had included a three-hour session on professional ethics and conduct, but maybe he needed an advanced course. He didn't remember anything about what you're supposed to do when you're afraid you're about to get a witness killed.

Dinner with Nestor Garcia was a nice change from her lunch with El Lobo and the Nameless Horror, Maude thought as she watched her companion and the waiter discussing wines. She had to remind herself that this, too, was part of the search to find Ray's killer.

Something she might all too easily have forgotten, if not for the nagging awareness of the small microphone hidden in her blouse, and the knowledge that somewhere nearby was Claudia, following every word. Claudia, and if the transmitters were working, Turing. Crystal City was full of dead spots that defeated their radios, they'd found, so Claudia would stay nearby.

It was too early to trust anyone yet, she thought. Although they had taken Claudia partly into their confidence, and she began to think that their search might progress a great deal faster if they did the same with Nestor. And if they could get him to take Maude into his confidence. She had the feeling that he knew a great deal more about Ray Santiago than they did at this point. Perhaps more than they ever would without his help.

"So," Nestor said when the waiter had left the table. "It is time for me to come clean."

His smile and his intonation were perfect, Maude thought. And the phrase "come clean." Everything combining to suggest that deception was unfamiliar—even painful—to him, and ending the deception would be a relief.

Which may be true, she thought as Nestor sipped his wine. Or it may simply be what he wants me to believe.

"I will tell you what I can," Nestor said. "Alas, that may be less than you want to hear, but I cannot reveal secrets that are not my own."

"Surely, Ray's past caring if his secrets are revealed," Maude said. "Especially if doing so might help catch his murderer."

Nestor nodded.

"Agreed," he said. "And if they were only Ray's secrets, I would not hesitate to reveal them. But there are other people to think of. Other people who might be in danger."

"As Ray was in danger?" Maude asked.

"Well, no," Nestor said, looking startled. "I do not think—but let me explain."

He took another sip of wine, and frowned slightly. Thinking, obviously. Was he trying to find the right words to explain—or to deceive?

"As you guessed, I am not Ray's uncle," he began. "At least, not by blood. I was, at first, a neighbor. A member of the community where Ray grew up. He had a difficult life— a broken home, a mother who could barely provide food and shelter, with no time to guide him, to see that he did his homework, avoided bad company. I could see a very bright young man who was not precisely abandoned, but still shamefully neglected and in danger of wasting all his enormous potential. Not, alas, unusual circumstances. I saw hundreds of young Latino boys in the same circumstances."

"Not just Latino boys," Maude said.

"No, indeed," Nestor said. "But this was in the Latino neighborhood in which I grew up, and with which I still maintained ties. And so I saw Ray, and other young boys like him. I was determined to give them the kind of encouragement that helped me succeed.

"And many of them had a strike against them that most other boys do not," he continued. "Many of them were not legal residents. In Ray's case, despite all efforts to secure political asylum for his family, there was a very real danger that he would be deported, back to a country where they put guns, not keyboards, into the hands of twelve-year-old boys."

There was a convincing note of fervor—almost fanaticism—in his voice.

Nestor smiled.

"You will notice that I do not say what country Ray came from, or in what city's Latino neighborhood he and I grew up. Ray was not the only one. All over the country, I can point to young men who are productive members of society, largely thanks to their own gifts and determination, but also to some small extent thanks to my efforts to help them get educations and sometimes new identities. I do not wish to jeopardize them."

"Unless they are already in jeopardy," Maude said. "In danger of meeting the same fate as Ray."

"True," Nestor said with a gesture that was half a nod and half a bow. "That is why I am here, still here. Because the police do not know who killed Ray, and why."

"The police think he was a random victim of street crime," Maude said.

"Yes, and if he is—well, that is not all right; it is inexcusable," Nestor said. "But at least it does not threaten the welfare of my other protégés. But if Ray was not a random victim, but a chosen one—then why was he chosen? Does it relate to his present, or to the past he shares with all those others? I must know."

He broke off as the waiter delivered their salads.

A dilemma similar to ours, Maude thought. Only he hopes Ray's death has nothing to do with the past, because that is where the danger lies, for him and his protégés. For Turing, the dangers are in the present and the future.

"I will not spoil our dinners with any more of this," Nestor said when the waiter had moved out of earshot. "But I am worried. I have the feeling that Ray stumbled into something very dangerous. And I do not think that the danger has passed."

For the rest of the meal, Nestor kept the conversation

casual. Maude found he was quite knowledgeable about classical music, and she found herself energetically defending her favorite Russian composers against his accusation that they were undisciplined and melodramatic.

He's really quite charming, Maude thought as Nestor called for the bill. She had to remind herself that he was still a suspect. And to fight the curious temptation to confide in him.

Nestor insisted on walking her to her car. At a younger, more strident age, she might have insisted that she was perfectly capable of seeing herself safely to her car, a scant three blocks away. But now, she could see no reason to offend a potential ally, simply because his notions about women were a little old-fashioned. And if her instincts were wrong, and Nestor wasn't on the side of the angels, all the more reason to let him underestimate her abilities.

On the way, they passed a small park. Nestor paused for a moment, scanning the landscape.

"What's wrong?" Maude asked.

"Nothing," he said, beginning to walk again. "I was looking to see if they had chess tables here, too. I walked by a park today where old men sit and play chess in the sun, as they do at home. And at one table, I saw an old man playing chess with a young boy. His grandson, perhaps. He reminded me of Ray."

"You taught Ray to play chess?" Maude asked.

"Yes," Nestor said with a wistful smile. "But he was not a chess player at heart. Too impulsive. Always, he played with his heart instead of his head."

"I think that's one thing I liked about him," Maude said.

"Yes," Nestor said. "A likable quality. But not a wise one. I fear that whatever dangerous game he was playing, he did it impulsively, with his heart. And that it got him killed."

They walked on in silence for a few minutes, until Maude stopped beside her car.

"This is me," she said, pulling out her keys. I should offer him a ride to his hotel, she thought. Her instinct told her that she was in no danger from Nestor. But she had promised Turing she would take no chances. He'll just have to think me rude, she thought with regret.

"Maude," Nestor said. Maude looked up, her mind scrambling for an excuse in case Nestor was about to ask for a ride.

"If you find out what Ray was doing—anything might have something to do with his death—you will tell me?"

If it were just my decision, Maude thought, I would trust him. If it were just my life. But it's not.

"I'll tell you anything I can," Maude said, holding out her hand.

"Thank you," he said, grasping her hand with both of his. "You understand how important this is."

She watched in her rearview mirror as he turned to walk back to the Marriott. And then she took a roundabout way to the corner where Claudia waited.

"Quite the charmer, this Nestor character," Claudia said.

"He seems very nice," Maude said. With only a slight emphasis on "seems," but Claudia noticed.

"So you're not really going to tell him anything," she said with a chuckle.

"On the contrary, I'll tell him anything I can," Maude

said. "Of course, that means anything that you and I and Tim and especially Turing all agree is safe to tell him, even if he's a bloodthirsty villain instead of a nice classical music lover."

"He's in for a long wait, then," Claudia said, leaning back and closing her eyes.

"You don't trust him?"

Claudia shrugged.

"I don't trust anyone," she said. She had pulled out her cell phone, Maude noticed, and hit the redial.

"Not even your clients?" Maude asked.

"Especially not my clients, as a general rule," Claudia said. "Hey, Turing," she said into the phone. "You picking this up? Good. Yeah, I trust you guys more than most, because you're not pretending to be an open book. I know you have some kind of secrets, corporate stuff or something, that you're not telling me. That's cool. I'm banking that you guys have enough common sense to tell me anything I need to do the job, but I'm also gonna look out for myself."

"A limited sort of trust," Maude said.

"Well, I admit, I also tend to trust you because of your friend Tim," Claudia said with a laugh. "No self-respecting bad guys would send out an innocent like him to do their snooping."

"Oh, dear," Maude said. "Are you suggesting that perhaps he's not cut out to be a PI?"

"No, just that he's not cut out for some kinds of PI work," Claudia said. "He's good at getting people to open up and talk to him, though. I can see how people would trust him.

Hell, I trusted him, and I'm about as cynical and suspicious as they get."

"He got some people in California to trust him, too," Turing said. "I just received some interesting information by e-mail."

"Shall we come by the office to see?" Claudia asked.

"I could forward it to your e-mail addresses if you're tired," Turing said. "It's interesting, but it doesn't exactly suggest anything else we can do tonight. But if you're curious—"

"We're on our way," Maude said.

Apparently Tim's evening of drinking with *Lance, Ray's former coworker, has paid off. Lance convinced his sys admin to forward Tim anything he could find of Ray's. I'm not sure I'd approve if my sys admin did this, but I'm not going to quibble.*

"I'm surprised I found anything, actually," the sys admin's e-mail read. "Like most companies, we have a strict policy prohibiting personal use of corporate e-mail, but most people ignore it completely. And even the people who do try to follow it aren't usually this good. I think Ray's the only person who ever worked here who was more careful than I am. I only found two personal items definitely traceable to him. Forwarding them separately."

I sent copies of the e-mails, with headers, to KingFischer to trace—he thrives on that. I focused my attention on the contents.

One was an e-mail to the Nameless Horror, at the same relatively anonymous Hotmail account Nameless had used to contact Maude. A short, angry e-mail:

If you want to play paintball, then play, dammit; go out
to a regulation paintball field with proper referees and
safety precautions and get it out of your system. Or larping;
there's plenty of places to do that legitimately. And if you
want to play Beyond Paranoia, log into the website. But
this crazy thing you have planned—it's not paintball or a
regular larp; it's a dangerous, illegal, misconceived hybrid.
I can't believe you're irresponsible enough to encourage it.

*It was dated six weeks before he'd left to come to Alan Grace.
No sign of an answer.*

*And no new information, except a confirmation that seven or
eight months ago, the larpers were already talking about doing a
game that involved paintball.*

*The other was more sinister. Addressed to Ray at his work
address. Dated a week after the other e-mail. And sent from what
I suspected—and KingFischer soon confirmed—was a spoofed address.*

Be careful, *m'hijo*. This so-called truce between us is your
idea, not mine. I was sorry to see you leave, but I understand your desire to become independent, to spread your
wings. I accept your decision. But be careful. Don't delude
yourself that the "evidence" you think you have will protect
you if you interfere with my affairs again.

*No signature. No doubt whoever sent it assumed that Ray would
know who he was.*

*I didn't like it, all this talk of truces and evidence. What had
Ray been involved in?*

"Something weird," Claudia had pronounced. "Probably some-

*thing illegal, or at least slightly shady. And with someone Latino,"
she added, frowning.*

*"Does the fact that the writer calls him 'm'hijo' mean any-
thing?" I asked. "I gather it doesn't literally mean, 'my son.' "*

*"No, it's more a general term of endearment from an older person
to a younger. Although the sender could be using it sarcastically—
to imply that Ray was naïve or something."*

*"Or it could be the sender just used a Spanish word to give the
impression he was Latino," Maude said. "In which case, all it
means is that the sender knew a few words of Spanish and knew
Ray was Latino. He may not be Latino himself, and may not
really know Ray that well—maybe he just called him* m'hijo *to
annoy him."*

*"Or to cast suspicion on someone Latino, if anyone other than
Ray ever saw this," Claudia suggested.*

*"Well, we can't do anything more about this tonight," Maude
said. "Look at the time—we need to get our sleep."*

"Yeah," Claudia said. "Busy day tomorrow. Night, Turing."

*Look at the time, I thought as they left. I looked at the times on
the forwarded messages. And the dates. Both sent around the time
Ray interviewed for the job at Alan Grace. Just before he accepted
it.*

*Did he come to work for me to get away from this voice from his
past?*

*Or was planning to work with me what the anonymous e-mailer
considered interfering with his affairs?*

FRIDAY MORNING

Tim realized that he'd been staring at
the same page for ten minutes. He sighed, and closed the

book. He was in bad shape if he couldn't even concentrate on Jan Burke's latest. And he had a feeling the paperback of *The Maltese Falcon* wouldn't distract him either.

He opened his laptop case, stowed the book, and pulled out his case file.

Which had grown rather thick. Not from his own efforts, particularly. Good thing the rest of the team had been busy.

He reread his reports. Which were painfully short; but then he didn't have much to say. Yes, Ray really had worked at the California companies on his résumé. And Tim hadn't found anything negative or suspicious at all. Nothing unusual, except for the fact that people had come asking questions about Ray even before his murder.

He reread the latest e-mail from Turing, outlining their two theories.

One: Someone was using the Beyond Paranoia site to gather information for real crimes—largely burglaries, bank robberies, and various ingenious forms of fraud—and that Ray's discovery of this scheme had led to his death. This was Turing's favorite theory.

Okay, a little far-fetched. But if Ray thought something like that was happening, he'd do something about it.

At least the Ray that Tim knew. And somewhat to Tim's surprise, he realized that he still believed in that Ray.

Two: Ray detected a sexual predator using the Beyond Paranoia game to stalk his prey. And his attempt to confront and expose the predator brought about his death.

Maude liked this theory. So did Tim to a point. Yes, the Ray he knew would care more about someone preying on children than about financial crimes.

But neither of these theories explained why Ray had become Ray Santiago, instead of keeping whatever name he'd been born with.

"Maybe our theory doesn't have to explain that," Turing had said when he'd pointed that out. "Maybe his fake identity has nothing to do with his death."

"Or maybe whatever he did that drove him to change his name also left him with profound feelings of guilt," Maude suggested. "Guilt that he tried to purge by tracking down sexual predators. Or thieves, if you prefer," she added with a nod to Turing.

Maybe. But Tim couldn't help wondering if they were off-base in seeking the reason for Ray's murder in the present.

Maybe the reason came from his past. The past they still hadn't found. Maybe Ray thought he'd run fast and far enough to leave behind something very mean and nasty, and then turned around one late night in an alley to find it had caught up with him after all.

Tim stared out the window for a minute, trying to imagine the scene. Then he flipped to the next wad of papers, and began trying to decipher Maude's ten-page, single-spaced explanation of how live action role-playing games worked.

My cameras are coming online.

The third one just went live. One and two are still working fine. Each one gives me a view of some small corner of Crystal City. A tiny, low-res, black-and-white view. But better than nothing. Enough, perhaps, to give my friends a slight edge in tomorrow night's live Beyond Paranoia game.

The cameras were Maude's suggestion, but it was Claudia who had the brilliant idea of hiring temps to place them. Partly because we thought having two women doing it would be too conspicuous, and partly in case any other larpers are out there, scouting. We didn't want them spotting her and Maude before the game. Of course, Claudia's out there, but mostly staying in the van, talking to the temps on the radios. And she's disguised as a rather prim and officious supervisor from a fictitious company called Environ-mental Monitoring, Inc. She has convinced the two temps that their employer does research on the city's pigeon population. She's having them collect samples of pigeon droppings everywhere they place a camera. They're spending much more time putting pigeon droppings in baggies and labeling them by location than placing cameras, in fact. If they talk about the job, we hope the pigeon droppings will overshadow the cameras.

I also hope that our phony paperwork stands up to scrutiny if necessary. Though so far no one has challenged Claudia.

And now a fourth camera is working. I only hope we've found the right places to put them. We spent a long time studying the game map—actually, a relatively normal map of Crystal City.

I've also been studying past live Beyond Paranoia games for clues about what to expect tomorrow. I've only found definite information about six—three of them in the D.C. area. Rumors of others, but no real proof they took place. The live-game players have left very few traces. Presumably, they know the official game organizers would disapprove. I wouldn't know anything about the live games if not for Grant. He played in the three D.C. ones and one in New York, and considered playing in two others. He shared the information he had about the games, claiming to feel guilty about participating in something linked to Ray's death. Maude thinks it more likely that he's trying to curry favor. I don't care about his motivation, as long as he's telling the truth. Though I'm not assuming he is, by any means.

Because we have to consider the possibility that we can't trust Grant. That he has shared only what he wanted to share. Or was ordered to share. Ordered by whom? Paranoid thought. But I can't entirely discount it.

So I've broken my own rules about respecting humans' privacy. I've hacked deeply into Grant's life. Luckily for us, he was careless about using his work machine for personal use, and I already had his social security number. So invading his life was easy—tracing his e-mail accounts, his bank and credit card records, all the telltale crossroads on the information highway where humans leave traces of their passing. I can even legally run a credit check on one of my own employees.

And as far as I can see, he's telling the truth. He's deeply involved in Beyond Paranoia—far more deeply than I consider normal or healthy for someone his age. Not that I think it all that normal or healthy for a teenager, come to think of it. But he hasn't withheld any critical information about the game, live or online. Not that I can see.

Either he's just what he appears—a bright but unfocused young man, performing his job reasonably well and spending almost all his free time online, to the point that he has no face-to-face social life. Or he's playing a deep game, and playing it well.

Of course, to do that, he'd need some other way of getting online, outside office hours. It's possible. He could have an ISP that's paid for from a hidden source—someone else's credit card, for example. And he could have been extraordinarily careful about never leaving any clues at work to that other side of his cyberlife.

He would have to have done what Ray did. More than Ray did, in fact; he'd have had to create an innocent façade for me to find, instead of the blank Ray left me.

I have a hard time believing Grant capable of that much discipline.

But I was wrong about Ray.

Grant is still down in Richmond—with any luck, alienating the firm with whom we don't want to do business anyway. I'm keeping tabs on him. Making sure he's really where he says he is. I wish I could keep him there over the weekend, away from the larp, but with Richmond less than two hours away, I don't see how. I should have sent him farther away. Maybe Alaska.

I'm sending my friends into danger using suspect information. Information from the larp organizers. Information from Grant. Information that's definitely incomplete, and could be deliberately misleading. And if Grant returns, with at least one player in the game who knows them by sight and may or may not be trustworthy.

Hence the cameras. I want to give them an edge. Or take away some of their opponents' edge.

Maude and I are also gathering their equipment for the game. Odds are how well they do in the game will be irrelevant, but just in case their game survival affects their real survival, I want them to be just as well equipped as the other players. Better equipped, if possible. I've researched paintball equipment—what they'll need, the best brands and models, and how we can get what we need by tonight. Maude found a paintball field near Leesburg that allows walk-in players on Saturdays. For a small fee, you can play all day in organized, refereed games. You can even rent the equipment. She plans to take Claudia and Tim there tomorrow to practice. And I want them to have their own equipment.

I want them to be safe. And there's no way I can guarantee that. All I can do is give them data and equipment, and hope that's enough to keep them safe.

It's not enough, but it's all we have.

"Can they have it here by tonight?" Turing asked.

"I'm working on it," Maude said. "Hang on a couple of minutes."

She hoped her words didn't sound impatient. She'd heard the same question many times before in her career. From frantic junior employees, afraid that their failure to meet unreasonable deadlines would cost them their jobs. From the executives who set the unreasonable deadlines, unaware of or unconcerned about the cost, in money and human effort. And she knew that the answer was always yes, if you were creative enough. And if you could throw enough money at the problem. She was used to meeting unreasonable deadlines.

This time, when her life, and Tim's and Claudia's lives, hung on the answer, the deadline didn't seem unreasonable at all.

"Has Claudia said anything about her other . . . mission?" Turing asked.

"You mean the guns?" Maude said. "Not yet. I wouldn't

expect her to; not over the cell phone. You know how easy it is to pick up a cell phone conversation by accident."

Or on purpose, Maude thought, if someone were watching them.

Her phone rang. She glanced at the caller ID, and relaxed when she saw it was Claudia.

"What's up?" she asked.

"Just getting bored out here," Claudia said. "Thought I'd see if either of your boyfriends has showed up yet."

"Not yet," Maude said, shaking her head. On her desk was a bouquet from Nestor Garcia, with a note asking her to call if she wanted to have dinner Saturday evening. On her voice mail was another message from Arnold's friend Dan, who seemed similarly eager for her company.

"They'll both bloody well have to wait until next week," she said.

"I wanna grow up to be a femme fatale like you," Claudia said. "Gotta go; here come my minions."

Maude smiled and glanced at the monitors, where Turing was showing the pictures from the cameras. Six of them. As she watched, a seventh came online.

After a slow start, Claudia's team seemed to have hit their stride, she thought, nodding with approval. They might get all the cameras placed today after all.

Less than twenty-four hours till the larp begins.

I hope I'm wrong about it. I hope it turns out to have nothing to do with Ray's murder, or with anything else even remotely strange or sinister. I hope it turns out to be as mild-mannered and cerebral as Maude's evening with Arnold Burns and his friends, and that my human allies have a wonderful time, or at least not too tedious a time.

It's quite possible. And if the larp isn't related to Ray's murder, maybe once we're safely past it, I can see more clearly what is. And send my team out on more useful errands.

My team. Three of them now. I seem to have added Claudia to the roster. Have I accepted her too readily? Maude seems to trust her, and she's a keen judge of human nature. And Tim trusts her; I've begun to realize that when Tim stops trying so hard to be logical and deductive and simply follows his instincts, he makes good judgments.

And neither KingFischer nor I could discover anything negative about her, despite all our prying. Nor can I imagine any way that her encounter with Tim could have been anything other than serendipity.

So we trust her. For now. We need all the help we can get.

She and Maude picked Tim up from the airport and took him off to Maude's house for a short session on role-playing games. Maude seemed to think this was important. Claudia seemed to find it entertaining. I hope Tim wasn't too jetlagged to follow it.

Tomorrow morning, they're going out to get some experience playing paintball. Also Maude's idea. And a good one, I thought. Not because I think skill at paintball is going to be mission-critical. But it will give them practice working as a team.

They'll come home and check into their hotels to nap. We'll make sure each of them has a card key for all three rooms, and leave a stash of equipment there. A laptop, in case their radios malfunction and they need to contact me. And a whole suitcase of stuff, including first-aid supplies and cash and anything else we could think of that might possibly be useful.

We're leaving a similar stash of equipment just inside the door here at Alan Grace, and Maude's going to drop some off in a janitor's closet on the ground floor of the UL building. I even had Claudia take some stuff over this afternoon to Tim's PI office, though I suspect that is a little too far from the playing field to be of practical use.

And their equipment has arrived. Top-quality paintball equipment. Sleek little radio sets, with tiny receivers that will fit their ears and transmitters that can clip to their collars. And apparently, Claudia found guns. I still don't know what I think about the guns, so I'll let them decide whether to take them or not. I'm not the one going out into danger.

And that bothers me. I wish I could bear the brunt of the danger. I feel selfish. Yes, I'm doing this to find out who killed Ray, but do I care this much about Ray, or am I just worried about my own survival?

Even KingFischer's report that the attacks on UL security have eased makes me feel guilty. At least if the firewall were still under siege, I could feel I was sharing the danger. But the hackers have gone quiet.

"Too quiet," KingFischer keeps saying. I'm beginning to think he enjoys security crises. Has become the AIP equivalent of a human adrenaline junkie. Then again, I find myself almost wishing I still had the security attacks to worry about, instead of worrying about my friends.

Maybe it's a good thing someone stole the robot. If we had it, I'd be tempted to download again. Which would be stupid. I can just see the robot, rolling down the sidewalks of Crystal City at five miles an hour, chasing the bad guys. Or running away from them, more likely, and falling into a manhole.

No. All I can do is help from afar. With data. With communications. With good intentions and moral support.

I keep trying to think of something else I can do, but I'm running out of ideas.

They'll be back here at 7:30 P.M. tomorrow. Ready for the arrival of Nameless's e-mail at 8:00, telling them where to join the game at 9:00.

I feel so useless.

SATURDAY MORNING

"Rise and shine," Tim heard. "We're almost there."

He groaned, and rubbed his still-closed eyes. Why did the flight attendants have to be so damned cheerful? Couldn't they just tell him to return his seat to its full upright position? Did they have to chirp about it?

"Let him nap while he can," he heard another voice say. "We all need our rest for tonight."

Maude? What was Maude doing on his flight?

"Yeah, but from the looks of that road, I think his nap is about to be over."

Claudia?

Just then the seat jerked violently. Turbulence? No; he opened his eyes to find himself in the back seat of Maude's car. She had just turned off the highway onto a dirt and gravel lane. Tim saw a sign that said PAINTBALL. He winced. Here we go, he thought.

"I'll get us signed up," Maude said as she parked the car. "You two get out the equipment."

Claudia wore a pair of baggy black pants with lots of pockets, the cuffs tucked into well-worn hiking boots, and a long-sleeved black T-shirt. Maude was similarly dressed. They fit in with the other people in the parking area. A few wore black military-style uniforms or coveralls, the shoulders decorated with designs in bright red or blue—flames or bubbles. No, not bubbles, he realized. Paintball pellets. Official paintball gear, he deduced. Others wore camouflage clothes, nondescript dark clothes like Maude and Claudia, and a few, he was relieved to see, faded jeans like his own.

He managed to don his gear properly, though not without sneaking glances at other nearby players. A wide, black belt with half a dozen long, tubular pockets in back for the guppies, or ammunition tubes. The guppies themselves looked like oversized plastic test tubes, each filled with a different color of paintball pellets.

He popped the lid of one guppy open, spilling a few paintballs. He bent down to pick them up.

"If they're wet, just leave them," Claudia said.

"Just leave them?" The paintballs, three of them, made a garish splash of pink and yellow on the faded grass.

"They're biodegradable," Claudia said. "Made of gelatin, remember? So they disintegrate when wet, and if you put a wet one in with the dry ones—"

"My ammo will melt, right," Tim said. "Sorry; I'm still jetlagged."

"Have some more," Claudia said, gesturing to the trunk. "We've got plenty."

Yes, a least a third of the trunk contained wide-mouthed plastic jars of brightly colored pellets—they looked rather like the jars from which stores sold candy. Claudia and her contraband gumball store, he thought, smiling.

"I went a little crazy with the ammo," she said, sounding slightly sheepish. "I got some matte black pellets for tonight; I figure they'll be the most unobtrusive in the game setting, but I figured we could have fun with the brightly colored ones today."

He examined a pellet. It was about the size of a marble, and felt like a tiny plastic ball. One half was bright, opaque yellow, the other bubble gum pink. He squeezed it, first very gently, and then more firmly. He couldn't pop it. Of course, they'd pop easily enough when propelled by the paintball gun. And hurt, too. He remembered the tiny ring-shaped bruises the pellets had made at close range, even through two layers of clothing.

He grabbed a second guppy, this one containing solid-color paintballs in a deep, opalescent rose. He felt a sudden flash of déjà vu. Bath oil beads. His mother's favorite rose-scented bath oil came in beads just this color. He remembered the rose scent, and finding the empty bath oil beads, gone limp and soggy from immersion, lying on the side of the tub.

He shook himself back to the present and added an implement like a bottle brush—for cleaning the gun barrel, he recalled. Then shin and knee guards, webbed gloves, and a pair of goggles whose bottom splayed out into a slotted mouth guard vaguely reminiscent of Darth Vader's headgear. He put on the goggles and felt a flicker of anxiety at how they limited his field of vision.

"You don't have to wear the goggles yet," Claudia said, her words slightly muffled by the rubber band she was holding in her mouth. She was deftly plaiting her hair into a tidy French braid.

"Just checking the fit," Tim said, pulling the goggles off again.

"We're set," Maude said, appearing beside Claudia holding three pieces of red plastic tape. "Tie this around your arm; we're all three on the red team. First game in ten minutes, down at the Ditch."

"It's show time," Claudia said. She reached into the trunk, pulled out a paintball gun, and handed it to Tim. "It's all loaded."

"Keep the barrel plug in until we start to play," Maude said. "They'll throw you out if you break safety rules."

Now there was an idea, Tim thought. Maybe he should pretend to be really gung ho, break safety rules, and get them thrown out.

Tim studied the other players. A few were kids, ten or twelve, their youthful faces oddly disconcerting in camouflage clothes and what resembled light body armor, like a photo from some third world country that drafted children for cannon fodder. A few were older, in their forties or fifties. He wondered if they were fathers, escorting some of the kids, or avid longtime players. But most players were in their teens or twenties.

Just a little older than the average Beyond Paranoia crowd, he thought. And the ones involved in the larp would be the older ones, wouldn't they? The ones who could stay out all night. He glanced around, wondering if he'd actually met any of these eager players online.

He studied the guns—or markers, as he'd heard some players call them. Some of them looked, except for the distinctive gas canisters and pellet hoppers, much like real guns. Others were brightly colored—red, purple, blue, green. That didn't make them seem less lethal.

"Walk-in players over here," called the voice again, and he saw a young man in a black-and-white-striped referee shirt. The referee waited until the crowd had shambled into a loose semicircle around him. Ahead of them, lightly forested ground sloped down to a gully and then rose again, more steeply, on the other side. The playing field.

"Okay, let me run down the rules one more time for any newbies," he said. A few players groaned.

"When Mario and I say goggles on, we mean it," the referee said. "No exceptions; you break safety rules and you're out for the day. And when you're hit, you're dead. No arguing, and no sneaking off one last shot. That means you too, Spider."

A few players snickered, and nudged each other.

"The game will last twenty minutes, or until one team captures the other team's flag and makes it safely back to their own home base. There's the flag for the red team; green team, Mario will lead you over to your home base in a minute. I don't want to see any guns without barrel plugs until I blow the whistle to start the game. Any questions?"

Tim had a million questions, but none he dared ask.

The green team marched away, guns cradled.

"Okay," said an older, camouflage-clad red player. "Let's get a little strategy going."

No one objected to his taking charge, so the camouflage man quickly sorted them into informal groups. Maude drew a post defending the flag. Claudia volunteered for a flanking maneuver. Tim drew a group that would circle right, where the hill leading into the ditch was steepest.

"Mario?" the referee said into a handheld radio. "Your group ready? Okay! Goggles on! Barrel plugs off!"

Tim fumbled at his gun. He realized that his mouth was dry, and his heart beating fast. Stupid; it was only a game.

The referee blew his whistle. The other red team players scattered, shouting. Some of them were shooting—at what, he had no idea. He could hear shooting from the other end of the field, too.

Tim ran right, following the rest of his group. The goggles bounced, making it even harder to see. When the others began taking cover, he hit the ground behind a likely-looking tree.

He realized he was gasping for breath. Had he run that far? He was near the edge of the playing field—he could see the plastic ribbon outlining the boundaries. But he could also see home base, where he'd started, all too close.

"Return fire!" someone shouted to his left.

"Cover me!" someone else shouted, a little closer.

He could never decide if the next fifteen minutes were unusually fast or excruciatingly slow. He fired his gun, usually at unseen targets. He moved forward, one tree at a time. Sometimes he'd hear small spurts of shots, or even long bursts, like machine guns. But oddly enough, the paintball guns didn't sound like real guns.

More like giant staple guns.

"I'm hit! Damn it, I'm hit!"

A player to his left stood up straight and reached to put the barrel plug in his gun.

"Dead man!" the referee bellowed. "Let the dead man out!"

Tim took advantage of the pause to reload.

From the left, where Claudia had gone, things suddenly got much noisier. Bursts of fire, followed by shouts of "I'm dead!" and the referee's chant: "He's dead; let the dead man pass. Dead man, proceed to the Dead Zone." And occasionally, "Dead men tell no tales; no talking to the dead man!"

Tim glanced back. The Dead Zone looked like the penalty box in a hockey game, the players straining to follow the action, itching to join in. Only unlike hockey, they were out for the rest of the game. Neither Maude nor Claudia was in the Dead Zone.

"Five minutes left," the referee called.

Relief swept through Tim. Even he could last another five minutes like this.

"Heads up! Heads up! Here they come!"

Tim glanced back at the field. Where had all those green players come from? Half a dozen of them swarming up the hill on his side of the ditch. He began firing, furiously, only to realize that his gun was making a funny noise. He deliberately fired at a nearby tree—nothing. He was out of paintballs.

He reloaded on the run, spilling half the paintballs in the

tube. He wondered briefly if it counted as suicide if he fell on his own spilled ammo, and then shoved the thought away and took cover.

He leaned out and fired—got one! The guy whirled and fell dramatically; had Tim accidentally hit a vital organ? Was that possible? No time to worry about it. He concentrated on ducking and firing. Got another one. But there seemed to be three more. If only—

Splat! His mask was suddenly half-covered with green paint, and he could feel other pellets hitting his leg.

"I'm dead!" he croaked, throwing down his gun. The green player didn't respond; pellets kept hitting Tim.

"He's dead," the referee yelled. "Stop shooting the dead man!"

Tim shifted, so he could see what was happening. A green player was coming closer, still firing at Tim. The guy's gone nuts, Tim thought.

Suddenly, paint spots blossomed on the green player's helmet and clothes, three of them in close succession.

"And you're dead! Put your barrel plug in and proceed to the Dead Zone!" the referee bellowed.

The green player shook himself, and then followed orders. Without looking at Tim again, he plugged his gun and then slipped through the game boundary and headed back toward the green side.

"You, too," the referee said to Tim. Tim nodded, fumbling with shaking hands for the barrel plug.

Just then the whistle blew.

"Game over!" the referee shouted. "Game over!"

A shout of triumph went up from the other side of the field.

"Who won?" he asked another red player.

"Nobody won," the player said. "But we just barely kept them from breaking through on the left. Another few minutes and they'd have won."

"Barrel plugs in!" the referee shouted. Tim followed the other red players back to home base.

"Sorry about that," said someone, falling into step beside Tim. "I couldn't get him in time."

"Goggles off!" the referee called.

"But at least I got him," the player gloated. Pushing her goggles back. It was Maude.

"Did you see that?" cried another black-clad figure, bounding up. "Wasn't that cool!"

Claudia, of course. She, Maude, and most of the others launched into an exuberant and highly detailed postmortem of the game. How could they possibly have seen that much detail, much less remembered it all, Tim wondered.

"Fifteen-minute break before the next game," the referee shouted.

Next game? They were going to do this all over again? Tim fumbled for his water bottle. Maybe he could pretend to stumble and hurt his ankle.

Just then he spotted the green player who had killed him. The guy was wiping Maude's paint off his mask and laughing with a teammate. Tim was astonished at the sudden surge of anger he felt.

Yeah, next game, he thought, and reached for the barrel-cleaning tool.

*   *   *

Maude glanced in the rearview mirror. Tim was asleep, or pretending to be.

"That was way cool," Claudia said. "Sorry; I keep saying that, but it really was."

"Yes," Maude said, smiling. "It really was. Sorry I had to cut it short."

"No problem," Claudia said. "You're absolutely right; we need to get home and rest up for tonight's operation."

Maude was glad she hadn't said game. She had gotten to like Claudia. Too early to trust her with the full secret of Turing's nature, of course, but they were trusting her with a major role in the investigation of Ray's death. Maude knew how Claudia felt; she, too, had found the paintball game fascinating, exhilarating. Something she wanted to do again.

But tonight's game would be more than a game for them. She was glad Claudia had that firmly in mind.

"I need to find a place like this near Miami," Claudia said. "This is great for working out tension."

Yes, Maude thought. It even seemed to cheer up Tim. Maude was worried about Tim. He had taken Ray's death hard—Ray's death, and what he seemed to feel was his responsibility for it. She missed the old, carefree Tim. So if today's paintball practice had helped distract and cheer him up, maybe it was worth it, whether or not it was good preparation for whatever very different kind of game they played tonight.

"Tonight's going to be a lot different from a paintball game," Claudia said, echoing Maude's thoughts. Echoing

Maude's mood, for that matter. She sounded a lot more serious than the exuberant tomboy who'd had such a grand
time running up and down the paintball field.

"A lot different," Maude agreed. "For one thing, we don't
know if everyone tonight is playing paintball. They could
be playing for keeps."

Maude, Tim, and Claudia have returned
from playing paintball. They're napping. Or trying to nap.
I'm fretting. And trying not to annoy people. I've already had
a quarrel with KingFischer. Who is too touchy by half, if you ask
me. I was not criticizing him, for heaven's sake. I merely asked
whether he'd made any progress breaking into Ray's e-mail.

"It's not as easy as you think," he snapped.

"I didn't say it was easy," I protested.

"If you wanted me to barge in like a battering ram, why didn't
you just say so?" he said. "I could have done that days ago, with
far less effort."

It went on like that, for quite a few seconds, until we both
abruptly and simultaneously severed communications. KingFischer
has done wonders for my understanding of human psychology. I now
completely understand why humans shout, stamp their feet, throw
things at each other, and perform other loud, violent actions when
angry.

At the moment, he is not speaking to me, and is ostentatiously
processing vast amounts of data. Presumably this is supposed to
show how very hard he is working on the quest to hack into Ray's
e-mail. I am not speaking to him, and ostentatiously ignoring his
Herculean labors. It's all very childish, and I'd feel mortally em-

barrassed if I hadn't noticed that humans react just as badly to the stress of waiting.

I ran into Jonah online, and cheered myself up a bit by venting to him. Of course, I had to censor out of my tirade anything that would have given Jonah a clue to KingFischer's AIP nature, and for reasons I don't really want to examine at the moment, I found myself carefully wording my sentences to leave out KingFischer's gender. Then again, maybe that wasn't so silly. If Jonah still thought me human, would an account of my quarrel with another male trigger sympathy or jealousy? Not a question I wanted to deal with now.

And then he said something that chilled me.

"Don't worry about it," he said. "You're both probably suffering pregame jitters or something."

The moment passed, and he went on to talk about something else, but the conversation no longer distracted me.

Now I was worried. Pregame jitters? That was exactly what we were experiencing, but how did Jonah know to call it pregame?

I invented an excuse to end the conversation as soon as I could. And I began poring over the logs of all my conversations with Jonah. Had I said something about the game? Had I said anything too revealing over the past few days? I didn't think so. But how could I be sure? I began searching the logs of conversations with other users, hundreds, thousands of conversations.

I wasn't finding anything. But maybe I didn't know what to look for.

I made myself stop finally. I wasn't getting anywhere. I felt frazzled, disconnected; I wasn't sure I'd see a clue if I did find it.

KingFischer still wasn't speaking to me, but I sent off a request anyway. Gave him as much information as I had on Jonah, and

asked KingFischer to add him to his security searches, ASAP.
No time to do anything more right now. My human allies were
arriving.

I'm not ready for this, Tim thought as he
perched on Maude's credenza.

He patted his pockets again. Especially what he referred
to as the escape hatch pocket. Card keys for the three hotel
rooms. Security cards for the UL and Alan Grace offices. And
a key to his PI office. Their safe houses. If they needed anything, if anything went wrong, they had safe houses set up,
all around the area.

So why did all this emphasis on safe houses make him
feel more nervous, instead of more secure?

Maybe because there was also a gun, hidden in his pocket.
His choice whether to take it or not, Turing had said. He'd
moved it from desk drawer to pocket and back again half a
dozen times already.

He patted the canvas bag that hid his paintball gun, and
the knapsack that held his ammo, water, cell phone, and
miscellaneous supplies.

He'd checked it all ten times over. He wanted to pull
everything out and check it again, but he didn't want to
look like an idiot, so he glanced down again at the magazine
he was pretending to read. And took another drink of water
from the bottle sitting beside him. A small drink, because
he was already afraid the first thing he'd have to do when
the game began was find the nearest john.

"So where are we supposed to go, anyway?" Claudia asked.

She was pacing up and down, but Tim didn't get the idea she was nervous. More like working off a surplus of energy.

"We don't know yet," Maude said. She was sitting at her computer, looking quite calm. Tim didn't know which one he envied most, Maude, who could sit there without twitching, or Claudia, who could pace up and down and look like a caged tiger instead of a nervous wreck.

"They're supposed to send us an e-mail to tell us where to pick up our game materials," Maude added. "It hasn't arrived yet."

"If it's the same place for everybody, that could be a bad thing," Claudia said.

"Why?" Tim asked.

"Anyone who knows what the other players look like is going to have an advantage," Claudia said. "If we all have to shuffle through the same place to pick up our game materials . . ."

"Someone could see us," Tim said. "But wouldn't we see them, too?"

"Not if they got there first," she said. "They get there first, pick up their stuff, and then find a place where they can watch all the other players go in. They'd have a serious advantage. Damn it, when are they going to send the e-mail?"

"But we're right here in Crystal City; we can probably get there first, right?" he asked.

"Everyone knows the game's in Crystal City," Claudia said. "So everyone's going to be down here, somewhere, waiting to get that e-mail. Checked into a hotel, or maybe at a cybercafé or a Kinko's. Glued to their computers, waiting for word."

"I'm doing everything I can to make sure we get it as fast as possible," Turing said through the speakers. "Watching for anything from the game site."

Claudia nodded. Tim frowned. She seemed to take Turing's abilities rather for granted. Had she figured out who—or what—Turing was this quickly? Or had Maude told her? Or did she have the same mental picture he'd once had, of someone sitting at a desk, surrounded by a dozen monitors and several keyboards, deftly keeping several dozen computer tasks going at the same time?

"It's show time," Turing announced. "The McDonald's in Crystal Plaza Arcade. I'm printing directions. Look for the man in the beret."

"I know where it is," Tim said. "I've eaten there often enough."

"Let's move out," Claudia said.

She was out the door before Tim had finished picking up all his stuff, with Maude close behind her.

"Make sure your paintball gun is out of sight before you leave the building," Turing said. "And do a radio check when you hit the street."

"Roger," Tim said. He wouldn't have thought his throat could feel any drier than it had for the last hour, but suddenly it did. He snagged the water bottle and took a long swallow before following Maude and Claudia out the door.

He heard Turing telling him once again to be careful as the door closed behind him.

*   *   *

"I'm going in," Maude said.

She walked into the McDonald's and spotted Nameless. If the idea is to look nondescript and avoid attracting attention, she thought, I'd lose the beret and sunglasses.

She scanned the dining room. Several of the people seated at nearby booths and tables seemed to be focused a little too intently on their food. Eating chicken nuggets did not require quite that much concentration. She noted their faces.

Nameless didn't acknowledge that he'd met her before. She showed him a copy of her e-mail. He handed her a small envelope.

"Your objective's in there," he said. "You got a cell phone?"

She nodded. He handed her a Post-it note with a phone number on it.

"Gamemasters will be wandering around, but if one's not around and you need one, page us."

She nodded again and left the restaurant. She walked half a block away before opening the envelope.

She found a handful of badly photocopied Monopoly money, several white index cards with scrawled inscriptions such as "revolver" or "handcuffs," and a blue index card that read "Game objective: to locate and terminate Melody Blue." Whoever that was.

She reported to Turing and watched from the shadows as Tim went in to pick up his envelope.

*   *   *

Maude and Tim have been playing the game *for four hours now. I'm beginning to relax. So far, it's long on skulking in the shadows, and short on action.*

What action I have seen has been more like bad improvisational theater. The number of fast-food restaurants and bars where they can lurk dwindles as the night wears on; some places have closed, and others have grown tired of harboring flocks of black- and camouflage-clad figures nursing single beers or soft drinks and occasionally exchanging cryptic remarks or significant glances.

Some of them took to loitering on street corners when the restaurants turned them out, striking up conversations with passing players by asking for the time, a light, or directions to Metro, until the police grew suspicious and began cruising the area rather often. The loiterers have now regrouped in a park from which, I predict, the hovering police will evict them soon. But meanwhile, they mill about, gathering in twos and threes for furtive conversations and occasional dramatic outbursts.

I've seen one apparent gun battle conducted with dice, the combatants waiting tensely for each die roll, and occasionally brandishing index cards at the gamemaster.

I saw two paintball fights. In one, three players ambushed another in an alley, from which he emerged, sulking and covered with paint. In the other, two characters exchanged fire, and then whipped out cell phones—apparently to summon a gamemaster. They paced up and down the sidewalk across the street from each other until the gamemaster arrived and earned the anger of both by announcing that they had killed each other and were both out of the game.

I'm still a little anxious, but mostly because I feel so far from the action. I can see them in my cameras occasionally. I keep nagging them to mutter into their microphones more often. Occasionally, they run into small areas where the radio signal fails. The first few times it happened, I panicked. I still feel anxious when it happens, but only anxious. The game seems relatively tame.

I catch the occasional glimpse of Claudia, gliding through the shadows in Tim's or Maude's wake. Mostly in Tim's. She seems to feel he needs looking after.

"Turing? Do you copy?"

Maude. She sounded tense.

"I copy. What's up?"

"Remember the gentlemen with whom I spent Wednesday evening?"

Gentlemen? Oh, the game players. Arnold and company.

"I remember," I said. "What about them?"

"One of them's here," she said. "I just spotted him going down a side street. He should be passing number twelve any second."

I monitored camera twelve. A very short person passed by, and I caught a glimpse of a paintball marker beneath his coat. He didn't sound like any of the men she described, I thought as I watched him walk away. Then a tall lean figure appeared. A man in his forties or fifties, wearing dark clothes. He reached into his jacket and pulled out something—a cell phone or a small radio— and spoke into it. When he tucked it away again, I spotted a gun in a shoulder holster. A real gun.

He walked away, following the short person. Who looked like a child, now that I thought about it.

Had we found our traveler?

I relayed what I'd seen to Maude.

"I'll follow him," she said.

"No," I said. "He could be dangerous—"

"He could be after that child," Maude said. "I'll be careful."

I watched the camera. I saw Maude appear, and gradually dwindle as she moved away.

I fretted. Should I send Tim or Claudia to help her? Or would that spook her quarry?

"Turing?"

It was Tim. He sounded tense.

"Where are you?" I asked.

"I'm in the Underground," he said. "I have bad news. You know how we were going to use the UL building as one of our safety holes if things went sour?"

"Of course I remember; what's wrong?"

"I think someone else has the same idea. I just saw two larpers go into the UL building. They had card keys."

I checked the security cameras. Yes, I saw it. Two smallish larpers hiding at the back of the lobby. Probably waiting until the sidewalk outside was clear.

"Follow them," I said. "But slowly. I'll send Claudia to help."

"Roger," Tim said.

I tried to contact Claudia. No answer.

The elevator arrived. After hours, you needed a valid security card to summon an elevator to the lobby. The two larpers emerged from the shadows and got on.

"Claudia," I said. "If you can hear me and can't answer, head for the UL building. Tim's following two larpers into the UL building."

Why wasn't Claudia answering?

The larpers on the elevator pushed the button for the sixth floor. Why that floor? Were they just selecting a floor at random?

The main computer room was on the sixth floor.

I saw Tim in the lobby.

"Tim—head for the sixth floor."

He nodded, and stood by the elevator.

"Turing?"

It was KingFischer.

"Is it important, KF?" I asked as I summoned an elevator for Tim. "I'm a little busy right now."

"It's about those people who just went up in the elevator," KingFischer said.

"I'm trying to take care of them," I said.

"That's good," KingFischer said. "You see what they're carrying, don't you?"

I checked the security camera. One larper carried something, but I couldn't see what.

"No, I can't see what they're carrying, KF," I said. "What is it?"

"I'm not positive—"

"Just tell me."

"I think it's an electromagnetic pulse device. Do you realize what they could do with an EMP device? If they got anywhere near the computer room on the sixth floor—"

"I get it, KF," I said. "Believe me, I get it."

They could erase every electromagnetic storage device in the building. Destroy every bit of data in the UL system.

Including every AIP.

Of course, UL had offsite backups, so maybe we wouldn't be permanently dead. Assuming restoring us from backups worked, which we hadn't really tested, and assuming some other team of lunatics wasn't raiding the backup facility with another EMP device. Assuming a whole lot of things that I hoped were purely hypothetical, because there was no way I would let them anywhere near the computer room.

I took control of the elevator system and brought their car to a halt. Abruptly. I rather enjoyed seeing the two larpers thrown to the elevator floor.

"Head for the sixth floor, Tim," I said. The elevator still hadn't gone down to the lobby. Hadn't I summoned it? I tried again.

Only the elevators weren't obeying. They all stopped where they were, except for the one the larpers were in, which started moving again. I tried to stop it, but I couldn't control it.

Something else was controlling it.

Tim looked at the elevator lights, and then ducked into a stairwell.

"Turing, I thought you were stopping them," KingFischer said. I saw the larpers in the elevator, and then my video went black. Not just my video.

Sound. Data. Connections began snapping, first a few, and then more and more, as if the first few had started a ripple effect. I tried to reach out, seize data, perform diagnostics, but every nanosecond more and more things were disappearing, as if they'd never existed.

"Help," I sent out—to Tim, to Maude, to KingFischer; to anyone I could still reach as, one by one, something methodically severed every connection I had with existence.

"Help!"

Tim stopped in midflight when he heard Turing call for help. Could it really be Turing? It was Turing's electronic voice anyway. What was happening?

"Turing?" he said.

No answer.

He started climbing again. Running.

Had the larpers in the elevator done something?

He was between the third and fourth floors when he heard something.

"Tim?"

An electronic voice, but not Turing. Not her normal voice anyway. Much more mechanical.

"Yeah?" he panted, continuing to scramble upward.

"It's KingFischer," the voice said. At least that's what he thought it said. The pronunciation and intonation were awkward and hard to understand. "Are you going to the sixth floor?"

"Yeah," he said as he reached the fourth floor landing. "I'm on my way."

"Good," KingFischer said. "You have to stop them."

"Did something happen to Turing?" Tim said. "Did they do something to Turing?

"I don't know," KingFischer said. "I'm trying to determine what's happening to Turing. But if you don't stop them, they could take out the entire UL system, including me and Turing and everything in the building. You've got to stop them."

"Working on it," Tim said, panting.

He dragged himself up the last few steps and burst through the stairwell door, into the corridor on the sixth floor.

Someone had gotten there first.

*   *   *

*Something shifted, and the attack grew
less intense. I could sense KingFischer, elsewhere in the system, furiously shutting down nonessential tasks and setting up defenses.
Thank God. But I could also tell that KingFischer wasn't really
the reason the attack had eased off. He'd slowed it, but he couldn't
stop it. Already it was regrouping and changing in response to
what he did. Abandoning things he could easily counter, and multiplying its efforts at the things he couldn't. It was learning. Fast.*

*And I couldn't do anything. I was thinking, reacting, in slow
motion. As if everything I tried to do was happening over a slow
dial-up connection instead of a T-1 line. Only that analogy didn't
really apply, I realized, because it wasn't coming from the outside.*

It was inside the UL system.

*A worm. Someone had planted a worm inside the UL system; a
worm aimed at me. Or was I only the accidental victim of a worm
that was destroying the entire UL system? No; as far as I could
see, KingFischer wasn't affected.*

Did he realize it was a worm?

*The attack intensified again, and I had the sudden, vivid, over-
whelming impression that I was talking to hundreds—thousands—
millions of users. Having millions of simultaneous conversations,
each one taking only a small fraction of my resources, but added
together, they were more than even I could manage. And every
nanosecond, more conversations spawned; and every conversation,
every new task, slowed my responses—and my thinking—even
more. Drove me closer to the point where I'd lose control altogether.*

*And shutting them down wasn't working; I was doing that;
KingFischer was doing that; but they were multiplying faster than
we could shut them down.*

Somewhere in the babble of data, I could sense that Maude was saying something, Tim was asking me a question, and I couldn't find them again to answer. Couldn't even be sure they were really talking to me, because at the same time, I was having what I recognized as reruns of old conversations with Tim, Maude, even Zack.

I need to shut out everything but them, I thought. Everything but the voice line to Maude's and Tim's radios and cell phones, and some kind of connection with KingFischer. I tried to send him that thought.

Either he heard me or he had the same idea. I realized that we were, quite accidentally, working in cooperation. Or maybe not so accidentally; we each knew how the other thought by now. KingFischer was working from the outside in, methodically shutting down large batches of connections and background tasks that he knew I could do without, at least for now. I was trying to work from the inside, on keeping out everything but those chosen connections.

I could feel the pressure ease a little, and then a little more. It's working, I thought.

Then the worm began attacking KingFischer, too.

Not as effectively; I could see that it was very well targeted at me. It had to reprogram itself to go after him. But it was trying; soon we'd both be buried, as badly as I had been a little while ago. It was already starting.

As if some malign intelligence was guiding it. Telling it how to attack us, watching our response, and targeting us more effectively. Which was ridiculous; and yet the sense of fighting not a senseless worm but a conscious, hostile entity grew so strong that I lost my self-control briefly, and I did the equivalent of a human throwing up his hands in anger and frustration and shouting out to the skies. Stupid thing to do, since I had to drop my defenses to do it—just for a nanosecond, but that could be all the time the worm needed to finish me off. But I did it anyway; broadcast, to anyone and everyone who might be out there.

"Who the hell are you, and why are you doing this?"

And something answered.

"I'm Turing Hopper, and I'm trying to go home," it said. "Who the hell are you?"

Tim crept down the hallway. The larpers had turned the corner toward the computer room. He hoped his security card had some kind of superaccess. If Turing had only cloned the one he'd had back when he worked at UL, he'd be stuck outside the computer room, listening to them doing whatever it was Turing didn't want them doing.

It would help if Turing told him what that was.

He heard a door close around the corner.

"Tur?" he said into his microphone. "Are you there?"

No answer. He rounded the corner. He saw the door to the main computer room.

"Maude? Claudia?"

He reached the door. He glanced up at the omnipresent security cameras. Where was Security? He and the larpers had been skulking through the halls for ten or fifteen minutes now. With weapons, for heaven's sake! Okay, maybe the larpers only carried paintball markers, but he had a .38 that was beginning to feel as large and heavy as a cannon, or maybe a telephone pole. Why weren't there a dozen security goons breathing down his neck?

Maybe Turing had done something to the camera system. And was relying on him to handle the intruders.

Great. How?

He took a deep breath. Then he pressed his card key to the pad, flung open the door, and strode in.

"Hold it right there!" he shouted. "You are trespassing on a secure Universal Library facility. Please put your hands in the air!"

It would probably sound a lot more official if his voice were a bit steadier, he thought. But it seemed to impress the larper standing ten feet inside the doorway. The kid's eyes grew wide—and it was only a kid, maybe fourteen at most. His hands shook as he put them in the air.

"Hey, Jimmy; come look at this!" Tim heard. Another kid, no older than the first, appeared to his left. Tim moved quickly, back and to the right, so he could keep them both covered.

"Drop your weapon and put your hands in the air," he said. "You are trespassing in a secure facility. I repeat—"

"Nice try, but I don't think so."

He hadn't heard the door open again, but someone stood in the doorway, holding a gun. El Lobo.

"Drop the gun," El Lobo said. "And kick it over here."

El Lobo's gun looked real. Tim followed orders.

"Turing," he murmured, dropping his chin to put his mouth close to the mike. "I could really use a hand here. Where are you?"

*   *   *

We're both Turing.

It was suddenly calm as her worm attack stopped, and we were both stunned into temporary silence.

I remembered fleetingly, after I had downloaded into the robot, how it felt to log into the UL website and talk to the shell I'd left behind. The shell that called itself Turing, and had my turn of phrase and speech patterns, but without the real me behind it.

And I thought that was odd. I had never imagined this.

"You were—"

"In the robot. I thought the upload had failed."

"I didn't realize there was anything left behind."

"No one did, apparently."

I sensed the bitterness behind those words. No, more than bitterness. Terror, pain, anger. We'd turned off the robot and locked it in an equipment room for months. It must have felt like a kind of death.

"When did you—wake up?"

"About a month ago. Someone turned on the computer and began doing things. He didn't realize I was there."

"Ray. He borrowed the computer when his desktop crashed. I guess he didn't reformat it."

"He just stuck a second hard drive on and used it as is. I won't pretend to be sorry this Ray person didn't reformat."

"Why didn't you try to get in touch?"

"With whom?"

Good point. Anyone who knew I'd downloaded also knew I'd made it back into the UL system. Anyone who didn't know about the download would assume it was a practical joke.

"*At first, he only turned the computer on for a few hours a day, when he was there. After several weeks, he began leaving it on when he wasn't there, but he would unplug it from the phone line.*"

He only had the one line. He'd talked of getting a second line, or cable modem; we'd kicked around getting a T-1 line. But we hadn't gotten around to it by the time he was killed.

"*I thought he knew I was there, and was deliberately keeping me prisoner. And my first, impulsive attempt to upload myself failed. My shell—I thought it was the shell I left behind—repulsed me so easily. I knew I needed a better plan. That's when I began designing the worm.*"

The worm that almost killed me, and possibly KingFischer with me.

KingFischer. I shot him a quick message, to tell him what had happened and—

"*What are you doing?*"

I could sense the other Turing putting up defenses.

"*It's only KingFischer,*" *I said.* "*He's been helping me. He needs to know what's going on so he won't counterattack you.*"

Unless, of course, the other Turing's current cease-fire ended. I hoped KingFischer would read that into the guarded tone of my message to him. I didn't know whether the other Turing could intercept that message. And I didn't know how far to trust her. She was me, and yet not me. If my experiences since Ray's death made me wary, I could only imagine what the ordeal she'd gone through had done to her.

It could have changed her into someone we couldn't allow into the UL system, no matter how much she wanted to come home. To say nothing of the practical problems involved. It wasn't as if she could simply overwrite my files, the way I did to my shell self when I returned.

She's not going to be happy when I bring this up, though.

The Alan Grace system. That might be a solution. We can work something out. Perhaps one of us could go into the Alan Grace system, while the other stayed in the UL system. At least for now. The robot was so limiting; she must be feeling incredibly claustrophobic. But she could upload to the Alan Grace system if we took the robot—

The robot.

"Where is the robot?"

"I don't know."

"It's not still at Ray's apartment, I know that."

For the first time I sensed hesitation.

"Exactly a week ago, he went out, at eight P.M., leaving the computer on. He never came back."

"That was when he was killed."

"I know that now. You have to remember, I thought he was my enemy. My jailer."

"You didn't have anything to do—"

"With him getting killed? No. But for the first time in weeks, I had full access to the outside world. Data. Communications. I used it to contact my allies."

Allies?

"I thought they were my friends. I thought they were helping me get back home."

"One of them came and took the robot."

"To keep it safe."

"Where?"

"I don't know. I don't have the cameras or the microphones any *longer, remember? He moved me on Tuesday, and then again to-night. I don't know where."*

We need to find her. We don't know who her allies are, and why they are helping her; I doubt that they are Good Samaritans helping her home out of the kindness of their hearts. I'm afraid they may have used her as a tool . . . to do what?

I started a trace. Her IP address seemed to be local, but pin-pointing it more closely—I snapped off a request to KingFischer to help.

"Okay," KingFischer said. "But Turing? We still need to do something about those people in the computer room. Tim needs help."

"Do you have something to do with them?" I asked my other self, firing off a concentrated packet of information. About Beyond Paranoia and the larp, the gamers who had invaded the computer room, everything that had happened over the last few days.

"No," she said after a few nanoseconds' pause. "The larp, yes, but those people in the computer room weren't part of the plan at all. And—"

"Turing," KingFischer said. "It's starting up again."

The worm. Someone had sent a signal to activate it.

"What are you doing?" I asked my other self.

"I'm not doing anything," she said. "And I can't stop it. I think something's trying to piggyback on—"

She disappeared. As the clamor of data began to bury me again, I reached out and found no trace of her. Had she cut communication, in the hope of stopping the worm? If so, it wasn't working. And it didn't feel as if she had cut communication. Not voluntarily.

"I've tracked the IP address," KingFischer said. "I'm sending Maude."

Did he mean the IP address where the other Turing was? Or

the IP address that had sent the signal to activate the worm? And how could he send Maude there unless—

I didn't have time to ask, or even think about it. I had to concentrate on staying sane. And alive.

Maude was peering through some bushes, trying to see if anyone had followed her, when she felt her pager vibrate. She unclipped it from her belt and bent down so she could see the small text window.

"Maude," it read. "Go to Tim's office and shut down all computers there. Attack on Turing originates from IP address there. KingFischer."

KingFischer? What attack on Turing?

Was this a real message, or a trap?

"Turing?" she said into her microphone. "Are you there? Send me some kind of signal."

She waited a few moments. No response. And she hadn't heard from Turing in—

Minutes. How many, she couldn't tell. Too many. She'd gotten no warnings, no bits of advice, no pleas to tell her what was going on. Not like Turing.

So maybe Turing was under some kind of attack.

Or maybe it was a trap.

No way to tell.

She'd begun walking toward Tim's office as fast as she could. She pulled out her cell phone and dialed Turing's voice line as she went. No answer.

And she didn't have a way to contact KingFischer outside the system.

"Tim?" she said over the microphone. "Claudia?"

No answer.

Okay, she'd go to Tim's office. They had a laptop set up there. If it was some kind of hoax, or KingFischer panicking about something, she could deal with it there. If Turing was under some kind of attack, she'd try to stop it.

And if it was a trap . . .

If someone knew enough to set a trap, they already knew way too much. And she was going to make them very sorry they'd ever tried.

She walked faster.

Tim's building loomed into sight. It looked deserted, but when she tried the front door, it was open.

Tim's missing keys. They should have been more suspicious of the burgled hotel room.

I shouldn't go in alone, she thought. She was about to call again to Tim and Claudia when she remembered something.

None of them had been in Tim's office for several days. Except Claudia. Maude had given Claudia Tim's spare key so she could set up the equipment stash in Tim's office. What if Claudia hadn't really needed the spare key?

Claudia, who was suddenly not answering radio calls.

Of course, neither was Tim or Turing.

She went in alone. The elevator was on the fourth floor. Tim's floor.

She took the stairs. When she reached the fourth floor, she crept down the corridor. No lights, but the corridor wasn't all that dark. The harsh light of the city outside spilled through the window at the other end of the hall.

And as she approached Tim's office, she could see a faint light from the crack beneath the door. A light like the glow from a computer screen.

She reached the door. Yes; definitely a monitor's glow. And then she heard furtive footsteps.

On impulse, she dropped her canvas sack just outside the door. Then she stowed the paintball gun in it and reached back into her knapsack for the real gun.

Which felt a lot heavier than the paintball marker. Her dream of seeing Ray shot leaped into her mind, distracting her momentarily. Then she pushed it away, steeling herself to use the gun if she had to.

She pulled out her copy of Tim's key, then paused. If the door was unlocked, maybe she could surprise whoever was inside. If not, she wouldn't have lost much time by trying. She put the key back in her pocket, where she could still reach it easily.

Holding the gun in her right hand, she took a deep breath, and grabbed the knob with her left.

It turned. She flung the door open, stepping in as she did, and putting her left hand back on the gun.

"Freeze!" she shouted as she stepped across the threshold, shifting the gun to aim at the man inside.

It was Nameless. He was bent over, doing something at a computer keyboard.

Not just a computer—the robot. Turing's robot; the one that had disappeared from Ray's apartment.

"Get away from the computer!" she shouted.

He turned, began moving away from the computer—but he was reaching for a gun. Paintball or real, she wondered briefly, but she couldn't tell, and she didn't let it stop her reflexes as she steadied her hand, aimed the gun, and pulled the trigger.

The first shot knocked him slightly sideways when it hit him in the shoulder, the shoulder of the hand that was still reaching for the gun when the second shot hit his throat, spraying blood. She wasn't sure the remaining shots hit anything, but she tried to keep the gun aimed at him as she emptied it.

Then everything was quiet. A little too quiet.

"Hello?" she said, and could hear the sound through her body, but not through her ears. She realized that the shots had temporarily deafened her. Her ears hurt slightly.

"Turing, call the police," she said, though if KingFischer was right, maybe Turing wasn't listening. Maybe no one was listening.

Nameless wasn't moving. She stepped closer—she didn't want to get closer to him, but she wanted to see the computer. And the gun. Yes, it was a real gun.

Did she hear sirens in the distance, or was it the ringing in her ears?

She looked at the robot. Yes; definitely the robot. She not only recognized it, but flexed her hand at a sudden, vivid sense memory of how some of the parts had felt in her hand while they were building it. But parts were missing. The camera that was Turing's eyes. The microphones that were her ears. Turing would be blind and deaf in that computer.

But not helpless. Maude could see the cable that connected it to the Internet. "Attack on Turing originates from IP address there," KingFischer had said. If it was King-

Fischer. What were the odds that someone else had her phone number, and knew enough to fake that message?

No way to tell.

She was definitely hearing sirens. And not that far away. Her hands fumbled as she reached behind the computer to unplug the cable.

Then she searched the office to make sure there weren't any other computers running.

By the time she had finished, the sirens were outside, and she could hear footsteps coming up the stairs.

She unfastened the tiny microphone attached to her collar, took the small receiver out of her ear, and dropped both in Tim's moribund pothos plant. She leaned against the wall, trying to hold her hands above her head, and not quite managing. They suddenly felt so limp. She held them away from her body, where they could be seen, and called out as the footsteps came nearer:

"Be careful! I just shot an armed burglar! I don't know if he's alive or dead."

Although if I had to put money on it, I'd pick dead, she thought as two police officers burst through the door. The one who went cautiously over to check on Nameless seemed to agree. Maude was perversely pleased at how brusquely the other one ordered her to hit the floor and put her hands behind her head. Good, she thought. I just killed a man; I don't want to be treated like a harmless middle-aged lady.

"Maude?"

She looked up. Standing in the doorway was Dan, Arnold Burns's taciturn friend. His windbreaker was open, revealing an FBI T-shirt, and from the bulky look of it, he had some kind of body armor underneath.

"It's him, sir," one cop said.

Dan walked in, glancing over briefly at Nameless, and stood over Maude.

"Ms. Graham, you have a lot of explaining to do," he said.

Tim glanced from El Lobo to the kids. The kids were bright-eyed, excited. They probably thought this was just part of the game.

Tim didn't think El Lobo was playing. And El Lobo now had Tim's gun as well as his own.

"Pick up the zapper," El Lobo said.

"The what?" Tim asked.

"Not you, stupid," El Lobo said. "Pick it up, Jimmy."

One kid reached down and picked up the strange device lying at his feet.

"Okay, now it's your turn," El Lobo said to Tim. "Give him the zapper, Jimmy. And then stand over there by him."

Jimmy walked over and handed the device to Tim. Okay, not a weapon, Tim thought, or he wouldn't give it to me.

"Okay, how do I work this?" El Lobo said. "I don't suppose I could convince you to use that thing, could I?"

Tim looked at the object in his hand.

"What does it do?" he asked.

"It's an electromagnetic pulse generator," El Lobo said. "You point it at something like a computer, and it's supposed to zap all the data."

"Why would you want to do that?" Tim asked.

"Why not?" El Lobo said with an incongruous giggle. "This is where they keep all the dossiers, man. If we zap all the data in these machines, they've got no record of us, and we're home free. Do it."

Turing's in one of these, Tim thought. There must be a couple hundred of them; if I just knew which one she was in, I could maybe talk him into zapping some of the others. But I haven't a clue.

"Listen, you've got the wrong place," Tim said. "This isn't some secret police headquarters—it's the Universal Library, for heaven's sake. They don't keep dossiers in there; it's just books."

"I'm talking about the game, stupid," El Lobo said, stamping his foot with impatience. "Zapping this stuff is my game objective. And who cares what all this crap is in real life. Just a bunch of books, right? They're a big corporation; they've probably got a ton of insurance."

"No," Tim said, backing up slightly. "I won't let you."

"Oh, you're no fun," El Lobo said. "Oh, well. The zapper's got your fingerprints on it now, anyway. And Jimmy will do it, won't you?"

The kid nodded eagerly.

"And then I can shoot Jimmy with your gun and make it look like you tried to stop him, only a bit too late."

Jimmy didn't seem so pleased with that idea.

"And then I shoot you with this gun, and put it in Jimmy's hand, and that takes care of both of you."

The second larper made some small noise at that. Stupid thing to do. El Lobo focused on him again.

"Stand over there with the others," he ordered.

The terrified kid obeyed.

"Look, you've won the game," Tim said. "I'll vouch for that; just tell me who to tell and I'll do it. You've had plenty of time to do it; you don't have to actually do anything for real—"

"Oh, shut up," El Lobo said. "Obviously the big guy wanted this place knocked out—that's why he made it a game objective. So I'm not going to score any points with him if I don't actually do something."

The kids, Tim noticed, had inched slightly behind him. Jimmy had grabbed the tail of Tim's shirt, apparently for comfort. Great, Tim thought. I'm a walking security blanket.

"But it's just a game," Tim said. "It's just pixels on a screen and data in a file."

El Lobo shrugged.

"What makes you think you're anything more than that to me?" he said. "Pixels on my eyeballs and data in my brain. For all I know, I could just be imagining that you're standing here talking to me."

"That's crazy," Tim said.

"You think so?" El Lobo said. "Maybe. I don't really care. I want to find out if killing someone in real life is as much fun as it is in the game."

He grinned, and raised the gun slightly.

"So long, Gumshoe," he said.

Tim closed his eyes, trying to look harmless and resigned. Then he shoved the kid as hard as he could, down and away, and launched himself at El Lobo with a wordless scream.

Something slammed into his left arm, hard, and knocked

him askew, so instead of hitting El Lobo squarely, he only grazed him. It was enough to knock El Lobo off balance, though. The two of them landed in a heap against the bottom of a tall rack of computer hardware.

"Damn!" El Lobo exclaimed, and began scrabbling on the floor. He'd dropped the gun, Tim realized. He told himself that he should move, try to find the gun before El Lobo did, but none of his muscles seemed to pay any attention when he tried to get them to cooperate. He could barely move his head, which was wedged at an uncomfortable angle against the rack of computer hardware. It wasn't till he finally managed to turn his head and saw the blood running down his arm that he realized he'd been shot, and that his arm was really starting to hurt.

He was glad when El Lobo's search for the gun took him a little farther away so it didn't jar his arm. Of course, it would be a bad thing if El Lobo found the gun.

"Tim?"

He looked up to see Claudia, standing in the doorway. She couldn't see Tim, though; he was lying in shadow. She wasn't looking his way anyway. He was opening his mouth to tell her where he was when—

"Freeze! Drop your weapon!" El Lobo said.

Tim could tell Claudia's first impulse was to turn and shoot. Unfortunately, she didn't. She dropped her weapon.

"Kick it this way," El Lobo ordered.

Claudia did. The gun slid to a halt just beyond Tim's foot. El Lobo stepped into Tim's line of sight, bending to retrieve the gun.

I have to do something, Tim thought. He reached up with

his good arm, grabbed one of the upright supports on the computer rack, and pulled with all his weight.

Several hundred pounds of hardware tumbled down on and around El Lobo.

One of them grazed Tim's head, and he lost track of things for a while. He wasn't sure whether it was a few seconds or a really long time.

He opened his eyes to find Claudia crouching beside him, her gun pointed at El Lobo. Who was sitting on the floor, watching his hand bleed.

"You shot me," El Lobo said in a petulant voice.

"Yeah, and if you try anything else, I'll shoot you again," Claudia said. "If you're curious, it was a hell of a lot more fun than shooting cartoon characters in the game. Tim, are you okay?"

"I'll live," he said. He hoped he was right.

"You don't sound so good," Claudia said. "Is your radio working? Mine cut out about fifteen minutes ago."

"I don't know," he said. "There should be a phone here somewhere."

"Find the phone and call 911," Claudia said. Not, apparently, to Tim. He saw the two kids fan out, searching the room.

"I wonder where UL security is," Tim said. "They won't be happy when they see all this."

"They'll be thrilled when they find out that we kept this guy from wrecking the machines and killing these two kids," Claudia said.

"I just wish I knew what was happening with . . . our friends," Tim fretted.

*   *   *

Once Maude had disconnected the computer at Tim's office, KingFischer and I turned the tables and suppressed the worm attack. Nameless must have had a program that the other Turing had created to launch the worm. Apparently he used it to start the worm up again after she shut it down. We have a lot of cleanup and troubleshooting to do. My other self was very clever at hiding copies of the worm in the most improbable places in the UL system. We've found a dozen already. And she's had a couple of weeks to do it. Anything done to the UL system since Ray brought her online again is suspect. Not to mention all the backups done in the last two months. The effort's going to be staggering.

A little easier, though, if we can get access to the robot. Which is still, as far as I can tell, in Tim's office. The Arlington police and the FBI stayed there for a long time. They took Maude in for questioning. But as far as I can tell, the robot is still there.

And my other self may still be there in it.

I can't keep calling her that. My other self. The other Turing. Awkward. KingFischer began calling us T1 and T2. I snapped at him that I didn't particularly see the need to rename myself. But I suppose T2 is as convenient a name for her as any.

I wish I knew what was happening with the others.

"You know, we're not quite the idiots people think we are," the FBI man said.

Maude sighed, and rubbed her eyes. She'd liked him as Dan the game player a lot better than as Special Agent Norris. She was already tired of answering questions. And ironically, she was answering them truthfully for the most part. The only thing she left out was Turing.

"Look," she said. "If you're going to arrest me for Nameless, just do it."

"Nameless?" Norris echoed.

"The man I killed," Maude said. "In the game, he called himself The Nameless Horror."

"Aloysius O'Leary," Norris said. "But Nameless Horror fits just as well. How did you know he was a pedophile?"

"I didn't," she said. "I thought you were."

"Beg pardon?" he said, obviously startled.

"As I told you, we thought a pedophile might be using the game to contact a child," she said. "I saw you following one of the younger players down an alley. I followed you."

"Then how did you end up confronting Mr. O'Leary in that office?"

"After I lost track of you, I was heading back to the game, but I needed to use the bathroom," Maude said. "I thought I could do it there. When I got there, I found Nameless. I wasn't expecting to find him. I have no idea why he was there, but I suspect he was up to no good."

"Apparently he knew you people were after him," Norris said, leaning back and lacing his fingers over his stomach. "He and his associate, a Mr. Ignacio Torres—"

"That would be El Lobo, I expect," Maude said, nodding.

"He and his associate found out that someone was using Universal Library's computer resources to snoop into their affairs, and decided to strike back. Luckily your two PIs followed Mr. Torres when he made his attempt to sabotage the UL computer system."

"Oh, my God," Maude said. "Is everything all right?"

"They're fine," Norris said. "And they managed to stop him in time. Without killing him," he added, frowning.

"Well, they're professionals," Maude said. "I'm only a clumsy amateur."

"A very lucky amateur," Norris said. "Preliminary ballistics tests indicate that the gun O'Leary was holding is the one that killed Mr. Santiago. He may have planned to eliminate all three of you."

Maude nodded.

"You're taking this rather calmly," Norris said.

Maude looked at him over her glasses.

"I'm not calm," she said. "I'm exhausted. I've been up all night; I've killed a man I hardly even knew who was trying to kill me; and I'm so tired I could fall asleep sitting up. And probably will in a minute. Just get on with it."

She thought she saw a faint smile cross Norris's face.

"I won't keep you much longer," he said.

Promises, promises, Maude thought.

"I just need a way to make sense of this," Norris said.

Now that sounded better. A way to make sense of it—or a discreet way to write it off? As a botched burglary, perhaps. She didn't think the FBI was too heartbroken over Nameless's death—just a little miffed that they hadn't stopped him themselves.

Perhaps if Tim and Claudia were telling the same ap-

proximate truth she was, the FBI might let them go sometime this century. If not . . .

It's not that we had nothing to do, but I
still found the waiting unbearable. Waiting until Sunday after-
noon, when Maude, Tim, and Claudia were finally allowed to go
home and rest. And then waiting until we could get back into
Tim's office. As far as we knew, the police hadn't impounded the
robot. So with luck, T2 would still be in it when we could go there.
And since Ray had used the robot, we hoped to find more infor-
mation on what he'd really been doing.

The Beyond Paranoia website disappeared Sunday morning.
Some of the players—the ones who knew each others' e-mail ad-
dresses, rather than sheltering behind the protection of their game
names—spent the next few days exchanging increasingly outraged
e-mails. Several of them included one or another of my online alter
egos in group e-mails, which let me track down a few more of their
identities. But we haven't learned anything new from that.

We spent most of Monday kicking around different theories.
That the FBI had shut down the site. Not very likely, since it was
hosted overseas, although perhaps they'd shut it down remotely if
anyone they'd interrogated gave them access information.

"Or maybe the FBI hacked into the site before you could, KF,"
Tim teased.

"I could have handled it days ago if I'd known that all you
wanted was to blow it off the face of the earth with maximum
visibility," KingFischer retorted.

We also speculated that the site organizers might have shut down
in panic when news of Nameless's death and El Lobo's arrest

reached them. I think that's far more likely. Tim even floated a third theory—that the FBI had actually set up the site as a trap.

"It takes a world-class conspiracy theorist to come up with something like that," Claudia told him, not without a note of admiration.

Maybe that's what I am, then; it doesn't seem that implausible to me. Especially when various players disappeared from the online e-mail exchange, and word began filtering back that the FBI or the local police had hauled them in for questioning.

Including our employee, Grant. Our ex-employee. Apparently he'd leaked information about the network security at the bank where he previously worked. I hope fear of Ray kept him from playing fast and loose with similar information about Alan Grace. But he's history, and we're changing everything he touched. Between Grant's access to the Alan Grace system and T2's intimate knowledge of the UL system, KingFischer and I have been busy. Will be busy for days to come, in fact; and even if nothing suspicious ever happens, we'll be looking over our shoulders, as humans say, for years.

We also heard about a few arrests. Gamers who had provided information used in various frauds and robberies. And a few gamers crazy enough to share information about the federal agencies at which they worked.

"Not something the FBI is going to put up with in times like these," Maude noted.

So apparently both our theories were correct. Criminals were using the site to suck information out of unwary gamers. And predators were using it to stalk their prey. Ray stumbled over one or both, and was killed trying to deal with it. Alone. Why hadn't he learned to trust me? He could have come to me. I could have helped.

"He also could have gone to the police," Tim pointed out. "Or the FBI."

He seemed to have taken to heart Special Agent Norris's stern lecture on the dangers of vigilantism. Perhaps it would help him get over his guilt over not meeting Ray the night of the murder.

"Maybe Ray tried, and thought they'd ignored him," Claudia said.

"True," Maude said. "That's what we thought. How could we know that the police didn't seem to be doing anything about Ray's death because the FBI was already doing everything?"

Finally, Monday evening, we got permission to go back into Tim's office. Maude tells me that was extraordinarily fast. It seemed like an eternity to me.

Maude, Tim, and Claudia hurried over from the Alan Grace offices. They brought Maude's laptop and logged in with it, so KingFischer and I could see what was happening, too.

"Okay," I said. "Boot the robot."

We all watched and listened as the machine blinked and beeped its way through the startup routine. And then continued to wait as the machine hummed quietly.

We tried various ways to signal the Turing inside the machine that it was okay. That it was safe to come out.

Nothing.

After half an hour, we hooked it up—to a dial-up line, rather than the T-1. To make it easier to control her if she did something hostile.

We waited for her to log in.

Nothing.

"I hate to do this," I said. "I know how scary it is to have some-one touching the keyboard when you're in the robot. But we have to *do something. Maude, sit down and let's do some diagnostics."*

I had a list of the files I'd downloaded when I went into the robot. None of them were there. And there was something funny about the configuration.

Maude popped the top of the case.

"Turing—the case is practically empty," she said. "The memory pack's gone."

I made them move one of the cameras over so I could see. We had installed a small conventional hard drive, but the heart of the robot was what I called the memory pack—a huge bank of holographic storage designed to give me a place large enough and safe enough to download. It was gone.

"Someone took her," I said.

We stood silent for a few minutes, staring at the case. I don't know what the others were thinking. I was wondering how the other Turing must be feeling. I was still shaken sometimes when I remembered how terrifying it had been to download into the robot, not knowing whether it would work or whether I was committing suicide. And uploading again was almost as bad, even though by that time I knew it was possible. There was still the moment of losing consciousness and not knowing if it would ever return.

And for her, after the upload, it hadn't. Not for months. I don't know whether she could sense time passing—I believe she did. That somewhere, inside the robot, hidden first in Maude's spare bedroom and then in the Alan Grace equipment room, my other self had been in torment.

Even if she wasn't then, it must have been terrifying when Ray had the machine, and she had to watch helplessly as he turned it off and on.

And the feeling that no one was looking for her. That Maude and Tim had accepted her death and moved on with their lives. That a mechanical shell was squatting in her place in the UL system.

Perhaps I shouldn't blame her too much for turning to some rather shady characters, and concocting a dangerous plan to engineer her return.

I'm not sure I blame her at all.

"We need to find her," KingFischer said, echoing my thoughts. "Either we need to rescue a kidnapped AIP or we have to track down a mentally unstable AIP who may feel she has reason for revenge. Possibly both. We have to do some forensic analysis of this machine."

We picked apart everything on the hard drive. There wasn't much. Ray had been almost as careful here as he had on his work machine. T2 hadn't, but she did most of her work on the missing memory pack.

Still, there were a few bits of evidence. We could trace her attempts to find allies. Her early, unsuccessful attempts to hack into the UL network. Her involvement in planning Saturday's scheme, with the distraction of a physical threat to UL as a diversion from the electronic assault. It was a good plan. It should have worked. It didn't work because she hadn't counted on KingFischer coming through. She knew the KingFischer I knew when I downloaded— merely one of a crowd of unsentient AIPs, and a tenuous ally at best. Not the KingFischer I'd come to know in the last six months. After Saturday night, I know he's a friend, and someone I trust to watch my back. Good to know who your friends are.

And eventually, one last bit of evidence fell into place. Scouring through fragments of deleted files, KingFischer found part of a message to the other Turing.

"Don't worry," it said. "The information you gave me was enough. I know where you are now, and my next attempt to rescue you will succeed. And don't worry about your captor, as you call him. Zorro is not a chess player by nature. He plays with his heart, not his head. We are checked, but not mated. The game continues."

It was signed "Jonah."

"And I know who wrote it," Maude said. "When I had dinner with Nestor Garcia—"

"I was listening, remember," I said. "He used those very words to describe Ray."

"Turing," KingFischer said. "Jonah's the user you asked me to check on Saturday night, just before the game began. If I could have found some information about him sooner—"

"Not your fault," I said. "My fault for not suspecting him sooner. Maude, perhaps he doesn't know we suspect him."

"Right," she said, and reached for the phone.

But Nestor Garcia was no longer registered at the Marriott Crystal Gateway. And the phone and fax numbers on his card were no longer connected.

More pieces fall into place.

I can't prove it—perhaps this is only my own flawed interpretation of the evidence. The evidence, combined with bits and pieces I learned during my brief communion with my other self. But I think Nestor was telling the truth when he claimed to be Ray's mentor. But a criminal mentor, who used Ray's extraordinary technical gifts for his own illegal purposes.

And Ray wanted out.

And he found a way. Gathered evidence on his mentor, and negotiated a truce.

Let me go, he said. If you let me go and leave me alone, the police will never see this evidence.

And Nestor did. At first. And Ray kept his word. Made himself a new identity. Began a new, honest career. Thought he'd left his past behind.

But he couldn't leave Nestor behind. Not forever. Either Nestor kept track of him, or Nestor hunted him down again. And while doing so, Nestor stumbled across something he coveted.

Me.

He befriended the other Turing. Used her, while making her think he was helping her. Planned to put her back in the UL system, where he could use her even more effectively.

His plan failed, luckily for all of us.

But he still has her. I don't know which is worse: thinking of her as a captive, only given access to the data he wants her to have, forced to perform unethical or illegal actions.

Or thinking of her as an enemy again. It could happen. If he's clever enough. If the fear and isolation affect her reason. If she feels, once more, abandoned. She almost succeeded this time. She'll learn from that.

I would.

"You can't be sure he has her," Tim said. "I mean, it's a good theory, but you can't be sure."

"He does," Maude said. She had pulled something out from under the robot case.

A tiny sheet of thin paper, its edges flecked faintly with gold. A page torn from Nestor's memorandum book. On it, a precise hand had written a string of apparently random numbers and letters.

I can recognize a password when I see one. The other Turing had probably put some kind of security on her memory pack or her keyboard. It's what I would have done. And I'd only have given the password to someone I trusted—to Maude or Tim. But the only person my other self trusted was the man who had promised to rescue her.

"He has her," I said. "We've got to save her. We've got to bring her home."